*C*LADY *Emma's* CAMPAIGN

A Regency Romance

OTHER BOOKS AND AUDIO BOOKS

BY JENNIFER MOORE

Becoming Lady Lockwood

LADY
Emma's
CAMPAIGN

A Regency Romance

JENNIFER MOORE

THE BEST-SELLING AUTHOR OF *BECOMING LADY LOCKWOOD*

Covenant Communications, Inc.

Cover images: *Emma* photograph by Picture This... by Sara Staker
Background Image: *The Battle of La Fere-Champenoise, on the 25th March 1814, 1891* (oil on canvas),
Willewalde, Bogdan (1818-1903) / State Central Artillery Museum, St. Petersburg, Russia / Bridgeman
Images

Cover design copyright © 2014 by Covenant Communications, Inc.

Published by Covenant Communications, Inc.
American Fork, Utah

Printed in the United States of America
First Printing: November 2014

20 19 18 17 16 15 14   10 9 8 7 6 5 4 3 2 1

ISBN-13: 978-1-62108-788-5

For my parents
You both taught me a passion for books.
Mimi, you gave me my love of romance.
Big Dog, my obsession with history.

Acknowledgments

Thanks to my family. For your support, laughter, and for giving me some alone time to do what I love. You five guys are everything to me.

To Ed Lunt for teaching me how to work a bayonet and sharing his collection of Spanish coins and military knowledge, Dave Lunt for telling me about guerilla warfare, and Carla Kelly and Sarah Eden for your willingness to answer questions, loan me books, and tell me where to find information I need.

I am so grateful for the hours Dr. Adam Schwebach spent talking with me, answering questions, and impressing on me the seriousness of PTSD. My heart goes out to those afflicted with this disorder.

Thanks so much to my critique girls: Angela, Becki, Cindy A., Cindy H., Jody, Josi, Nancy, Ronda, and Susan. I love you girls, your brainstorming ideas, good advice, and encouragement. You make me reach higher and work harder.

Amanda Kimball, Penny Lunt, Josi Kilpack, and Nancy Allen, thanks for being my beta readers and for understanding when you found out how terrible a first draft can be.

Stacey Owen is the world's most patient editor. She makes sentences flow and the story shine. An editor does more than just correct grammar and punctuation. She comes up with ideas and gives excellent feedback and encouragement when it got tough. I completely love working with her and the lovely Kathy Gordon and everyone else at Covenant. It is truly a pleasure.

Prologue

LADY EMMA DRAKE SMILED AS she tied the last ribbon. She stood on tiptoe upon a chair in the great hall, reaching to arrange a garland over the mantel on Christmas Eve morning. She had risen early, before anyone else in the family, and while it was still dark, persuaded the steward to help her collect the wreaths and evergreen boughs from the stable. For the last few days, she had secretly gathered and fashioned greenery to decorate the Manor House.

It had only been three weeks since her older brother William, the new earl, had returned from sea with his wife, Amelia, and his closest friend, Sidney Fletcher. For the first time in her life, her home was filled with love and laughter, and Emma was determined to make this Christmas special for her family and their guest. Her mind spun with thoughts of the Yule log, the warm cider, and a few remaining details needing attention when a voice startled her from her reverie. Not just a voice, *his* voice.

"Why, Emma! I do not believe I have ever seen such splendid decorations."

Emma turned and saw Sidney smiling up at her; the twinkle in his brown eyes caused her heart to trip. He reached to take her hand and, for a moment, touched her waist to help her balance as she stepped down from the chair. The brief contact nearly stole her breath, and she ducked her head to hide the blush that immediately covered her cheeks.

He tugged on one of her braids playfully. Emma thought it could be time to begin following her mother's advice—sleeping with her hair in papers and trying to coax a bit of curl out of her stick-straight unmanageable locks. Perhaps then Sidney would not tease her as if she were merely a little girl. She was seventeen after all.

"Happy Christmas!" Emma was thrilled that he had been the one to discover her.

Since Sidney had arrived, she had found herself yearning for his attention, while at the same time paralyzed when he spoke to her. Her heart had beaten faster each time she heard his voice and saw his smile. She lay awake in her bed at night thinking of witty anecdotes that might make him laugh, though she knew she would never be brave enough to actually say them.

Sidney tucked her hand into the crook of his elbow and led her around the hall, admiring and commenting on the decorations and even opening the front door for a closer inspection of the holiday wreath. They stopped beneath the archway that led to the dining room, and Sidney turned to face her.

Emma kept her gaze on the floor, though her heart had begun to race. They were standing directly beneath the kissing bough.

"How, indeed, did you accomplish such a thing before the rest of the household even awoke, Emma?" He lifted her hand off his arm and pressed it to his heart dramatically. "Truly, this has the makings of the best Christmas in my memory."

Sidney glanced upward and then stepped back for a closer look at the cluster of greenery that hung from a ribbon directly above them. He studied for a moment the evergreens, apples, paper flowers, and dolls representing the figures of the nativity that Emma had so carefully bundled together.

Emma's heart had risen into her throat and threatened to choke her. She did not dare meet his gaze.

"Finding myself beneath the kissing bough with such a beautiful young lady is not a responsibility I take lightly." Sidney's voice carried a note of mock gravity that would have normally caused Emma to laugh, but under the circumstances, she was attempting to control the heat that flared over her face and neck.

Sidney crooked a finger beneath her chin and lifted her face until their eyes met. He winked and smiled, which did nothing to relieve the trembling in her knees. "Be assured that I shall not fail in this important duty." Bending down, he placed a very tender and very chaste kiss upon Emma's cheek.

Emma felt as though someone had lit her heart on fire and replaced her legs with gooseberry jelly. Her mind tumbled, and her pulse raced. She wondered if Sidney could feel the shaking in her hand, which he still held.

If he could, he didn't acknowledge it. Hearing someone's throat clearing, they both turned to see William descending the stairs with Amelia.

"Good morning, and happy Christmas!" Sidney called out.

William looked between Sidney and Emma. His eyes narrowed when he saw their joined hands, and he heaved an exaggerated sigh, looking up to the heavens. "And this is what happens when I sleep late, I find my houseguest kissing my sister." He turned to his wife, and Emma recognized the teasing in his voice. "I knew we should not have invited him to our home, Amelia."

Emma had often wondered how Sidney tolerated her brother's rudeness, even though she knew it was usually contrived. The two men were like brothers. They had sailed together in the navy since they were boys. Sidney constantly teased and provoked William with his cheerfulness, and William invariably responded with feigned bad temper. And yet they still remained the closest of friends.

Amelia ignored the men. "What a beautiful surprise. The house looks wonderful. Thank you, Emma." She pulled William toward the dining room doorway. "And look, my dear, a kissing bough."

"Emma and I have put it to the test and have concluded that all of the holiday décor, *especially* the kissing bough, is in excellent working order." Sidney squeezed her hand conspiratorially, and Emma felt the heat rush back into her cheeks.

"And naturally you have exploited my hospitality—and my sister. I shall have to keep a closer eye on you, Mr. Fletcher," William said. The lines around his eyes softened in an expression that most people would not have even noticed, but Emma recognized it as humor.

"I understand. But you must admit that I am not in the least to blame, finding myself quite by accident in such a circumstance and with a lovely girl so close at hand." He winked at Emma again.

She attempted to smile back. She was, after all, a grown woman, and a simple kiss on Christmas Eve should not elicit such overwhelming emotions.

"Shall we leave these two alone to assess the kissing bough themselves, Emma? Come, I can smell breakfast, and I should not wish to remain in such a vulnerable location in case Mrs. Hatfield happens by and attempts to extract a kiss as well." He tucked her hand back into the crook of his elbow and led Emma into the dining room.

As she walked with Sidney, she lowered her head and touched her hand to her cheek, wondering how she could possibly still feel warmth from his kiss. She wished that he would have shown some bit of discomfort when William had found them beneath the kissing bough. But he had acted as easy as if they had simply been discovered playing at cards. She glanced his way and wondered what he was thinking. Had he noticed that she'd grown up?

The first time Emma had met Sidney was five years earlier. William and Sidney had traveled to the Manor House on shore leave. Lawrence, Emma's and William's elder brother, had been the earl then. Like his father before him, Lawrence had had a violent temper and a propensity to drink too heavily and lose too frequently at the gaming tables. While William and Lawrence argued and yelled in the study, Sidney spent time with Emma and her mother, regaling them with stories of his travels and playing card games when he could just as easily have left the contentious house and occupied himself elsewhere. Emma had committed each moment in his company to memory, and by the time of his next visit, she had admitted to herself that she was utterly smitten with the dashing sailor. Yet his attentions toward her remained that of a brother, albeit a kind and silly one. Had he not noticed that she was a young woman? Would he have kissed her five years ago just as he had today?

When William and Amelia had finished admiring Emma's handiwork and making use of the kissing bough, they took their places at the dining table, followed by Emma's mother, whom Amelia and Sidney affectionately addressed as Lady Charlotte. Emma listened to the conversation and commented in the appropriate places, but she was distracted by Sidney's close proximity beside her and extremely conscious of the way his sleeve occasionally brushed hers. She was a hopeless case. She sighed and took a bite of egg.

"And what plans do you have in store for us tomorrow, Emma?" Amelia asked. "You seem to have arranged everything to perfection. I even overheard cook saying something about a roasted goose."

"Yes, Christmas dinner will be a grand feast: boar's head, plum pudding, gingerbread, and more pies than you can imagine," Emma said. "Then, of course, we shall have games and music."

William groaned. "Please do not say we will be forced into any type of play acting."

"Certainly we will," Amelia said. "And, my dearest, you shall partner me in charades."

William put his hand over his eyes.

Sidney laughed. "Maybe I shall demonstrate my expertise at snapdragon, if you are up to a challenge, Emma." He snatched a bit of scone from her plate to prove his skill at the competition that required exceptionally quick movements.

"Please do not allow her to play such a game, Sidney." Lady Charlotte wagged her finger at him and smiled. "She has a Season in a few months, and how would it look if she were to be presented at court with scorched hands?"

Emma refrained from rolling her eyes. When would her mother realize that Emma was nearly a grown woman and stop treating her as if she were made of glass?

William pushed his chair back from the table. "It's *Christmas*. Must you remind me that we are soon to be inundated with mantua makers and forced to attend balls and concerts in the hope of finding my sister a husband?"

Emma could feel Sidney's gaze on her. She focused on running her fingers over the stitching of the napkin in her lap. Any mention of her Season left her feeling vulnerable and nervous.

"Lady Emma is to be presented," Sidney said slowly. "The young men of the *ton* do not know how fortunate they are." He flipped one of her braids playfully over her shoulder. And when he spoke next, his voice regained its usual note of good humor. "She shall undoubtedly be the loveliest young lady in London. And it is probably fortunate that I am to return to sea after Epiphany. I should not want to ruin Emma's debut by occupying her entire dance card or to cause a scandal by chasing away men that I deem less than worthy of my dear friend."

Emma's stomach felt as if it were filled with lead. Her brother Lawrence's death last year had delayed her debut, as the family was in mourning. At seventeen, she would be one of the oldest ladies presented, but she felt the least prepared.

The meal ended after a change of conversation, for which Emma was immensely grateful.

William stood, and Sidney followed suit. "If you ladies will excuse us," William said. "I am to make a few tenant visits this morning, and Sidney has agreed to accompany me."

"Even though a sea captain has no business upon a horse," Sidney added with a grimace that caused the three ladies to chuckle. He started to follow William but turned back, meeting Emma's eye. She straightened in her chair and wished—again—that her hair was not in braids this morning. "Emma, do make certain that you find a husband that will make you laugh. The sound is too delightful to be wasted on a man who does not appreciate it." He winked and reached over to tug on her braid one more time before leaving the room.

Emma knew of only one man who fit that description, but it was folly. Even if he *had* thought of her as more than his best friend's little sister, Sidney would return to sea, and she would be launched into society. She pressed her hand once more to her cheek, marveling at the emotions that had been stirred by such an innocent kiss and fearing that every other man on earth would pale in comparison. Her heart was lost to Sidney Fletcher.

Chapter 1

Eighteen Months Later

LORD DEWHURST WAS WITHOUT A doubt one of the most eligible bachelors in London. His manners were exemplary, his dancing graceful, his waistcoat a la mode and perfectly fitted. He was an attentive conversationalist, classically handsome, charming nearly to a fault. And Emma hoped desperately that he would not propose.

This was the fifth time he had called at the Drakes' London residence since he and Emma had been introduced a few weeks earlier. He'd appropriately limited his visit to thirty minutes, conversing about such easy topics as the weather or the events of the Season. But today, instead of being contented to remain in the drawing room where Emma could depend on her mother or Amelia's presence, Lord Dewhurst had insisted that it was a pity to waste such a lovely afternoon indoors. He had waited while she fetched her bonnet and gloves, and now the pair strolled through the small garden behind Emma's family's town home.

Her mother's roses perfumed the air around them, and ivy covered the wrought iron trellis above a garden bench, which was picturesquely situated in the shade of a willow. Birds sang in the trees. The garden was one of the most beautiful in town, and the early summer displayed it splendidly.

Tilting her head the slightest bit, Emma glanced up beyond the edge of her bonnet to find Lord Dewhurst looking directly at her. She looked away quickly, casting her eyes about for something—anything—to focus on in order to avoid meeting his gaze.

"Do you mind very much if we sit for a moment, my dear?" He gestured to the bench. "There is something I should like to ask you." He caught her hand and held it for an instant as he led her from the path.

Emma was disappointed to note that his touch did not send her heart fluttering. It was the same with the other men she had met in her two Seasons. She had briefly clasped hands as she stepped from a carriage or partnered in a dance, but as usual, the sensation was no different than what she would experience if her mother had taken her hand, or William.

Emma sat upon the edge of the small bench with her back straight, her head tilted demurely, and her lips curled in the slightest bit of a smile, casting her eyes downward in the manner expected of a proper young lady.

Despite her outward appearance of serenity, Emma's mind raced. How could she distract Lord Dewhurst from the question she was sure he intended to ask? "I do believe you told me you meant to purchase some new horses, my lord," she said. If there was anything to divert a man's mind, it was the mention of horses.

Lord Dewhurst smiled, and his eyes took on a dreamy aspect. "Why, yes. It took a bit of persuasion, but in the end, Baron Wilkinson and I managed to agree upon a price. And I must admit I feel as though I got the better part of the bargain . . ."

As he launched into a description of the animals, Emma began to relax. Perhaps his equine report would occupy the remainder of his visit. She glanced up at him again while he spoke. He was indeed one of the handsomest men she knew, and she did enjoy his company. She had already refused four suitors in her two Seasons but thought that it would be more difficult this time, as she did have tender feelings for Lord Dewhurst. She had hoped that if she spent enough time with him, her affection for him would grow into something deeper than friendship. But even though their association was genial, the idea of becoming his wife produced a sour taste in her mouth.

Her musing was brought to an abrupt end when Lord Dewhurst turned toward her and laid his hand upon her shoulder. "I also inquired after a smaller mare. A gentle mount more suitable for a lady. Which brings me to the reason I had intended to speak with you."

Emma began to feel an uncomfortable sort of sinking feeling in her stomach.

"My lady, or if I may call you, *Emma*," he paused a moment, possibly waiting for her to acknowledge his request, but she kept her gaze firmly upon her gloved hands folded tidily in her lap.

"From the moment you entered the Chanceworths' ball, I was impressed with your gentle and reserved nature. It was not long after making your acquaintance that I was certain I would not rest until I knew you better." He shifted his position, leaning forward and tilting his head in an attempt to catch her eye.

Emma did not look up.

"The weeks we've known each other have done nothing but firm my conviction that you are a person I would feel comfortable sharing a life with and the one who shall make me happier than any other. You are a beautiful, gentle young woman who needs to be taken care of, and I should like to be the man to see to your comfort. I have, of course, spoken to your brother who insists—even though you are not of age—that the decision is entirely yours." He took a deep breath. "Lady Emma Drake, would you do me the honor of becoming my wife?"

Emma would have been a fool to expect a declaration of love which they both would have known was untrue. Marriage to Lord Dewhurst would be a marriage of convenience. So many of her friends had formed practical connections, marrying for a title, money, or out of desperation because it was a well-known fact that marriage—even a loveless marriage—is much more desirable than becoming an unwed spinster. Lord Dewhurst's offer was possibly the best she'd received, and the Season was nearly over. Her *second* Season. If only she felt more for him than a friendly affection.

She tried to tell herself that she was simply being childish, dreaming of true love. But then she thought of William's face when he looked at Amelia: as if she were the most precious creature in the world. How Amelia smiled when he entered the room, and the way William touched her arm when he passed or kissed her cheek when he thought they were alone.

It was a stark comparison to what her parents' relationship had been— an arranged marriage filled with violence and tears and ugliness. She did not imagine that Lord Dewhurst could be cruel like her father. She had never seen anything in his manner besides kindness. His reputation as well as that of his family was beyond reproach; but even so, she longed for a relationship like William's, and she'd tried again and again to find it.

The truth of it was that Emma had enough people determined to take care of her. Her mother, especially, treated her as if she were still a child. Would her entire life be filled with people pampering her and never trusting her with anything more difficult than pouring tea or choosing curtains?

How could she possibly expect to spend her life with a man with whom she had merely exchanged a few sentences while they had danced, ridden through the park with his mother, and visited a few times in her drawing room? She tried to remember whether Lord Dewhurst had even heard her laugh. Would he ever try to make her laugh? Or would such a thing ruin his opinion about her gentle and reserved nature?

Only when he took her hand did Emma look up at him, realizing she had remained silent far too long. "Please forgive me, my lord, I am contemplating."

"Of course, my dear. And you must call me Maynard."

Maynard?

Still pondering on the fact that she'd not even known Lord Dewhurst's Christian name until this moment, Emma was quite taken by surprise when he leaned close and kissed her on the cheek. It was a feat that required some agility, as he was compelled to negotiate the brim of her bonnet. She froze, waiting to feel something magical, but his kiss did not send her heart racing any more than his grip upon her hand.

Obviously believing her pause to be the result of her pleasure at his romantic gesture, Lord Dewhurst bent closer to kiss her again.

Emma rose to her feet quickly. "I am sorry, my lo . . . Maynard. I need time to consider your offer, and I must speak with William and my mother before I can reply to your request."

He stood with her. "I understand, my dear. Farewell. I believe I shall call upon the earl right now, myself." Inclining his head in a bow, he added rather as an afterthought, "And I shall, of course, visit you tomorrow."

Emma dipped in a curtsey, holding her hands behind her back to discourage any further familiarity as they parted. Once Maynard, Lord Dewhurst, had gone into the house, she settled back upon the bench, relieved for the time alone with her thoughts.

Removing her bonnet to enjoy the gentle breeze, she looked around the garden. It was truly a work of art. The small bench was a splendid setting for a proposal. She attempted to further unravel her feelings. Lord Dewhurst would make an amiable husband. He was wealthy and kind and respected. A position as his wife was quite possibly the best situation she could hope for.

Lord Dewhurst would give her everything she could ever desire: gowns, jewels, children. He possessed all the attributes she had ever wanted in a husband. Except one. He was not Sidney.

Emma sighed. She indulged for a moment, permitting her mind to travel down a path that it took more frequently than she should allow. She touched the bracelet on her wrist; her fingers traced the familiar flowers carved in the jade. She had found it upon her pillow the day Sidney had departed, accompanied by a note which Emma had read so often that she could see his script when she closed her eyes.

Emma,

I purchased this bracelet in Macau. The Chinese use jade to represent all that is pure and beautiful, and I cannot think of a more worthy recipient than my lovely young friend.

Yours, Sidney

P.S. Ensure that you are selective about the men you choose to stand with beneath the kissing bough. Most of us are not deserving of the honor.

Emma pulled her gaze away from the bracelet and looked at the roses instead. It was unfair to compare the kiss of the man who could soon be her husband with that from a man she might never encounter again. She had only received correspondence from Sidney twice since he had returned to sea a year and a half ago, general inquiries about her health and brief accounts of his journeys. It was quite obvious that he did not consider her in any sort of romantic capacity. While he had been thoughtful and diverting during the time they'd spent together, she knew her infatuation was quite one-sided. He no doubt thought of her only as a child.

But she wasn't a child any longer. If only Sidney could see her now. The baby fat that had plagued her was long gone, leaving her body filled out in all the right places. The fly-away, unmanageable hair that she had kept in braids had been trained by her lady's maid and a fair amount of pomade to curl softly around her face.

Her second Season was even more exciting than her first had been, and she was currently swept up in a never-ending flurry of gowns, invitations, balls, concerts, luncheons, intrigues, card games, and on-dits. Her dance card was always filled, and the bowl in the front hall overflowed with calling cards and invitations. She moved in the best of circles and found herself at the center of attention at every event she attended. The Season was nearly perfect—or would have been if only she had managed to fall in love.

She stood, brushing off her gown, and picked up her bonnet. She had dallied long enough. Clarice, her mother's dresser, would soon be searching her out to settle upon an ensemble for the concert that evening. Emma had it on good authority that Olivia Dewitt intended to wear a peach-colored frock—although the pale color would wreak havoc with her horrid complexion—in which case, Emma needed to alter her own wardrobe plans. She would consult with her mother and Clarice as soon as she spoke with William. Lord Dewhurst would undoubtedly have left by now.

Emma walked toward the house slowly, wondering what William would say. She had rejected three other offers this Season and one last. Would William be impatient? She did not think so. He would not insist that she marry Lord Dew—Maynard. While William presented a rather bad-tempered exterior, she knew him to be kind and fair. He had made it clear that she would be allowed to choose her husband and was strongly supported by their mother and Amelia, though Emma's unwillingness to form an attachment likely frustrated them all. If she did not accept this offer, she would most likely require another Season to secure a husband, and she did not imagine that William would be overly thrilled with the idea.

Emma's shoulders drooped. Another Season would bring the same men and the same parties. Perhaps she should save all of them the aggravation and not put her family through it again.

Emma stopped with her hand upon the doorknob as thoughts began to fill her head. A plan was taking shape. She could not in good conscience accept Lord Dewhurst when her attachment to Sidney was still so strong. Her breath came heavily as she pondered what she must do. She would confess her feelings to William and ask for his assistance. Amelia would support her. If Emma explained that she had rejected so many offers because she longed for a relationship like theirs, William would naturally understand.

Emma smiled as she imagined it. It would be a simple thing for her brother to invite Sidney to the Manor House for a visit; then Emma would have the chance to see if there would ever be the possibility of a relationship. Could she turn his head now that she was a woman? She must try. And if in the end, Sidney did not feel the same, she would be at peace, knowing that she had made her best attempt. Then she would be free to accept the next proposal that came her way.

Emma entered the main hall and started up the stairs. She would probably find William reading the papers, following the latest news from the war in Spain, and trying not to wish that he was a part of it. The last they had heard, his old ship, the HMS *Venture*, had sailed with the fleet in the campaign to free the Spanish city of Cádiz, which the French had held under siege for more than a year. William had been in the navy for eighteen years prior to the title falling on his shoulders, and Emma knew he was frustrated to read weeks-old news in the soft chairs of his library while his former shipmates were in the midst of the action.

She knocked softly on the door before stepping into the library, expecting to see William behind his desk. His chair, however, was empty. Hearing a sniffle, she turned to the other side of the room, and her stomach sank. William sat upon the sofa with his arms around Amelia as she wept against his chest.

"What has happened?" Emma cried rushing to them. It seemed certain she must be the reason for such a reaction. Perhaps her unwillingness to settle upon a suitor had been harder on her family than she had considered. "What did Lord Dewhurst say? Was I too dismissive of his offer?" She stood on the carpet in front of them, wringing her hands. "I am sorry; I know I was not as kind to him as I should have been. I promise I'll make it right. Please, Amelia, do not cry."

William raised his gaze to meet hers. His eyes were red-rimmed, and his hair was tousled as if he had run his hands through it. He squinted for a moment in confusion. "Lord . . . Oh, yes. He did ask to speak to me. I am sorry I could not receive him today." He turned his attention back to Amelia, patting her shoulder and whispering words of comfort.

"Then what is wrong, William? Is Amelia ill?"

Instead of answering, William reached for the newspaper that lay on the small table next to the sofa. He swallowed and cleared his throat as he handed it to Emma.

She took it from him and saw that it was folded to the daily list of dead and missing soldiers. Numbness spread from her chest as she looked down the list, knowing what she would see even before she found it:

Captain Sidney Fletcher of the HMS Venture *killed at Cádiz, Spain. April 25, 1811.*

Chapter 2

IT WAS NEARLY A WEEK later when Emma peeked into the small parlor and saw her mother sitting in her favorite chair next to the window overlooking the garden.

"You look lovely, my dear." The dowager countess reached to take her hand.

Emma stepped closer, sitting on the stool at her mother's feet, just as she had when she was younger.

"Are you certain you won't join us this evening, Mama?"

"I am afraid I still have a bit of a headache. I'm off to bed in a moment. And you young people will have a much more amusing evening without an old lady dogging your steps."

"You are hardly old. And I would be happy to remain here with you. I don't know how I can smile and laugh and enjoy myself as if everything is normal."

"Emma, it has been nearly a week since you were out in society. It will be good for you and William and Amelia to be back among your friends instead of . . ." Lady Charlotte reached to touch Emma's cheek. "Sidney would not want you all to remain like this. He was always cheerful and full of life." She sighed. "Trust me, dear. The pain does not last forever."

Her mother had endured so much in her lifetime, and there were times when it seemed almost as if she closed herself off from emotions. Emma made sure to protect her as much as possible from things that might be upsetting.

"And I would imagine Lord Dewhurst will attend the concert tonight as well." Lady Charlotte raised her eyebrows and smiled. "We've still not spoken of his visit last week . . ." She allowed her voice to trail off, inviting Emma to speak.

After a week of keeping to her room, Emma felt she owed her mother the truth of what had happened in the minutes before learning of Sidney's death. "Lord Dewhurst made me an offer," Emma kept her gaze on her mother's hand. The women had a strong connection, forged through years of her father's abuse. They had sought comfort and found strength in each other, and it saddened her to think that she might marry and leave her mother's home to become part of a family she hardly knew and wife to a man she did not love.

"And did you accept him?"

"I told him that I required time to come to a decision."

"That was wise, my dear." The Dowager Lady Lockwood placed her other hand over her daughter's.

"I do not love him, Mama."

"I know."

"Yet he would make a good husband. What should I do?"

"Emma, it is for you to decide. I was not given the choice, and I am determined that my only daughter shall not enter into marriage unwillingly."

"But I had so wanted to marry a man I love." Emma did not think she could possibly have any tears left, but one still managed to make its appearance and slide down her cheek until her mother brushed it away.

"And now he is gone," Lady Charlotte said softly.

Emma lifted her gaze to her mother's face. Had her feelings for Sidney been so very obvious? She wiped away the remainder of the moisture on her cheek and breathed deeply to regain control of her emotions. Emma did not want her mother to see her upset. She stood and wrapped a blanket around Lady Charlotte's shoulders. "I do wish you would change your mind about this evening." She pressed a kiss to her mother's cheek before she turned to leave the parlor.

"Emma, I heard some wise advice once that I believe bears repeating, though I do not remember the words exactly: find a husband who will make you laugh—"

"The sound is too delightful to be wasted on someone who will not appreciate it," Emma finished quietly. Her eyes burned, and her throat constricted. She left the parlor and walked slowly down the stairs. Was a life with a husband she did not love better than a life alone? She knew she would always have a home with her brother's family, but the longing for a family of her own, for someone to love her, for *Sidney* was nearly unbearable. She still did not know how she would answer Lord Dewhurst.

The letter she'd sent him a week ago simply told him that the family was adjusting to the loss of a close friend and that she would not be able to see him for a few days. It was unfair to expect him to wait indefinitely for her answer. She sighed as she walked down the stairs, still unsure of what to do.

She was surprised that William and Amelia were not waiting for her in the entry hall. Perhaps they were having a difficult time feeling ready to venture back into society as well.

Just as Emma had made up her mind to walk back up the stairs to retrieve them, the door knocker banged—rather loudly.

Emma stepped out of sight into the Morning Room off the entry hall. Who would call at such an hour?

Dawson, the butler hurried past, unaware of her presence, and opened the front door.

Hearing the sound of voices and activity, she peeked through the opening and was taken aback when she saw a group of sailors on the doorstep. A man who was apparently the leader asked to speak to "Captain Drake."

"His lordship is preparing to leave for the evening," Dawson said, "But if you would call back tomorrow—"

"It is extremely important, sir. If you would please tell him that Lieutenant Wellard of the HMS *Venture* is—"

"Mr. Wellard." Emma jumped as William's voice echoed through the entry hall. She turned to see him striding down the stairs.

Dawson stepped aside, opening the door wide for the men to enter. The sailors crowded into the hall. Two of the officers were dressed in navy blue uniforms, and the other two soldiers wore the red jackets of marines. They were accompanied by a young boy, who could not be older than thirteen.

Emma stepped back into the shadows where she wouldn't be seen but had a clear view.

William greeted each man by name. "Lieutenant Wellard, Corporal Ashworth, Corporal Thorne, and I see that you've received your white lapels, Mr. Fairchild. Congratulations, Lieutenant." He shook their hands before turning to the boy and clapping him on the shoulder. "And Master Riley. Welcome." William's tone was subdued.

Emma imagined it was difficult for him to see his old shipmates, who were also mourning for their captain.

Lieutenant Wellard spoke. "Sir, I apologize for the lateness of the visit. But we felt that it could not wait. We have come about Captain Fletcher."

Hearing Sidney's name, Emma felt a fresh wave of tears rush to prickle behind her eyes.

William's face fell. When he spoke, his voice had taken on a monotone sound. "Yes, I read of it in the *Times*. Thank you for coming yourselves to inform me of his passing."

"No, sir. It is a mistake." Riley said. "We need—"

The boy was interrupted by a cry from the top of the stairs. Amelia rushed down into the entry hall. "Corporal Ashworth! Riley!" She embraced each of the men in turn. "What a wonderful surprise. Please, come up to the drawing room. Dawson, have Mrs. Hatfield send tea and cakes for our guests."

The lieutenant looked to William, who nodded, and the group made their way up the stairs.

Emma followed, curious about the visitors, and even more curious about their news. What had the boy, Riley, meant when he said it was a mistake? Was he referring to Sidney? Was there more information concerning his death? When she stepped into the drawing room, the men stood, and Amelia motioned for her to join them.

"Please, may I introduce my sister, Lady Emma Drake," William said.

Emma nodded to the men and then quickly took a seat near Amelia.

Mrs. Hatfield delivered tea, and Emma and Amelia set about pouring and distributing cups and plates.

William did not wait for the guests to be served their refreshment. "Let us dispense with the formalities. What news do you bring?"

Lieutenant Wellard began to speak again. "Sir, we have come for your help. We believe Captain Fletcher is not dead."

Emma jolted, and she quickly set down the cup that she had been about to hand to William as her hand started to shake. She blinked and pressed her lips together to keep from crying out. Could the others hear her heart pommeling in her chest?

Lieutenant Wellard continued, "When it was discovered that the numbers of French troops stationed at Cádiz were being reduced as more and more departed—"

"Yes, to assist with the siege of Badajoz," William interrupted. He nodded and rotated his hand, indicating for the lieutenant to speed up his account.

"A relief army was sent to Tarifa to attack the French lines from the rear. We were part of the campaign under Sir Thomas Graham, and we found ourselves marching to Fort Matagorda on the Trocadero Peninsula near Cádiz. As the battle progressed, we were commanded to fall back to the town of Chiclana, tend to the wounded, and reassess our strategy. Captain Fletcher was unaccounted for and assumed either dead or captured."

"But I saw him taken." Riley's words burst forth in a rush he'd likely been holding back since his arrival. "Captain Fletcher was with me on the battlefield. He was covering my escape, sir, when he was cut off from the remainder of our company and relieved of his weapons. They surrounded him and took him into the French fort at gunpoint."

Emma's stomach turned over. The image of Sidney struggling while being dragged by French soldiers into a building with metal armaments arose in her mind. She blinked, remembering herself, and returned to the task of serving the tea.

"An inquiry was made, of course." Lieutenant Wellard nodded his thanks to Emma as she handed him a cup and saucer. "But we were told there was no prisoner by that name."

Amelia pressed both hands to her mouth, and William put his arm around her shoulders. "And what of your new captain? Was he informed of this? Did he not investigate?" William bit off each question.

Lieutenant Fairchild folded his arms in front of his chest and lowered his eyebrows. "The acting Captain Mitchell is . . . reluctant to look into the matter."

"You believe that he does not wish to locate Captain Fletcher, as it would not only reflect badly upon him for not doing so sooner but restore him to his former office of first lieutenant." William's scowl matched the lieutenant's.

"Sir, I cannot assume such a thing without being accused of disloyalty to my commanding officer," Lieutenant Fairchild said. "However, if *you* were to assume it, I would not find myself inclined to argue with you."

Emma held her hand to her throat. Her mind swam, questions tumbling over one another. Was Sidney really alive? If so, was he injured? Ill? Had he been tortured? And why was there no record of his imprisonment? How was it possible that his own men could not find him?

"We have even spoken to my uncle, the Duke of Southampton, who appealed to the Lords of the Admiralty for a more formal investigation to be opened," said the tall, gangly Corporal Ashworth. "But without a ransom demand or evidence that he is indeed a prisoner, they declare that there is nothing they can do. We have run out of options. The commander of our fleet, Admiral Griffin, suggested that, as the matter cannot be officially pursued by the navy, we should speak to you."

Riley set his plate on the table next to him and leaned forward. "Captain Drake, we must return to Spain. We cannot abandon Captain Fletcher, and you are the only one who can rescue—Do you have access to a ship?"

William's agitation apparently became too much to contain. He rose and began to pace around the room.

Emma wished propriety would allow her to join him.

"Lieutenant Wellard"—William stopped and turned back toward them on the heel of his boot—"how long are you in port?"

"At least a month, Captain."

William was silent a moment longer before he resumed his pacing. "I do have a ship, a clipper. She is berthed in Greenwich but could be made ready to sail in a matter of days. We could reach Spain within a week." He turned to the men. "How fast can you gather a crew?"

William and his shipmates immediately began to plan the rescue mission. They would meet at Greenwich in two days and sail at high tide.

Emma's heart pounded as she leaned her head back against the chair. The idea that Sidney could be alive made her shaky and lightheaded. It was nearly too much to hope that William and these soldiers would reach Spain and find him. Was it possible that he was whole and well? She felt as if her chest were being squeezed in a clamp when she thought of Sidney spending months in an enemy prison.

As the men continued to plan, Emma's fingers traced the jade flowers on her wrist. She would be forced to remain in London, pretending to enjoy the festivities of the Season, while her heart would be across the sea with William and his sailors. How could she possibly bear the wait?

And while she hoped for news about Sidney, the dilemma of Lord Dewhurst would remain. He would not be content to wait another month for her answer. It had already been more than a week since he'd asked for her hand. But could she in good conscience accept him when, at this very moment, Sidney could be languishing in a prison? And just the possibility that Sidney could be alive was no guarantee that he would return home with William and fall into her arms. She thought of Amelia and her journey upon a naval frigate when William had escorted her to England from Jamaica.

She had done it. So why not Emma?

As the men concluded their visit and took their leave of her, Emma remained in the drawing room while Amelia and William accompanied them into the entry hall. She heard the front door close and walked to the top of the stairs, but when she heard William and Amelia talking, she stepped back, not wanting to intrude.

"Absolutely not," William said.

"But it is *Sidney*. If there is even a small chance of finding him alive, I cannot sit home and wait, left behind like a helpless child while you—"

"It is not an option, Amelia. I will not take you to a battlefield. Do not even entertain the idea."

"Is there a chance that he could be alive?"

"There's no way of knowing. The circumstances are not normal. The enemy obviously does not realize who he is or arrangements for his ransom would have been made. He must have his own reasons for concealing his identity. I fear it will not be easy to find him, let alone rescue him."

William lowered his voice, "Amelia, I know you could do this. You are my brave shipmate." Emma imagined him touching Amelia's cheek tenderly or kissing her hand. "But in your . . . condition. I am sorry; I will not risk it."

"You are right, of course." Amelia's voice was soft. "But I shall worry about you."

"I do not expect to be gone longer than three weeks. Surely you will find plenty to occupy yourself with my mother and Emma in that short time." William's voice lightened. He obviously wanted to change the topic.

"Attending champagne breakfasts and piano concerts will not distract me enough from missing my husband and worrying every moment about your safety. But I understand." Amelia's voice was resigned but still carried a note of petulance.

"I will need to send a missive immediately to the shipyard," William said.

"I shall find a nice book to read in the parlor until you are finished. And then I would like to go to bed. All of this excitement has quite worn me out."

Emma moved into the parlor and waited for Amelia to join her. She wished again that she could pace about the room—her nerves were quite close to becoming completely unraveled—but she steeled herself and, balling her fists in her lap, took a deep breath. This was her only chance.

Amelia entered the room and spotted her. "Emma, I am sorry about the concert. In all the excitement, it completely slipped my mind . . ."

Emma put up a hand to stop her. "I must go to Spain." She rushed through the words while she still had the courage to say them. "Will you help me?"

"Emma," Amelia sank onto a divan and patted the seat next to her. Amelia's eyes were tired and her face drawn. "I know you are fond of Sidney—"

Emma sat beside her. "I am in love with him." Her heart lurched as she actually said the words aloud. "I have been in love with him since I was eleven years old."

Amelia's face softened. "Emma, I consider you every bit my sister. I care for you, and I understand. Truly I do, but I cannot in good conscience allow such a thing. And William certainly will not."

"William cannot know. Please, Amelia. I am determined to go. I must. If I were to conceal myself aboard his ship . . ."

Amelia shook her head.

"Your experience, your adventure changed you, as you have told me often. How can you deny me this?" Emma nearly choked on the lump that was swelling in her throat. Her voice was getting higher, but she did not care. "Am I expected to remain here and marry a man I do not love when Sidney could be out there alive?"

"You have no idea what you'd face," Amelia said. "Nothing I tell you could come close to describing the horrors of war."

"But I shall be with William. He will protect me."

Amelia opened her mouth, but Emma kept speaking. "Please, Amelia. You must understand. I want what you have with my brother. This is my last chance to discover whether . . ." The look on Amelia's face made Emma realize that she would not be moved. "I am sorry to have put you in this position. I thought, out of everyone, you would understand." Emma squared her shoulders and brushed away her tears with shaking hands. "My mind is quite made up. I will go with or without your help." She stood and turned to leave. Amelia's refusal to assist her was a blow, but she would find another way. Perhaps she could dress as a man and—

Her thoughts were cut short by Amelia's hand on her arm.

Amelia blew out her breath. "Emma, I do not agree with this, but if you are resolved to go through with it, let's do it right."

Chapter 3

EMMA STEPPED OUT OF THE carriage, gazing across the shipyard before she turned her attention back to the high masts of the clipper that rose above them: the *Lady Jamaica*. Her mouth instantly went dry. She followed Amelia and William across the pier and up the swaying gangplank, attempting to keep her face from revealing the apprehension that was tumbling about her insides.

The marines, officers, and sailors alike saluted as the boatswain whistled, announcing the captain's arrival.

William gave the women a quick tour of the vessel, and while they walked through the hull, Amelia and Emma exchanged a glance. A small cubicle, tucked away in the shadows and hidden by sacks and barrels, would be the perfect place for Emma to hide. The women had both smuggled a few essentials beneath their petticoats, and while William's attention was focused elsewhere, Emma took a bundle from Amelia and added it to her own.

When the tour was over, Emma said her good-byes. Then, under the pretense of returning to the carriage while Amelia bid her husband farewell, Emma stole down the companionway into the hull and secreted herself in the tiny space, climbing over and nestling between sacks of grain. Her stomach constricted, but it was not seasickness. She traced her jade bracelet with one gloved finger, finding strength as she focused upon the reason she was doing this. She knew Amelia still disapproved of the entire venture, but once committed, she had not wavered. Emma had found a new connection with Amelia as they'd planned and worried and created scenarios late into the night. She even caught a look of mischief in Amelia's eyes when they discussed Emma's inevitable discovery.

Emma adjusted her position, trying to judge whether any part of her was visible to the main area of the hull. Finally deciding that the shadows sufficiently concealed her, she sat perfectly still, accustoming herself to the movement of the vessel, with muscles clenched and ears strained. She startled at each creak of the boards or snap of the sails until she was able to distinguish the regular sounds of the ship from the sounds of the men. As they hurried about making preparations to cast off, some of the sailors approached uncomfortably close. A passing man dropped a barrel and let out an exclamation quite near to Emma's hiding place. Tingles of fear shot down to her fingers when she imagined that she had been discovered. But he simply retrieved his burden and hurried on his way, leaving Emma to sink back in relief as her heartbeat returned to normal.

Once the excitement of stowing away had subsided, Emma's breathing calmed, and her muscles relaxed. Unwelcome feelings of doubt began to niggle at her mind. What on earth would William say when she was discovered? It was an understatement of immense proportions to assume that he would merely be angry with her. Would he turn the ship around and return her to London? Amelia had assured her that if she managed to remain hidden until the morning, the voyage would be too far underway to turn back.

A bell sounded, and footsteps pounded on the deck above. With a lurch, the motion of the ship changed, and she knew they had left port. The sacks of grain were quite comfortable, the belly of the ship dark, and the rocking motion soothing. Scooting down, she rested her head upon a bundle of clothing and allowed the pitching of the waves to lull her to sleep.

✳✳✳

Emma didn't know how much time had passed before she awoke, stretched, and turned to see a man's shocked face peering over a stack of barrels. She screamed and jumped up, knocking her head upon a low beam as her mind—still sluggish from sleep—tried to make sense of her surroundings.

"Cap'n Drake!" the man yelled, hobbling toward the companionway, leaning on a crutch to make up for a missing leg.

The realization of where she was—and the fact that William would be here any moment—crashed over her. Emma tried to stop the man. "Please, wait." She rubbed her head and climbed back over the small barricade of supplies that had hidden her. "Sir."

At that very moment, the ship lurched, and Emma lost her balance. She reached out, pulling down a few of the unsecured barrels as she tumbled to the ground. One of the lids separated from its container when it hit the deck, spilling rice across the boards. Emma stood and attempted to steady herself just as William, followed by a group of men, crowded down the companionway.

"What the blazes is going on here?" William roared, his gaze taking in the mess. "Who is responsible for—" His gaze met Emma's, and he froze, his eyes widening and his jaw going slack. "Emma?"

"In the larder she were, Cap'n." The man who had discovered her leaned on his crutch, pointing to the small space that Emma had crawled out of. "Near scared the wits out of me, sir."

"Emma?" William's gaze did not leave his sister.

She wrung her hands together, wishing she could disappear. Seeing her brother's anger directed at her was so much worse than she had imagined.

William's face regained its look of authority. He stood as tall as he could beneath the low ceilings. "Emma, follow me. The rest of you clean up this mess," he barked.

"Aye, aye, Captain." The sailors sprang into action, darting glances at Emma as she walked past them.

She followed William up the companionway to the room that served as both the captain's office and the officer's dining room. With each step, her heart sank further. William seemed much angrier than she had expected, and she began to fear her plan wouldn't work.

William closed the door through which they had entered then crossed the room, closing the door leading to the main deck. When he turned back around, his face was hard, and Emma found herself wanting to shrink beneath his gaze.

"Emma, what on earth are you thinking? You have cost us two days since we are now forced to turn around and return you to London. Why would you do this?"

"I came to help find Sidney and—"

"Find Sidney? What are you talking about? You're a girl, a child. How could you think that hiding aboard the ship would help anybody?" William's face was flushed, and he worked a muscle in his jaw.

Emma stood straight and lifted her chin, trying to project a confidence she did not feel. "I am sorry, William, but I knew it was the only way I would be able to accompany you to Spain." Seeing the question in his eyes, she continued, "I would like to assist in Sidney's rescue."

William knit his brow, studying her for a long moment. "I am trying to understand, but for the life of me . . . Why, Emma?"

She rubbed her forearms, looking at the ground. "Because I am in love with him," she whispered, unable to meet his eyes.

William began pacing. When Emma dared to look up, she saw that his face had turned red. "And how long has this been going on? Last Christmas? And under my very roof! That traitor. If the French have not flayed him, I shall—"

"William, nothing—what I mean to say is, Sidney knows none of this, and I do not know if . . . I do not know how he feels about me." Confessing such things to her brother was painful, but she knew that if she did not convince him that this was of utmost importance to her, he would turn the ship around.

He stopped pacing and burrowed his fingers through his hair. "And this is the reason you have accepted none of the offers of marriage that have come your way."

Emma nodded, feeling a hardness in the pit of her stomach.

William's hand moved to rub the back of his neck. He stared at a painting upon the wall, speaking quietly. "We are operating under the suspicion that he is still alive, but there is no way of knowing until we reach Spain. And if by some miracle, we do find him, Sidney will quite possibly never leave the sea. He has obligations to his family and the navy." William's eyes narrowed as he looked at Emma for a long moment. "Does he return your feelings? If he does, I shall . . ." He paced again and stopped, his eyes widening and his face becoming, if possible, more flushed. He spluttered the words. "If he does *not*, that unworthy piece of shark chum will regret—"

"William!" Emma cried, horrified at the idea of her brother forcing Sidney to declare his love for her. "No, William, please give me your word that you will say nothing of this to him."

"No, of course not." William sat, and for the first time, her brother looked lost. "I . . . am not handling this well. These types of things are outside my realm of expertise." He shook his head and stood, resuming his pacing and his authoritative tone. "But all this is beside the point. Spain is embroiled in the middle of a bloody war. It is not safe for anyone, least of all, a young woman. If Sidney *is* alive—and I cannot guarantee he is, Emma—" William's voice softened considerably, "I will return him to London as quickly as I am able."

Emma took her brother's hand in both of hers. "We cannot afford the delay. Two days may very well be the difference between life and death for Sidney. I will stay out of the way and help when I am able. I will not be a burden." She shifted her feet; her throat constricted as she tried to pour every ounce of feeling into her words, praying that he would understand. "Please, William. I must do this. I have never felt so strongly about anything. I must know once and for all if he is alive, and if there is a chance that . . ."

William was silent for a long moment. He stared at her hands clutching his own. Finally he cleared his throat. "Emma, I have lived with Sidney Fletcher for nearly my entire life—in very close quarters much of the time—and I will warn you he is annoyingly . . . cheerful. Constantly. But if you wish to torture yourself with that man's exasperating good humor, I'm afraid there is nothing else I might say to dissuade you from this course." His expression was resigned, but his eyes had a softness as he cocked his eyebrow ever so slightly. "Although I do question your taste in men."

Emma laughed and threw herself into her brother's arms, waves of relief flowing over her.

"But you must know this. Cádiz—and all of Spain, for that matter—is filled with soldiers. I will not allow you out of my sight for one instant."

"Thank you, William," she whispered and felt him brush a kiss upon her head.

Chapter 4

EMMA ATTEMPTED TO FIND THINGS to occupy her time aboard the ship. The crew avoided her—whether it was because of her brother or because she had stowed away, she wasn't sure. William had told her once that sailors considered it bad luck to have a woman aboard, and she thought that could account for the less than gracious behavior.

She perused the book cabinets in the ward room, disappointed to find the collection consisted only of naval books depicting ships, ensigns, maps, signals, and the Articles of War. She made a mental note to purchase some novels for her brother and the officers when she returned to London. Surely they tired of reading about ships.

She did not venture below into the cargo hold again, after her incident with the rice. And she avoided walking above decks since she had no parasol and did not want her skin to become too brown or her nose to develop freckles. She wanted to look her best when she saw Sidney. The majority of her time was spent in her cabin, turning the pages of dull books, airing out her gowns, and daydreaming. She took meals with the officers and looked forward to the time she spent with William.

During the few days they spent together aboard the ship, she glimpsed bits of what his life must have been in his years at sea. This voyage strengthened their relationship, providing a chance for them to spend time alone together, something that rarely happened. Emma did feel a slight twinge of guilt, however, when she thought of the displacement of some of the officers so that she would have a private cabin next to her brother's.

Emma was delighted to be included in a planning meeting one evening after supper, when William had decided that their course of action upon reaching Cádiz would be to appeal directly to Henry Wellesley, the ambassador. William reckoned Wellesley would provide their best chance of leaving the besieged city and gaining access to Matagorda, as he was likely the one responsible for negotiating prisoner exchange.

Less than a week after they'd set sail, Emma stood on the deck as they neared the port of Cádiz. The voyage had been surprisingly pleasant. It was a relief to focus on something aside from breakfast parties and gown fittings and balls, which typically took up her time. And it was possibly just a few hours until they would find Sidney.

Corporal Ashworth approached and leaned one hand on the gunwale, following her gaze to the Spanish shoreline. "We're nearly there, Lady Emma." He turned around, leaning his back against the rail, and indicated a group of officers who stood quietly on the deck. One man had removed his hat and held it over his breast. "I was not in the navy then, but the captain and some of the lieutenants are no doubt remembering the battle of Trafalgar. The conflict took place not distant from here, just a bit farther south, almost six years ago."

Emma looked back to the quarterdeck, where her brother stood near the helm, gazing at the sea. As usual, his face was unreadable. She wondered if he was indeed remembering the great battle: cannons booming, men fighting and dying.

Emma inhaled the warm sea air. She looked up at the friendly face of Corporal Ashworth. He had been welcoming and kind to her, unlike most of the sailors who had acted uneasy around her. She wondered what they thought about her sneaking aboard the ship. Emma had mulled over her astonishing course constantly on the voyage. Her actions went completely against every bit of ladylike conduct that had been ingrained in her since she was a child. But she did not feel any remorse about the deception or the gossip that was sure to follow once she returned. She only knew that nothing in her life had ever felt so absolutely correct.

The corporal regained her attention as he pointed to the coast. "The opening to the bay is guarded on the north by the French. I shouldn't wonder, my lady, if you would prefer to go below decks until we are safely past the harbor mouth. They will no doubt fire upon us."

Emma's heart jolted. She spread her hand upon her breastbone as if attempting to hold in her breath. "Are we in danger, Corporal?"

"Captain Drake knows to make for the south end of the harbor. But cannons firing upon the ship can be . . . upsetting. Come, I will accompany—"

His words were cut off by the sound of explosions, followed by the whistle of cannonballs. Emma's head whipped around, but the men aboard the ship continued about their duties, not even acknowledging the threat, except for the boy, Riley, who shook his fist and yelled something at the French that Emma was certain was not meant for a lady's ears.

As Corporal Ashworth had predicted, the shots did not reach them, splashing into the sea yards away, but Emma's hands still shook. Up until that moment, the threat of the war had seemed so distant. The idea of enemies and danger had sounded exciting, even romantic. But the flashes from the shore as the French army attempted, albeit halfheartedly, to sink their ship suddenly cast the journey in a different light. Emma began to feel a wary sort of anxiety that she was entering into a situation she wasn't prepared for.

Ahead of them was a walled city at the tip of a peninsula. Emma had read for months about the city of Cádiz. The French army had effectively cut the city off from the rest of Spain by setting up siege lines upon the narrow bit of land attaching Cádiz to the continent. It was an attempt to dispel the influence of the Spanish parliament—the Cortes—upon the rest of the country, which was in upheaval after Napoleon had removed King Fernando and crowned his own brother, Joseph. The continual supplies brought into the harbor by the English ensured that the city remained fortified and supplied with the necessities to ensure the residents' survival.

"You are a bit pale, my lady." The corporal recaptured her attention. "It won't be long now. Isla de León." He indicated a small island south of Cádiz. "That is where we shall go ashore."

William ordered the small boat to be lowered, and Corporal Ashworth helped Emma climb over the side and settle into the tottering vessel, situating herself among the crew of men.

As they rowed closer, Emma looked up at the tall stone walls of the city. Spires and domes shone against the clear sky. The water of the harbor was a deep blue with bright glints of light sparkling on the waves. It was beautiful and peaceful. She almost couldn't believe this land was even now plagued by war.

"Ya should have seen it, your ladyship," Lieutenant Fairchild said to Emma as they bounced over the waves. "After Trafalgar, the entire harbor here was filled with bodies washed in by the tide. Bobbing up and down in the surf, bumping into the walls like a—"

"That is quite enough," William said, cutting him off.

"Sorry, Cap'n." The lieutenant looked appropriately chagrined. "I thought the lady might be interested in a bit of history, it being her first time in Spain and all."

"It is all right, William. I do not mind hearing about the battles," Emma said, even as her stomach turned. She scooted away from the side of the boat, shivering, and refrained from looking into the water.

The small town of San Fernando upon the Isla de León was filled with British and Portuguese soldiers and mosquitoes. The men slept in tents but inundated the taverns and streets in their leisure time. William kept his sister close to his side as he led his group of marines through the town and across the sandy isthmus that joined the island with Cádiz. On her right, hundreds of white mounds shone in the sun, and upon questioning William, Emma learned that they were made of salt harvested from the sea.

Massive gates flanked by guards and fortified by bastions barred the south entrance of the walled city. Emma's eyes darted to the armaments above them, and she moved closer to her brother when the armed guards peered down at them.

One of the Spanish guards approached, and William spoke at length with him, explaining their mission and asking to speak with the ambassador. The guard conferred with his associates and eventually permitted them to enter Cádiz.

Four Spanish soldiers accompanied them through the winding, narrow streets. Emma craned her neck, looking up at the white stone buildings looming above them. Many of the roofs were either domed or flat with terraces atop them, reflecting the Moroccan influence in their design. They passed a cathedral which William told Emma was under construction. He explained that the canvas sheets covering the unfinished roof were actually sails from the Spanish Armada, which His Majesty's Navy had all but obliterated at Trafalgar.

The fact that the British were now Spain's closest allies attested to the destruction wrought by Napoleon's army in the past six years.

"It seems that war creates and destroys more alliances than gossip among the *ton*," Emma mused, glancing up at her brother.

"That assessment is extremely astute." William responded with a wry smile.

Upon reaching the embassy, William, Emma, and their company were shown into a courtyard surrounded by arches and columns interspersed with palms and greenery. Wrought iron chairs, tables, and benches clustered around a large fountain. An exotic mixture of flowers and spices perfumed the air.

Emma sat on a bench next to William. "It's difficult to believe that something as terrible as war can touch such a place," she said.

"I wish you could have seen this country before it became a battleground. It was perhaps one of the most picturesque settings in the world. But now, armies have trampled fields, burned villages and orchards. The people, once so hospitable, have become hardened and distrusting of outsiders." William spoke softly; his voice sounded heavy.

"It is heartbreaking," said Emma. The sound of the fountain, the low murmur of men's voices, and the cool breeze were beginning to take their toll upon her. She closed her eyes, just for a moment, and rested her head upon her brother's shoulder. They were so very close to finding out what had happened to Sidney. She imagined how delighted he would be to see her. In her mind, Sidney sat upon a dirt floor in a cold dungeon. William and his soldiers would storm into the prison, subduing the guards, but it would be Emma who found Sidney. And when he laid eyes upon her, he would fall weeping into her arms declaring that the memory of her face was the only thing that had sustained him through his incarceration. He would gently lower his lips to hers—

William stood, startling her out of her daydream.

Emma blinked and looked around, wondering if anyone noticed the color in her cheeks, but everyone's attention was on a man who had entered the courtyard. Though he was an Englishman, he wore a mustache in the Spanish style and, in the place of boots, buckled shoes.

"I apologize for keeping you waiting, Lord Lockwood." He inclined his head and shook William's hand.

"It was no wait at all," William responded. "Thank you for meeting with me, Your Excellency."

"There is no need to stand upon ceremony. My elder brother is the Duke of Wellington, but I am simply Henry Wellesley. I am delighted to meet you."

"May I present my sister, Lady Emma Drake, sir."

Emma dipped in a curtsey.

Henry took her hand. If he had any opinions about William bringing his sister into a besieged city during the middle of a war, he kept them to himself. "It is a pleasure, Lady Emma."

William introduced Lieutenants Wellard and Fairchild, Corporals Thorne and Ashworth, and Riley.

Henry Wellesley sent a servant for drinks and tapas, which turned out to be a variety of finger foods. Most were completely foreign to Emma, but she was pleased to find them all delicious. While they ate, Henry made arrangements for the company to remain at the embassy for the night, and servants were sent to the ship with the corporals to retrieve essentials. Emma was relieved. The idea of walking the entire distance back to the island and then taking a boat out to the ship was exhausting.

"Thank you for your hospitality, sir," William said, when they had finished eating.

"It is always a delight to receive visitors from home. You can imagine I do not have the opportunity often."

"I do not wish to impose more upon your time, so I will come to the purpose of our visit."

Henry nodded and leaned back in his chair, crossing one leg over the other and waving his hand as a signal for William to continue.

"Captain Sidney Fletcher of the HMS *Venture* was imprisoned at Fort Matagorda two months ago. Upon inquiry, the prison denied the existence of any prisoner by that name. We are unsure whether he has given an alias for a purpose unknown to us or if the French are denying his presence for another reason."

"And are you certain he was captured?"

"Yes, we have a witness. A trusted soldier who would not mistake the fact."

Emma saw Riley sit up a bit taller.

Henry Wellesley rubbed his chin. "Technically, I am the envoy to the court of Spain. My interaction with the French is limited, for obvious reasons." He stared at the fountain for a moment as he apparently contemplated the situation.

Emma began to feel sick. What if the ambassador was unwilling or unable to assist them? Did William have a contingency plan? "Please, sir. Is there anything you can do?" she asked.

Henry looked at her for a moment and finally spoke again. "I do believe, in this case, it would be entirely appropriate and within my rights to launch an investigation. I shall send an emissary tomorrow morning to the prison at Matagorda to inquire after Captain Fletcher."

"Thank you," Emma breathed.

William's shoulders relaxed, the relief upon his face obvious.

"However," the ambassador continued slowly, his eyes still on Emma. "I do not know if my emissary would be able to discover information about the captain if he is using an assumed name. Perhaps, it would be prudent to send someone with him who would recognize Captain Fletcher."

"Of course," William said. "I would not think to send your man alone. I shall join him."

"Naturally, you would be an excellent choice, my lord. However, I do not believe the French are likely to allow a man of your standing and military experience behind their siege lines. Especially with the British forces massing for an attack at any moment. You would be suspected as a spy." Henry looked at each of the men. "As would all of you. I believe that even you, Master Riley, would be considered a potential threat by our enemies."

Finally, the ambassador turned to Emma. "Lady Emma, however . . ."

"Out of the question." William shook his head.

"Her ladyship is the sister of a nobleman. Even the blasted French respect such a thing as rank. They can be trusted to act honorably toward a young gentlewoman, my lord. And I have had some dealings with the prison under its previous leader. He was quite reasonable when it came to prisoner exchange. My man would keep the young lady safe."

Emma's heart raced as feelings of fear and hope tumbled around in her chest. "I would be careful—"

"I will not even discuss it," William said.

"But if it is the only way . . ." Emma began, but a look from William quelled her words.

The ambassador nodded his head in acquiescence. He made arrangements for the group's meal to be served in the courtyard and excused himself, as he had a late supper with the Dons to prepare for.

Emma did not bring up Henry Wellesley's suggestion again. She knew William would not entertain the idea, and it would surely anger him to discuss it further. They ate and were shown to their chambers. She found the gown and slippers that had been fetched from the ship. It was one of her very loveliest dresses—Emma knew it showcased her figure and complexion perfectly. She had specifically brought it on the voyage and saved it to wear when she saw Sidney. Laying the dress over a chair, she gazed out her window at the garden and began wrapping her hair in curling papers.

Her emotions battled with each other. She balled her fists in frustration at the annoyance she felt of being so completely underestimated by her brother, and at the same time, her heart filled with love for him. He truly had her safety in mind.

She felt a pang of regret when she thought of how furious he would be in the morning when he discovered that she was gone.

Chapter 5

THE HEAVY METAL DOOR CREAKED and slammed shut, plunging the dank cell into darkness. Sidney breathed a sigh of relief as he lay upon the hard floor and then wished he had not when the pain shot through his side. He pressed his ribs gently with his fingers, attempting to determine the extent of his injuries. No bones broken. He touched his face. His lip was cracked, blood filled his mouth, and one eye was beginning to swell. He vaguely wondered whether it had been hit by the wall or his assailant's fist.

Finally pulling himself into a sitting position, he moved to lean against the damp wall, wincing as the back of his head bumped against the uneven stones. It was definitely not the worst beating he had received since his capture, and truth be told, Sidney preferred Lucien's fists to *le creux*, which was by far the warden's vilest method of torture. Sidney had spent two separate weeks in le creux: a pit too shallow and narrow to fully stand or extend his legs. The pit was sealed by a metal grate, leaving him exposed to the scorching sun and freezing rains, which flooded the small space. Each time, when he was finally released, it had taken days for his leg muscles to stop cramping and finally bear his weight. Although he knew his body could survive another week in the pit, he was nearly certain his mind could not.

He had tried, at the beginning of his incarceration, to document the time that passed, but the dark dungeon where he spent days without food or light had disoriented him so badly that he could only guess how long it had been since he had lost his freedom. Perhaps two months? No doubt everyone he cared about thought him dead.

He touched his fingers to his lip and winced at the stinging. He thought of the continued beatings and interrogations, hoping an opportunity to escape would present itself soon.

Sidney had been occasionally allowed out of his cell into the common area with the other prisoners and had formed an alliance with two other inmates. The three of them were plotting an escape. Sidney spent every opportunity studying the movements of the guards and the layout of the prison. His mind was constantly occupied with devising a way out. Being able to focus on that one task and finding ways to communicate with his partners gave him a sense of purpose and hope that he would not die in a French prison. The only thing keeping him from going mad was the knowledge that he had a job to do. He knew that he must keep his brain active, or he would lose the ability to control it.

And Sidney could not bear to lose his mind. His memories were his only companions—aside from the rats—during the long days. They were his alone, the one thing the guards and warden couldn't take from him.

He shifted his position on the hard floor, bending his legs and resting his arms upon his knees. He willed his mind to concentrate on anything that would keep it active. He mentally thought through the equations he'd used every day at sea to determine latitude and created scenarios to calculate a ship's speed. He thought of his shipmates, forcing himself to recite the name and rank of each officer, the ship's schedule, and every man's job.

He smiled as he remembered the time he had spent aboard the ship with Amelia. William had been his closest friend, and Amelia had quickly become equally so. He missed them terribly, especially William. The two men had grown up together at sea, closer than any brothers. William had been a natural leader, and Sidney trusted him implicitly. He'd had limited correspondence with his friends for the past year and a half. He thought they may have a child by now, and he spent some time contemplating whether it was a son or daughter, and even smiled at the thought of William chasing twins around the Manor House. His mind wandered to the memory of the Christmas they had spent together, of kind Lady Charlotte and adorable Emma. It was incredible to think that the charming little girl had grown up and been launched into society, and equally unimaginable to suppose that such a young woman as she had not been snatched up quickly by a man of some consequence, as she deserved.

It was with a familiar heaviness in his chest that Sidney thought of his friends marrying. He knew he never would. Sidney's eldest brother was the Viscount of Stansbury, a longstanding title that had been inherited with a longstanding debt. Sidney's two elder brothers and their families lived on the family land that Sidney had seen only a handful of times since he'd joined the navy. While he was fond of his family, none of them had a mind for business, and they spent more than the estate brought in each year. Sidney was the family's salvation. His income kept his relatives afloat and provided for their lifestyles. The honor of preserving his family name was something that he did not take lightly. He had accepted the fact that, for their sakes, he could never leave the sea and the living it provided.

Without warning, the door swung open, banging into the wall and echoing throughout the dark tunnels. Sidney jumped and squinted against the light of a lantern. Fighting to control his trembling, he kept his face impassive and his muscles relaxed. He would not give the warden the satisfaction of seeing his fear.

Sidney stretched one leg out on the floor slowly in an effort to look as casual as possible. "Monsieur Trenchard. My favorite warden. Might I assume that you are responsible for the lovely visit I had an hour ago?"

The warden narrowed his eyes and set the lantern upon the floor. Eerie shadows moved across his face. "Insolent Englishman," he said in the slurry French accent Sidney was so weary of. "I grow tired of your mocking. If Lucien was not forceful enough to convince you to talk, perhaps another week in le creux will."

Sidney forced his face into an easy smile which belied the jolt of terror the suggestion produced. "Monsieur, we are beginning to sound like an old married couple, arguing about the same thing over and over." He sighed loudly. "I will tell you once again that I am not keeping a secret from you. I have no notion of where one might find the lost treasure of de la Cruz. As I have explained numerous times—often under an uncomfortable amount of duress, I should add—I found the coin merely by accident. The greatest regret of my life is putting the blasted thing into my pocket. I should have thrown it as far away as possible, but I thought perhaps I could use it to buy a croissant. I do so love croissants, don't you?"

Lieutenant Trenchard took another step toward him, but Sidney held up his hand. "Please, allow me. Now you will raise your voice, demanding that I tell you the truth. Perhaps you will rant and threaten, telling me that nobody knows of my whereabouts, there is no hope of rescue, et cetera. You may deliver a few weak blows to my head or kicks to my ribs. Might I just say that I am particularly not fond of that aspect of your personality? After that, you will, no doubt, take the coin from your coat pocket and wave it in front of me while you scream and your face grows crimson with anger. The spittle that forms in the corners of your mouth is particularly unattract—"

The warden's slap came so fast that Sidney did not register the movement until his head hit the wall and light exploded in front of his eyes.

Sidney sucked in his breath and let it out slowly, stifling a moan as he allowed his mind to clear. "I did not realize you would be changing our regular routine," he said, acting as if the pain in his head was not making him nauseated. "If you had explained that earlier, I might have been able to skip ahead to my role of writhing in agony. We do need to coordinate our parts better."

A kick to the stomach knocked him onto his side, and he groaned aloud. "Now that's just bad manners."

The warden pulled back his foot to deliver another blow but stopped when they heard voices in the passageway outside the cell. He dragged Sidney to his feet, pushed him against the wall, and leaned his face close. "I will not be deceived forever. Every man can be broken. I will find a way to convince you to tell me the truth." He shoved Sidney once more, and Sidney wondered if there would ever be a time that his head did not throb.

"I would recommend speaking with your chef, Monsieur, concerning the amount of garlic in your diet," Sidney ground out, determined to maintain his belligerency to the last possible moment. "Perhaps chewing on a sprig of parsley after you dine . . ."

The warden ignored him and stepped into the passageway to investigate the voices, which were growing louder.

In all of Sidney's time at the prison, he had not seen another person in the underground dungeon beside the warden and an occasional thug sent to "assist his memory." Sidney could not make out the words, but he thought he heard a woman's voice among the deeper male ones. He was obviously mistaken, no doubt a result of the blow to his head. No one, not even the warden, would allow a woman into the dungeon.

The voices came closer, and Sidney listened as the warden argued with another guard. It was a woman's voice, and she was speaking English.

"I will see Captain Fletcher this moment."

Sidney's brain was fuzzy; he must be hallucinating. The guard continued to apologize to the warden, but the woman was determined.

Sidney searched his mind. Could someone have found him? Who?

He looked toward the opening as the flickering light grew brighter. The warden stepped back into the room and held the lantern aloft.

Immediately behind him appeared what Sidney could only describe as a vision. Her figure was silhouetted as she stepped past the lantern and cast her eyes about the small cell until they landed upon him. It must be his imagination. The woman looked remarkably familiar.

"I am afraid there has been a mistake," she said. "I asked to see—" She tilted her head and peered closer. Her eyes widened in shock. "Sidney?" She rushed to him but quickly took a step back. He assumed his stench was the cause of her quick retreat, but she had come close enough for him to get a better look.

It could not be her.

She hesitated only for a moment before stepping forward and laying a gloved hand upon his face. "Oh, Sidney. What have they done to you?"

Reaching up, he placed his hand over hers where it rested upon his cheek. Surely his mind deceived him. He had been thinking about William's family earlier, and now his imagination had conjured her. Was he finally going mad?

"Emma? How . . . ?" Finally his brain seemed to come back to life, and the rejuvenation was accompanied by an expansion in his chest. He had been found! Surely he would finally be free. He should have never doubted his friends. "Where is William?"

Emma reclaimed her hand. Her eyes shifted, not meeting his. "William is at Cádiz. Soldiers were not permitted behind the siege lines."

"He sent you alone? To an enemy prison in a combat zone?" The feeling of elation began to ebb. This did not sound like anything William would allow, even for his boyhood friend. "Lady Emma Drake, what are you doing here?"

"I have come to rescue you, of course." She lifted her chin. "And I am *not* alone. I traveled with an escort. He will arrange your ransom, and we shall leave as quickly as possible."

"Does William know where you are?"

She lowered her lashes. "By now he does."

Oh, Emma . . .

"Perhaps, mademoiselle, you would be more comfortable continuing this conversation above ground?" the warden said.

Sidney felt an unexplainable surge of anger when the man took her arm. It was quickly followed by the burst of panic that overcame him whenever he was left in the cold cell alone.

"*Merci*, Lieutenant Trenchard," Emma said.

"And Captain Fletcher, you will join us, *oui*?" The warden wore a shrewd expression that caused Sidney's heart to sink.

Lieutenant Trenchard carried the lantern and led the group through the tunnels and up the narrow staircase. The other guard followed closely behind Sidney, who was attempting to walk without feeling the jarring pain of each step in his head and ribs. In just a moment, the warden had unlocked the gate at the top of the staircase, and Sidney breathed in the fresh air and raised his face to the blue sky that he'd seen only rarely since his incarceration. Even though the bright sunlight caused a stabbing pain in his head, he would never take such things for granted as long as he lived. He looked to the tops of the garrison walls, where guards stood at their posts, keeping watch on the inmates as well as on activity outside the stronghold. Instinctively he assessed whether any changes had taken place, noting an increase in guards upon the battlements pointing at the fields outside the fort. They spoke more animatedly than they normally did. He wished he could see what was drawing their attention.

He glanced toward Emma. She stood quietly, her hands folded in front of her. She was studying his face, and he wondered what she saw. The poor lighting in the cell had likely hidden the worst of his injuries. But now she would be able to see that his clothes were filthy, his face was unshaven, and he was covered in an abysmal mixture of bruising and blood. It was a fair assumption that his appearance was just shy of horrifying. The complete reverse was true when he looked at her.

Little Emma had grown up. Her figure had filled out into that of a woman. Her blonde curls were freed from their braids and pinned to her head beneath a stylish bonnet, a few escaping to frame her face and neck. She stood straight and tall with an air of confidence that he had not seen in her before. It was quite becoming. Emma was the epitome of a British beauty: light coloring, large eyes, and a heart-shaped face with pink bow lips. Sidney found himself in awe as he wondered when the cute little girl had become so supremely beautiful.

He was jolted back into reality when he saw Lieutenant Trenchard's gaze moving back and forth between the two of them. The hairs on the back of Sidney's neck rose at the Frenchman's smirk.

Sidney stepped closer to Emma, angling himself to exclude the warden from their conversation. "Emma, you should not have come. This is not a place for you."

"Nonsense." Emma raised her chin. "My escort is an emissary from the ambassador at Cádiz. He awaits us at the gates."

She took a step to the side to face the warden. "Lieutenant, I must insist that Captain Fletcher accompany me back to Cádiz. His treatment has been absolutely abominable, and I shall report this abuse to His Excellency, Henry Wellesley, as well as to Lord Wellington. I am aware of the rules governing the treatment of an officer, and I insist that the *parole d'honneur* be granted based on the courtesy of Captain Fletcher's rank. And furthermore—"

"Emma. Stop," Sidney said, taking another step to obstruct her view of the warden. His jaw was clenched, and he struggled to keep his voice calm. "This is our enemy's domain. You do not have the advantage here." He took her arm, leaning closer. "Such talk is dangerous. You must return to William." A heaviness grew in Sidney's gut. Emma had no idea how serious this situation was.

Emma pulled her arm from his grasp. The expression on her face was determined. "I shall not leave without you."

Lieutenant Trenchard stepped around Sidney. "The mademoiselle is correct. She shall not leave, though I will do my best to ensure she is quite comfortable while she remains."

Emma gasped.

Hot anger shot through Sidney's chest, leaving him dizzy. He lunged at the warden, only to be seized by the guards. His own punishments had caused him a great deal of agony, but that was nothing compared to the anguish he felt at the idea that Emma would come to harm because of him. He strained and fought against the guards, but reinforcements arrived, and even the strength borne of panic could not free him from their restraints.

"How could I allow her to depart when I have finally been given the tool I have searched for? I do not think it will be difficult to extract information, Captain, when you would no doubt wish to keep the lady from harm." The warden's eyes bore into Sidney's. "Do not fear, *mon ami*, I shall remain ever the gentleman—until you give me reason not to." He lifted a curl that hung at Emma's neck.

Emma jerked away, her eyes wide with fear. "*Monsieur!*"

"Do not touch her," Sidney said through gritted teeth. He thrashed against the men holding his arms but was unable to break free. This man did not obey the rules of engagement. The warden was no gentleman. He acted on his own and was accountable to no one. The man's obsession with the treasure and his belief that Sidney was concealing it from him had obliterated any honorable actions. Sidney's fear of what the man might do—or allow others to do—to Emma caused him to see red. Digging deep, he clung to every bit of discipline drilled into him by the navy.

"*Oui*. I think she will be very effective, Captain."

Chapter 6

EMMA'S HEART POUNDED AND HER knees felt weak. This was impossible. This lieutenant would be sorry for treating her this way when she returned with William and the ambassador and Lord Wellington and possibly the entire British army.

"I must leave now, Monsieur Trenchard," she said, attempting to sound firm. "My escort is waiting."

The warden smiled rather as a shark might before he took a bite, and Emma cringed. He called to a guard and spoke rapidly in French to him, ordering him to fetch the señorita. The guard saluted, hurried down the stairs, and disappeared through a doorway.

Emma took the opportunity to move toward the entrance. She was determined to rejoin her escort and find a way to get Sidney out of this horrible place. However, she had taken no more than three steps before Lieutenant Trenchard stopped her. He gripped her arm so tightly that tears sprung to her eyes.

"Monsieur, you are hurting me," Emma said, stunned that the man would touch her in such a coarse manner. Her mouth went dry, her mind wavering between outrage and fear. She glanced once more toward where Sidney struggled to free himself. While she watched, one of the soldiers raised his musket and drove the butt into Sidney's stomach. He groaned and bent over. The guard followed with another blow to the back of the head.

Emma's mind raced. She must get Sidney away from this place. She was torn between running to him and running for help. She looked toward the entrance again, but her escort was nowhere in sight. Where there had been merely a few guards earlier, it seemed that every soldier in the garrison had begun to assemble at the gates. Some men distributed weapons, speaking excitedly. She heard the sounds of a commotion outside the fort—yelling and what she thought might be distant gunshots. Was her attempt to rescue Sidney the cause of all of this activity?

She was struggling to pull her arm from the warden's painful grasp when she heard a woman's voice.

"Captain Fletcher!" A young woman ran across the courtyard followed by the guard the warden had spoken to earlier. The woman wore traditional Spanish peasant clothing: A mantilla attached to her hair by a comb, and from it draped black lace which spread over her shoulders like a shawl. Her blouse was white cotton, her skirts full and colorful, and a red sash wrapped around her waist, accentuating her curvy figure.

The woman held on to Sidney's arm and helped him to stand upright. She placed her hands on his shoulders, leaning her face close to his. The two of them spoke quickly to each other in Spanish before the woman was pulled away by a guard. Based on the familiar way she touched him and how they had spoken together, the woman and Sidney had a relationship that went beyond mere acquaintances. The thought shot a pang through Emma's heart.

The warden stepped closer. "Señorita, I have a companion for you. Please show her to your quarters."

Numbness spread from Emma's chest to her fingers. Her throat began to close, and she was having difficulty breathing. She did not want to follow this señorita anywhere. Her mind tumbled as she tried to grasp any sort of plan, but she came up with nothing.

The woman looked at Emma then back at Sidney. Cocking an eyebrow, she nodded and motioned for Emma to follow.

"No!" Emma yelled, trying to make her voice sound as if she were not on the verge of tears. "I will not remain here any longer. I—"

A pain erupted in her head, and Sidney yelled something that she did not understand. For a moment, Emma didn't know what had happened. She spied her bonnet a foot away and realized that the warden had slapped her with enough force to knock it to the ground. She pressed her hands to her cheek, biting back tears and fighting the image of her father striking her mother in precisely the same manner. She picked up her bonnet, staring at it, wondering why her mind would not work properly.

The Spanish woman tugged on her arm urgently, pulling her toward the passageway on the other side of the courtyard.

Sidney! Emma turned back toward him. She didn't even attempt to contain her tears now.

He continued to struggle with the guards who were pulling him back to the underground tunnels. "Emma," he called. "You can trust Serena."

She looked at the woman next to her. She was beautiful, and Sidney had called her by her Christian name. Emma's tears flowed freely now. "Serena?"

"*Sí.*" Serena glanced back at the warden and, taking Emma's hand, began to lead her quickly toward the stairs. "Come. *Que estará bien.* You will be all right."

The warden followed. His expression twisted into a cruel sneer, no longer hiding behind a mask of civility.

Emma felt cold—and foolish. Had she truly thought she would be able to carry out such a thing? It had seemed so simple when she'd envisioned the amazing rescue and triumphant return to Cádiz. William would have been so proud. Sidney would have been so grateful. She was a fool, imagining he would have dropped to one knee and proposed as soon as they reached British soil. She had never dreamed the French would not follow the rules of polite society, but the bruises and cuts on Sidney's face and the blow from Lieutenant Trenchard confirmed the reality—she had underestimated the true severity of the situation. The fear intensified at the thought that she may have placed Sidney in even more danger.

As Serena continued to pull Emma away from the courtyard, Emma fully grasped that she had made a botch of her rescue attempt, recklessly inserting herself into a situation where she had become a liability instead of an asset.

Sidney had said to trust Serena. Emma glanced toward her, studying her profile. If she had to guess, she would assume the young woman was close to her own age, perhaps a bit older. Beneath the black lace of her mantilla, thick, curling dark hair poured over her shoulders and surrounded a high cheek-boned face. Her features were bold and exotic: plump lips, long lashes, brown doe-eyes, and ivory skin. Next to her, Emma felt plain and dull.

Emma followed Serena, walking quickly down the dark passageway. She could hear the footsteps of the lieutenant behind her and hurried her pace. Serena tightened her hold, giving Emma a little tug when she stumbled over the rough stones.

Soldiers hurried past them, calling to each other in French, and Emma felt the tension in the air. Was this regular procedure in the fort? Or was something amiss?

Serena stopped in front of a heavy wooden door, pulling Emma to the side while the warden took a large key ring out of his pocket.

Emma attempted to replace her bonnet, but the warden's blow had torn the ribbons, rendering it impossible to attach. She pulled her silk shawl closer around her shoulders, feeling even more vulnerable with her head bare.

Without warning, the explosions of gunfire sounded from outside the fort. Even muffled as it was in the passageway, it was deafening. Emma covered her ears.

Serena's gaze darted around. Her eyes were shrewd and intelligent.

"The prison is under attack. This is our chance for escape," Serena whispered. She looked pointedly at Emma, motioning toward the keys.

Emma squinted her eyes and shook her head, not understanding.

The warden opened the door, and the sounds of gunfire and men yelling hit Emma like a wave. The room's small window high up on the wall was the source of the noise. Lieutenant Trenchard hurried between a bed and a small table to peer out the window.

Serena touched Emma's hand, motioning again toward the ring of keys that hung forgotten in the door. *She wants me to get the keys!* Emma's heart clenched in terror, but with her hands shaking and her pulse pounding in her ears, she turned her back to the room and attempted to extract the key from the lock as silently as she could.

A crash startled her, and she jumped away from the door, ducking from the blow the warden was sure to deliver. But when she turned, Emma screamed and quickly clapped her hand over her mouth. The lieutenant was lying upon the floor, bits of pottery around him. Serena knelt next to him, pulling off his uniform jacket.

Emma could not move for the space of a breath. She stood, shocked, one hand gripping the key ring and the other pressed to her mouth.

Serena looked at her, raising her eyebrows and tilting her head in an expression that could only be described as irritation. "*Ayúdame.* Help me. For Captain Fletcher." Then she went back to wrenching the unconscious man's arm from his coat sleeve.

Emma finally regained her wits and closed the door. She stepped closer and, with her fingertips, gripped the cuff of the sleeve while Serena reached inside the jacket and pulled the warden's arm, finally managing to bend his elbow. Emma shook the jacket, and the arm fell out, hitting the ground with a slap. She hurriedly pulled on the other sleeve, and once the jacket was free, Serena tore a long strip from a bed sheet, indicating for Emma to help her bind the man's hands and feet. Emma gingerly pulled at the strips, not wanting to touch Lieutenant Trenchard's wrists and certainly not his ankles. She might be trapped in a dirty prison, but she was still a lady.

Serena gave her another look of exasperation, blowing out her breath and flipping her hair out of her face.

The sounds of battle continued outside the fort, and soldiers ran down the passageway sporadically. Emma tried not to think about what would happen when someone discovered what they had done.

Serena took the keys, handed Emma the warden's jacket and hat, then carefully opened the door and peered outside.

Emma rolled the jacket into a bundle and nervously watched Lieutenant Trenchard for any signs that he might awaken.

Finally, Serena darted out of the door, pulling Emma behind her. She turned the key in the lock and, without releasing Emma's hand, walked quickly down the passageway.

When they emerged into the courtyard, chaos surrounded them. Soldiers fired weapons from the battlements above while more men ran to the gates with muskets or led horses from the stables near the main entrance. A few groups operated cannons, and Emma nearly collapsed in terror when the massive weapons fired.

Serena continued to pull her through the smoke and confusion toward the archway that led to the below-ground dungeon she'd been taken to when she'd first arrived.

Emma's mind began to clear, and she focused on the task that had brought her to this terrible place: rescuing Sidney.

Once they reached the gate, Serena shoved a key into the lock, wiggling, twisting, and finally pulling it out and trying another.

Emma looked around, hoping they were not attracting any attention, but the fighting caused enough of a distraction that nobody seemed to notice the two women.

The gate finally opened on squeaking hinges. Emma grabbed the lantern and the tinderbox next to it before following Serena through the opening.

Serena closed and locked the gate while Emma set about lighting the lantern. She had only ever seen servants and men use a tinderbox, but she didn't think it could be too difficult. Holding the u-shaped steel over the box, she struck it repeatedly with the flint. Nothing happened.

Serena joined her, and they moved away from the gate into the semi-darkness of the stairwell.

Emma continued to strike the steel and was eventually rewarded with a spark or two, but she was unable to direct them into the chamber to ignite the tinder. Frustrated, she handed the tinderbox to Serena, whose efforts were equally unproductive.

The women looked at each other for a moment.

Serena glanced behind them at the dark stairway. She pressed her lips together, "I have not been in the dungeon. You can find Captain Fletcher in the dark?"

Emma nodded then shook her head. "I do not know."

Serena's eyes held Emma's, her brows were knit together anxiously, but after a moment, her expression softened. She smiled encouragingly and took Emma's hand again, but this time, it felt like a gesture of support rather than exasperation.

Emma led the way down the steep staircase, deeper into the darkness. Before long, she moved the bundle of the warden's jacket into the crook of the arm that held Serena's hand and began feeling her way, with her fingers upon the rough wall. Once they reached the pitch dark of the passageway, Emma walked blindly, testing the space before her with sliding feet. She wished she had remembered the passage more clearly, but the way had been shadowed and she'd been so anxious to find Sidney and bask in his gratitude for her rescue that she had not paid close attention to the number of doors they'd passed. Both girls jumped when something scurried across their feet, and Serena pressed closer to her.

"I think it is just a bit farther. I do not remember which door," Emma whispered.

"We must hurry." Serena's voice shook slightly, betraying her anxiety.

Emma didn't know what would happen if they were caught. The very idea of facing the lieutenant again made her chest feel tight. She ran her hand along the damp stone wall and stopped when she reached an outcropping that she thought must be a doorframe. Moving her fingers a bit farther, she touched a wooden board.

What if it was the wrong door? She had no idea what sort of things were hidden in the dungeon. And though she assumed it held only prisoners of war, the thought that she might accidentally release a Turk or Ashanti warrior or, even worse, a savage American into the dark hall with them terrified her.

Emma debated whether or not to try to open the door. She gripped Serena's hand tightly for courage and ran her fingers over the rough wood, searching for the handle. She took a steadying breath and pressed her ear against the boards.

Chapter 7

SIDNEY PACED THE EDGES OF his dark cell. He had checked every stone and searched the corners for something, anything he could use to escape. He knew his endeavor was fruitless, having done it hundreds of times before, but he had to busy himself with something. He had thought there was no way his situation could have become any worse. His own incarceration and torture was one thing, but he didn't know what he would do if something were to happen to Emma.

His breath hitched as he remembered Emma's expression when the warden struck her. He felt an overwhelming need to protect her. It must be a brotherly feeling, he reasoned. William had spoken rarely about his father, but from the few things he had said, Sidney knew that the old earl had been cruel and abusive to his wife and children. Because of that, Sidney had been careful never to raise his voice around Emma or do anything that might cause her to feel threatened.

How would he ever face William if anything should happen to her? If only Emma hadn't thought that a French prison in the middle of a battle zone operated with the same rules of politeness as a London drawing room.

Again he mentally kicked himself for picking up that blasted coin. And what kind of pitiful officer allows himself to be captured? Balling his hands into fists, he pounded on the door and finally rested his forehead against the thick wood. Only then did he register the pain from where his hands had made contact.

A soft tapping sounded upon the door. He was either imagining it, or the warden had returned to taunt him. He had resolved to ignore it, though it would do no good, when he thought he heard his name spoken through the heavy planks.

Emma. A quiver of dread moved through him and settled heavily in his gut. Had the warden brought her down already to force information from him? Information that he could not provide. He gritted his teeth. He had no weapon, but he would not allow Emma to come to harm.

"Sidney? Are you in there?" Even muffled by the thick door, he heard the fear in her voice and hastened to try and dispel it.

"I am here, Emma. It will be all right."

A key turned in the lock, and Sidney tensed his muscles, preparing to spring at the warden.

The door squeaked open slowly, but there was no lantern light. What was Lieutenant Trenchard playing at? He heard footsteps and the rustle of skirts.

Sidney's senses were heightened almost to the point of pain. He strained to locate the warden in the pitch darkness. "Emma. Do not be afraid," he said as steadily as he was able.

"Where are you?" she said.

Sidney reached toward the sound of her voice. "I am here."

"We must hurry." Emma's voice drew nearer to him.

Sidney found her in the darkness and pulled her behind him, stepping between her and the door.

"We could not light the lantern," Emma said. "Here is Lieutenant Trenchard's coat. There is a battle happening outside." Sidney felt something soft pressed against his arm, and when he took it, his fingers brushed Emma's gloved hand. He clasped her fingers and noticed that she was trembling.

Sidney's mind began to churn as he attempted to understand Emma's hurried words. "Where is the warden? Are you harmed? Are you alone?" He attempted to speak calmly through his confusion.

"Serena . . . hit him. On the head, and then we bound his hands and feet. I do not know how long it will be until he wakes up."

"Where is Serena?" Sidney asked.

"I am here," Serena answered.

"And Jim?" He turned blindly toward her voice.

"I believe he is in his cell. We must release him. And we must hurry. You can light the lantern?"

Sidney felt something pressed against his chest. He released Emma's hand and took what he recognized to be a tinderbox. "Is there tinder in here?"

"Bits of cloth," Emma said. "But it is difficult to . . ." her words trailed off as Sidney struck the flint and shook a shower of sparks into the chamber. He blew softly until a small flame grew, and he hurriedly lit the lantern.

"Much better," he said once he could see the women. He was, at the same time, overjoyed at this chance of escape and terrified as the full magnitude of the situation settled upon him. Emma and Serena had both risked their lives for him and placed their own into his hands. He could not allow anyone to hurt them, and recapture was not an option. He set the lantern upon the floor then quickly slid his arms into the warden's jacket and placed the bicorn hat upon his head to complete the disguise. The French uniforms with their silly tri-colored rosettes and plumes were utterly ridiculous.

He picked up the lantern and looked between the two women. He could see the fear in their eyes and spoke lightly, hoping to set them at ease. "Well, one could certainly not ask for lovelier rescuers, although in the future when I describe our gallant escape, my ego may demand that I embellish my role somewhat."

His own naval jacket lay carefully folded in a corner of his cell. He snatched it, handed it to Emma, pocketed the tinderbox, and led the women out into the passageway.

They followed the tunnel as it wound back toward the stairs, and Sidney commented, "I cannot believe you navigated your way in the dark."

"It was Emma who found you," Serena said, and Sidney felt a glow of pride, as an elder brother naturally would, he told himself.

Once they reached the staircase, Serena handed him the keys, and he quickly opened the gate, following Serena's instructions to Jim's cell. He knew he would never be able to navigate the Spanish countryside without Jim's help.

In the French uniform, Sidney was able to move through the fort unnoticed. Although he kept his eyes straight ahead, Sidney scanned the courtyard for any threat. He was conscious of each man that passed and how he would defend himself and Emma and Serena if they were stopped. When they turned a corner, he glanced at his companions. Serena's face was tight with worry, but Emma looked terrified. Her gloved hands clenched the jacket she held pressed against her chest, and her eyes darted nervously around.

He smiled and lifted his brows, hoping he looked encouraging.

Sidney leaned back around the corner and surveyed the courtyard behind them. He tried not to allow his surprise to show as he observed the soldiers running and yelling throughout the fort. The British army would never allow its troops to behave in such a way. Discipline was key. Each man knew his duty and moved to his position in an orderly fashion. Even though Sidney was an enemy wearing a poorly fitting uniform jacket and leading two women through the stronghold, none of the French soldiers spared him a glance, making him grateful for the shoddy French training.

When they found Jim's cell, Sidney glanced through the barred window in the door as he turned the key in the lock. Jim sat on his cot and raised his head when the door opened. If the man felt any surprise at seeing Sidney dressed in a French uniform, accompanied by two ladies, he did not show it. The fact that he simply stood, put on his red regimental jacket, and followed Sidney into the courtyard attested to his faith in their partnership. Sidney hoped he would not let his friend down.

Sidney looked around the fort, determining quickly that the stables seemed to be quiet. The group crossed the courtyard and slipped inside the stable door, crouching behind a low stone wall that sectioned off the individual stalls. He moved Emma to the innermost corner, where he hoped she would be safest, as she was the smallest and weakest of the party, not to mention the least experienced. Sidney removed his hat, certain that the colorful plume would show above the wall and give away their position.

Serena moved closer to Jim, and he gave her a small nod and a pat on the arm. It was the closest Sidney had come to seeing the man show any emotion in the time that they'd known one another. "Colonel Jim Stackhouse, Lady Emma Drake," Sidney whispered, motioning between the two by way of introduction. They nodded at each other. Jim studied her for a moment, and Emma looked decidedly uneasy at the severe expression she received from the colonel.

Sidney had come to trust Jim through their months of planning and interaction, but seeing him through Emma's eyes, he realized that the man was quite intimidating. Jim looked to be in his late forties. His skin was weathered from a lifetime of army campaigning. Lines stretched from his eyes and formed parentheses around his lips. His expression, to those who did not know him could be interpreted as cruel. Sidney could not imagine what a smile would look like on Jim Stackhouse's face. It would be positively bizarre, he decided. But Jim was nothing if not steady and honorable, which is why he had been entrusted with Serena's care in the first place.

Sidney and Jim slowly rose and peered over the wall before ducking back down and squatting in the hay-strewn dirt.

"How would you recommend we proceed?" Jim asked. "We'll not be able to follow our original plan."

"I think a diversion is the thing. I'll distract the soldiers at the gate," Sidney responded. He turned to Emma and Serena. "Stay with Jim." He took Emma's hand as he spoke, hoping he sounded confident enough that she would not be afraid. "No matter what happens. Can you do that?"

Both women nodded.

"Rendezvous in the grove west of here and over the hill. You know it, Jim?"

"Aye," Jim said. The steadiness in his bearing showed none of the nervousness that Sidney felt. He attributed it to the colonel's years of discipline in the British army.

Sidney was suddenly aware that he still held Emma's hand, and he was surprised at how natural it had seemed to grasp it in the first place. How it comforted him to feel her near.

"Jim, wait fifteen minutes, then take the women to Tarifa with or without me and find a British ship. Any will bring you to Cádiz where—"

Emma jerked his hand, cutting off his words. "What do you mean, *without* you?"

"Emma, we're escaping into a battlefield. There is no guarantee that any of us will survive."

The color drained from Emma's face, and her eyes darted between her three companions. Sidney wished he had not frightened her, but she needed to know the truth. The chances of escape from the fort were slim, and making one's way through a battlefield . . . treacherous.

"But I came here for you. I cannot leave without you." Emma's chin began to quiver.

"Emma, I will join you as soon as I am able. Please trust me."

Her gaze moved to Jim and Serena and then back to his. She nodded her head reluctantly.

Becoming sentimental would only impede his decision making, so Sidney forced his mind away from Emma's wide eyes. He began emptying the pockets of the warden's coat and slipping the contents into his own, hoping there might be something useful since they had no other supplies. He needed to remove the foul-smelling French jacket as soon as possible. He would be a target for the British sharpshooters and rifles if he were to run through the gates of the fort in an enemy uniform. He would rather try his luck with the poor aim of the French muskets. He handed his jacket back to Emma.

"Jim is your best chance. Trust him."

"Colonel Stackhouse, he will protect us," Serena said, taking Emma's hand from Sidney's and putting an arm around Emma's shoulders. Emma clutched Sidney's jacket to her chest.

Sidney gave his companions one last glance before making his way across the stable, stooping behind a two-wheeled cart filled with straw. With the help of the tinderbox, it took only a moment to start a blaze and shove the cart out through the stable door toward the other side of the courtyard. By the time it reached the armory and smashed into the entrance, huge flames completely engulfed the cart, threatening the store of weapons and gunpowder. The duty of guarding the main gate was forgotten as the guards panicked and ran about attempting to put out the fire.

From the corner of his eye, Sidney saw Jim lead the two women through the chaos, slipping past the guards and out of the fort. He nearly sagged in relief. But the sensation did not last long. It was quickly replaced by tension as he began to calculate how he would get himself through the entrance.

Still wearing the warden's jacket and hat, Sidney strode toward the gate, taking note of his surroundings and the movements of the soldiers as they scurried back and forth pouring water upon the blaze. His heart was pounding in his ears, but he moved purposefully, as if he had every right to be there.

The guards had reorganized themselves and stood in front of the entrance, though their attention was still on the attempts to extinguish the fire and not the battle taking place outside the walls. Sidney stood near them for a moment, feigning interest in the proceedings. He casually turned toward the gates, pushing calmly against the one that was still partially ajar.

When it had moved enough to allow him to pass through, Sidney turned sideways and began to slip into the crack. The tight space pressed upon his ribs causing a burst of pain through his side. He heard a yell behind him and recognized the voice of the warden. Resisting the urge to turn back, Sidney thrust himself through the opening, shedding the jacket and hat as he ran, hoping his filthy clothing would still identify him as a British officer.

He ran steadily through the battle, dodging bayonet points and sword skirmishes. The field was littered with the dead and dying. Smoke hung heavy. Blood turned the hard dirt into mud and made the ground slippery. Sidney stumbled and nearly fell. He was completely defenseless and began to look around for a weapon. Veering slightly off course, he pulled a sword from a fallen soldier, strapping the sheath onto his belt as he ran.

Sidney blocked everything out: his own pain, the gunfire, the war cries, the moans and screams of men and horses. He remembered the sights and sounds as clearly as if it had only been yesterday that he had fought upon this same battlefield. The sick feeling created by the memory of his capture months before hung over him, but he pushed it away. He concentrated his entire energy upon the hill and the grove of trees beyond, searching for any sight of his companions.

At last he saw them. They were nearly halfway up the slope. His chest tightened painfully. Emma and Serena were attempting to lift a seemingly unconscious Jim. When Sidney caught up to them, he saw that both women's eyes were wide with alarm. Jim's face was covered in the blood that flowed from a gaping wound in his forehead. Sidney tried not to show his panic, but he knew that getting himself and the women to safety without Jim's help was nearly impossible.

Chapter 8

EMMA'S HEART MELTED WITH RELIEF when Sidney joined them, whole and unhurt. She and Serena had begun to panic when they found that they could not budge an unconscious Jim, let alone carry him to the top of the hill.

Sidney lifted Jim over his shoulder, staggering a bit. He looked back at Emma and Serena, yelled for them to follow, then ran to the top of the hill. Emma clutched Sidney's jacket tighter beneath her arm, lifted her skirts, and forced her tired legs to move. A soldier was struck by the sword of a passing horseman a few yards away, and he turned, lurching toward her. Blood sprayed from his neck, landing in droplets across the bodice of her dress.

Emma staggered backward, tripping over the broken body of another man. Nearby, a dying horse writhed and thrashed on the ground. Pushing her hands to her ears to block out the shrieks and blasts around her, Emma clenched her eyes shut. She didn't realize she was screaming until Serena gripped her shoulder and shook her until her teeth rattled.

"Stop, Emma. Stop!" Serena jerked her to her feet. "You must follow me. If we remain here, we will die!"

Clutching hands, the women ran up the hill together. They reached the crest, emerging from the heavy smoke. Without pausing, Serena led Emma to a wooded area. Once they were in the cover of the grove, they walked slowly, allowing their eyes to adjust to the shade and their breathing to calm. Sidney called from a cluster of trees, and they pressed through clumps of undergrowth to join him. The clearing where Jim lay was fairly well concealed, but there was no escape from the crashes and screams of the battle.

Sidney knelt over him, pushing aside his hair to assess the damage. "Are either of you hurt?" he asked when the women joined him. His gaze moved over them to assess for injuries. "What happened?"

"A horse fell in front of us, and Jim pulled us out of the way," Serena explained. "He was hit by a musket ball."

Guilt squirmed in Emma's chest as she realized that Serena deliberately left out the fact that Jim had been struck as he had stopped to assist her when she had lost her balance. Her stomach lurched as she remembered the sight of him holding his head and collapsing while blood dripped between his fingers.

Serena moved to kneel on Jim's other side, helping to remove his jacket to cushion his head.

Emma turned away. She sat on a log, certain that it would catch and snag her fine muslin skirt but knowing that her legs would no longer hold her. How had the simple task of finding Sidney become such a nightmare?

Behind her, Sidney and Serena murmured together, but Emma did not even attempt to listen. Her heartbeat continued to pound in her ears, and she grasped Sidney's coat, shutting her eyes tight in an attempt to block out the images from the battle that continued to fill her mind.

"Emma."

She opened her eyes. Sidney was crouching in front of her. He put his hands on her arms.

"Serena and I must find help. Can you remain with Jim?"

Alarm rose inside her as Emma glanced toward the man lying upon the ground. Serena held a bunched cloth against the wound in his head.

"Must you both go?" Emma attempted to speak through her constricting throat.

"Yes. He needs a surgeon, and there is no telling who we will meet. If he is Spanish, he will respond better to Serena, and a British surgeon will listen to me. The two of us will attract much less attention than a young Englishwoman in a lace-trimmed walking dress. You will be safest here."

Emma looked toward Jim. Blood had painted a thick trail down the side of his face. The sight of it caused her head to swim. She shut her eyes again. How could she possibly remain here alone with him?

"Please, Emma. Jim needs you." Sidney squeezed her shoulders, offering a smile. He gently pried her fingers from his jacket and then slipped his arms into the sleeves.

Emma inhaled and nodded. She moved to sit next to Jim, removing her gloves and tentatively pressing her hand on the cloth bundle where Serena indicated.

When Sidney and Serena had gone, Emma cast her mind about, searching for anything to take her thoughts away from the battle and the bloody man next to her. She began to notice the pain in her feet. The lace-lined kid slippers with satin ribbons that she'd chosen to complement her gown were made for indoor or fine-weather walking. She sighed as she lifted a limp ribbon and ran her finger over a mud-covered tear. Surely the cobbler did not intend his creations to be used so roughly.

Emma lifted the rags to peek at the wound upon Jim's head and immediately wished she had not. It was quite deep, his skin peeling back from a gash directly above his forehead, and she saw the white of bone within. Her head swam, and she quickly replaced the makeshift bandage. As she did, she realized the cloth must have been torn from Serena's petticoat. The Spanish women wore layer upon layer beneath their skirts. Emma was grateful she did not have to tear her petticoats. She didn't have many to spare.

In an effort to distract herself, Emma assured herself that the worst was now over and imagined how the day would end. She thought how wonderful it would be in a few hours when they returned to Cádiz, and she was able to change into a fresh gown and clean slippers. If they found a carriage to take them on the same road, they would be at the ambassador's home in time for supper. William's anger would soon be forgotten when they returned. Emma thought about sitting in the lovely courtyard, watching the fountain with Serena while Sidney and William talked and laughed as they used to. She wondered if Sidney had ever eaten tapas.

The sound of Jim's moan jolted her from her daydream. She tensed, pondering what she should say to him.

He stirred and shifted his weight as if to sit up. "What the devil happened?" he said in a raspy voice. His eyes opened and rolled back into his head before closing again.

Emma stifled a gasp at the man's vulgar language. "You have been wounded, Colonel Stackhouse. Do not attempt to rise. Captain Fletcher and Serena have gone to retrieve a surgeon."

"And they've left the screaming debutante warrior to guard me, eh? Splendid."

Emma was unsure whether to take offense at the man's words. Undoubtedly his pain caused him to lose any good humor he might have possessed. Perhaps he was not even aware of what he was saying. She resolved to forgive his rudeness. "Yes, sir. Is there anything I can do to make you more comfortable?"

"Water," the colonel said.

Emma looked around the little clearing. The noises of the battle, though muted slightly by the trees, still crashed through the air. The fighting was not far enough distant that she dared leave the grove.

"I am not certain I shall be able to find water, sir. Perhaps if we wait until—"

"Water," he croaked, more loudly attempting again to rise.

"You must remain still, Colonel."

"If you did not intend to help after all, next time it would be best not to offer."

Emma did not know what to do. Certainly he would only injure himself further should he move about. "Captain Fletcher and Serena will return soon. Perhaps they will bring some water."

"My lady, I'm sure you do not know the first thing about battlefield medical procedures. But allow me to enlighten you." He spoke slowly in the same raspy voice. "With a wound such as this and the amount of blood I am losing, I will not survive without water, so it is not as if I am simply asking you to enter the battleground and fetch me a refreshing beverage. If I don't get water soon, I will die."

Emma's heart rose into her throat. Sidney and Serena were at this moment risking their lives for this man; she could not allow him to die when they had trusted her with his care. She swallowed and nodded, even though the colonel's eyes were shut.

Emma placed her palm upon his chest. "I will find water, sir. But you must remain here, and do not move your head."

She searched quickly for something to hold the bandage in place and finally lifted Jim's hand, showing him where to press to slow the bleeding.

Emma stood and brushed at her dress nervously, then she scurried around the edge of the clearing, making sure to remain in the shadows. Pushing aside the thick bushes that caught on the train of her gown, she stepped into the trees, wondering which direction she should go. Back toward the battlefield? She discounted the idea immediately. It would be far safer to remain in the cover of the trees. Her body began to tremble as she worried that she might encounter another skirmish or meet a band of renegades or any number of other dangers that might befall her.

Emma walked around a large tree, her ears strained for any sound of a stream or peril. She was an earl's sheltered daughter and had no idea where to find water in a forest. And if she did find it, how would she bring it back to Jim? She made certain to remember her path, to ensure she could find her way back to the clearing.

She had only walked a bit farther when she heard a noise. Creeping toward it, she came upon a soldier in British regimentals. Relief swept over her. Here was someone who could help her. He sat against a log with his back to her.

Emma swallowed her nervousness at finding herself alone with a stranger.

"Pardon me, sir. I wondered if you might have some water for my companion . . ." Her voice trailed off as she rounded the log and saw that the soldier was not merely relaxing but had obviously dragged himself to this spot. His jacket was open; his shirt shredded and crimson with blood. A tangle of inner workings spilled out of a wound on his torso, despite his attempt to hold them in with his hand. A pool of blood grew on the ground beneath him. Her stomach threatened to lose its contents, and Emma clamped her hand over her mouth.

Inside her mind, a battle raged between the urge to flee and the possibility that she might be able to assist him. Emma's legs began to tremble; her mind swam. She remained frozen in place until the man opened his eyes and reached his hand toward her.

Without a thought Emma turned and ran blindly through the trees. Any plans of remembering her direction flew from her mind. She pushed through thick branches that caught at her clothing and tangled in her hair. Attempting to climb over a fallen log, she tripped, landing upon her hands and knees and surprising a group of men who all rose to their feet when they saw her. They had been crouched around a soldier who lay upon the ground. They themselves were not soldiers, and Emma was instantly wary.

She scrambled to her feet, her pulse racing.

A man wearing a bandana around his neck took a step toward her, and Emma shrunk back. Her knees felt weak. The log was behind her and the men before her. She was trapped.

She looked at the man on the ground. He lay dead with his mouth open. Next to him was a piece of cloth with a pile of jagged red and white rocks on it. Whatever were they doing?

The man with the bandana took another step toward her, and Emma glanced at his hand. He held some sort of a tool, and Emma tried sort through her muddled mind to remember where she had seen such an instrument before, but it seemed as if her brain had ceased to function.

"Señorita," he said, his gaze darting to the men behind him before he stepped even closer. One man grabbed the cloth with the pile of rocks, and the other moved to stand in front of the body.

Emma's heart jolted. She recognized the instrument he held as one she'd seen carried by a dentist, and she instantly knew what had been happening. Those had not been rocks. The men were stealing the dead soldier's teeth!

The man reached for her, grabbing her wrist.

Emma screamed.

He was startled but pulled her closer speaking rapidly in Spanish; whether he was talking to her or the men, Emma was not sure.

She hit his chest with her fist and continued to scream.

The man put his hand over her mouth but just as quickly released her when Sidney bounded from the trees brandishing a sword.

In an instant, the men bolted, and Emma collapsed in a heap upon the ground. She closed her eyes, pressing her hands over them, but could not banish the vision of the dead man with a gaping hole for a mouth or of the wounded soldier lying in the woods, entreating her for help. Her throat felt thick, and her eyes would not focus.

Sidney took her hands and helped her to stand. He turned her gently away from the body. "Emma, what on earth are you doing? What if I had not found you?" His voice trembled, obviously with suppressed fury, and the back of Emma's eyes prickled with tears.

"Colonel Stackhouse needed water, then I saw . . ." Her stomach churned as guilt flooded over her. Why had she fled when the dying man so obviously needed comfort? If she could only go back; but by now, it was certainly too late. She was proving to be a useless rescuer. She raised her gaze to Sidney's and saw that he was working a muscle in his jaw, just the way William had when he had found her hiding aboard his ship. Only the expression looked so much more terrible on Sidney's bruised and whiskered face. He must be furious. The tightness in her throat threatened to choke her, and she blinked against the stinging in her eyes. "I am sorry I made you angry," she said, hanging her head and swaying, her knees still a bit shaky. "I've made everything worse, haven't I?"

"I am not angry, Emma. Not at you. Terrified, perhaps." Sidney's voice was low. He held on to her arms to steady her, pulling her from the clearing into the cover of trees. "Are you all right?"

Emma nodded and sniffled as she rested her head against his chest, beginning to relax. Sidney was here, and soon everything would be all right.

Even though the sounds of battle still surrounded them and she and Sidney were both filthy and nothing had gone the way it should from the moment she had walked through the prison gates, Emma found that being held in Sidney's arms felt every bit as wonderful as she'd always imagined.

Chapter 9

HOLDING EMMA'S TREMBLING BODY NEXT to his had the curious effect of calming Sidney's unexpected surge of anger and terror.

"How did you find me?" Emma asked against his chest.

He glanced down at her blonde curls. When he and Serena had returned with a surgeon and discovered that Emma had gone, Sidney had been nearly apoplectic. He'd immediately run into the woods to search for her, anxiety nearly causing his heart to explode from his chest as he imagined her bound and flung over the saddle of an enemy soldier.

He tried to speak lightly and ease the horror she was undoubtedly still feeling. "Well, Emma, as it turns out, you are in possession of an excellent set of lungs which can take full credit for leading me to you."

He closed his eyes, not wanting to remember how desperate he'd felt. Hearing her screams and imagining her headed toward a fate worse than death, his caution had flown, and all he could think of was reaching her. It was lucky that he'd not run into a group of enemy soldiers, as he would have been completely vulnerable, having taken no thoughts for his own safety. His rage when he'd seen the man holding Emma had scared him nearly as much as his anxiety for her. The men had made a blasted good decision when they fled because Sidney was afraid he would have skewered the lot of them otherwise.

When had he lost control over his emotions? As a soldier, he'd been trained to approach dangerous situations with restraint, make split-second decisions, and not allow his feelings to play any part in his actions on the battlefield. The torture he had endured in the prison had certainly changed him, and he feared he would never be the same.

Sidney held Emma tighter and felt his heartbeat returning to its normal rhythm, even as she continued to tremble. He'd seen a flash of something in her eyes, and for an instant, he thought her fear might have expanded to include him. His heart sank at the mere thought that he might have put some of that distress into her eyes.

"Are you quite all right now?" he asked.

Emma nodded her head against his chest, and he found himself reluctant to release her. *And blast, if she did not smell like vanilla.*

"We must return or Jim and Serena will be concerned," he stepped back, immediately feeling the loss of her warmth.

Once he was certain she was steady on her feet, Sidney surveyed the soldier on the ground, carefully positioning himself in front of Emma to block the sight from her.

"We can at least be grateful to this soldier for the use of his supplies," Sidney said. He picked up the musket, removed the bag of musket balls and bayonet case from the man's belt, then handed Emma the soldier's canteen.

Emma tried to lift the knapsack that lay a few yards from the dead man, but she could not move it.

Sidney hefted it easily onto his back.

Emma's eyes continued to dart around, and she held the canteen so tightly that her knuckles were white.

Sidney wanted to tell her they were safe now, but such a thing was far from the truth. So, silently, he led her through the underbrush, back to the clearing where the surgeon was at work sewing up Jim's wound. The sounds of the battle continued in the distance, and Sidney was becoming more anxious to move the group farther away from the action.

When they arrived in the clearing, Serena rushed to Emma, embracing her.

"Doctor Sharpe, allow me to introduce Lady Emma Drake. Lady Emma, this is Doctor John Sharpe of the Twenty-Ninth Regiment," Sidney said.

The surgeon and Emma exchanged greetings, and Sidney couldn't help but think how absurd it was that social niceties were still observed in such a situation.

"How do you find him, Doctor?" Sidney stepped closer.

"He'll have a mighty headache for a while, that's certain. But the ball did no damage to his skull." He produced a bandage from his haversack and wound it around Jim's head.

"And when do you think he'll be able to travel?" Sidney asked.

"The lot of you can stop talking about me as if I'm deaf." Jim pushed himself up into a sitting position. His face grew even paler, but he did not lie back down.

"Here is some water, Colonel Stackhouse," Emma said, walking closer and handing him the canteen.

Jim took it, opened the cap, and took a long drink.

The sound of an explosion nearby caused all of them to turn toward the direction of the battlefield. Jim held his hand to his head, the quick movement obviously painful.

Emma instinctively covered her ears and ducked down.

"You will want to rest, sir," the doctor told him.

Jim ignored the man, turning instead to Sidney. "If you are ready to depart, let us put as many miles between us and that cursed prison as we can before nightfall."

"I would not recommend travel for at least a day, Colonel," the surgeon said. "It would serve you better to accompany me back to camp. And you, Captain. You are injured as well. Judging by the way you are holding your side, I wonder if you've some cracked ribs."

Emma turned away from Jim and studied Sidney for a moment, and he determined the worried expression on her face was nearly worth the throbbing in his side. Nearly. "Just a bit sore," Sidney said, endeavoring to stand in a manner that didn't betray his pain.

"I'm grateful for your expertise in these matters," Jim said to the doctor, "but I've my orders."

Emma stiffened her spine, holding her head up. "It should not be long back to Cádiz, Colonel," she said in a comforting tone. "We shall have to wait until the fighting stops, and the horses will have to move slowly, of course, so as not to jostle you and Captain Fletcher too much. Doctor, do you know where we might arrange for a carriage?"

The entire group stared at Emma, stunned by her naiveté. Jim was frozen with the canteen halfway to his mouth. In any other circumstance, Sidney might have laughed at the man's expression.

"Emma, we cannot return to Cádiz. The French still hold it under siege," Sidney said as gently as possible.

Emma blinked rapidly. "I am sure when we explain to them that we are merely passing through to William's ship, they will . . ."

Sidney shook his head. "We must travel to Tarifa. We will find a ship there to take us to Cádiz by sea."

Emma looked at each member of the party. "And how far is Tarifa?"

"Fifty miles," Jim grunted, shifting his position and still holding his head with his hands.

"No," Emma said, crossing her arms. "I cannot go. William must be sick with worry. I cannot travel fifty miles. Even with a good carriage, it will take us at least two days, and what if we are unable to find a suitable inn? We may be forced to lodge above an ale house or some other sort of disreputable place." Her voice was beginning to rise in octave, and she was breathing heavily.

Jim snorted.

Serena reached for Emma's hand and led her to a log a short distance away to sit, speaking softly to her and leaving the men to discuss their plan.

The doctor looked truly worried. "Surely you will avoid the roads and the major cities. There is not much that the French have not destroyed in their path. It will be quite dangerous this far behind enemy lines with no army for protection . . ."

"Colonel Stackhouse knows the region," Sidney said. "Thank you again for your offer, Doctor. But we cannot remain in hopes of joining a detachment that may or may not take us to Tarifa. The colonel's orders are clear, and I can do no other than assist him in his assignment, as well as ensure Lady Emma's safe return to the care of her brother. Our best chance lies in secrecy. But I thank you again for the equipment you were able to procure on such short notice, sir."

"Yes, of course, Captain. If you will excuse me." The doctor rose and shook Sidney's and Jim's hands. "I have a long day ahead." He nodded to Serena and Emma. "Señorita Alvarez, Lady Emma. A pleasure."

Once the surgeon had left the clearing, Sidney moved to the pile of supplies. "Emma, these were the smallest boots we could find." He offered them to her, but she did not take them.

"I am sure my own slippers will suffice a bit longer." She eyed the boots suspiciously. "Where did you find . . . ?"

Serena took the tall boots from Sidney and set them next to Emma's feet, motioning for her to put them on. "Come, you must wear strong boots for walking so far."

"I will not." Emma stood. She curled her lip. "These boots are dirty and made for a man. And it is not too far to walk to . . ." She looked from Serena to Sidney, and he could see the moment the truth of the situation settled upon her. "We are walking to Tarifa." Her voice was quiet, almost a whisper. She sat back down upon the log, her shoulders slumped.

Serena sat next to her, raising her eyebrows at Sidney and tipping her head toward Emma, indicating for him to say something to reassure her.

Sidney crouched down to Emma's eye level. He nodded to Serena and tried to think of encouraging words. All he could manage was, "Yes. I am sorry, Emma, but we must make the journey on foot."

Emma studied the dirty boots, nudging one of them with her toe, and then turned toward Sidney, opening her mouth to say something. She tensed, making a sound somewhere between a choke and a sob as she looked past him with wide eyes.

Sidney jumped to his feet, pulling out his sword as he whirled to see what had frightened her.

Chapter 10

A MAN STOOD IN THE clearing with his hands raised.

Sidney shoved him to the ground, knelt upon him, and squeezed his throat with one hand. In his other hand, Sidney held his sword, poised above the man's face.

The man's eyes were wide and terrified. His words were strained because Sidney's grip on his neck was quite strong. "Señor, please. I did not mean to startle you. I was a prisoner also. You must remember me. Enrique Luis Trevino-Reyes at your service."

Sidney's heart pounded. It frightened him how close he had come to killing this man who had done no more than surprise him. His time in the prison had obviously made him skittish and distrustful. Didn't this man know better than to creep up on a soldier? He pressed his lips together, frustrated at his lack of control.

"I heard you speak of Tarifa—" Enrique said.

"Then you heard too much," Sidney brought the point of the sword closer to the man's neck.

"Tarifa is my home. I only want to join your party."

He studied the man's face. Enrique Trevino certainly looked familiar, but he obviously hadn't been at the prison long as he did not look gaunt and pale, and his clothing was relatively clean.

Sidney looked to Jim, who had leapt to his feet as well and now leaned heavily against the trunk of a tree. Jim shrugged.

"Do you recognize this man, Señorita Alvarez?" Sidney spoke without turning around.

"Sí," Serena answered. "He tells the truth. He was at the prison also. But I do not know why."

The man had no doubt been eavesdropping on them if he knew their destination. Sidney wondered exactly what he had heard and why he had not made himself known sooner. He loosened his hand upon Enrique's throat but did not lower his sword. "How did you escape from Matagorda, Señor Trevino?"

Enrique gesticulated with his hands as he spoke. "In the confusion from the fire and the battle, I followed the guards as they chased you through the gates of the fort. I saw the direction you ran and hoped I would find you."

Sidney narrowed his eyes. The man had followed him unnoticed? Had the guards been so intent upon recapturing Sidney that they had not spotted another prisoner escaping? They were poorly trained if this was the case. Enrique's story was odd but not impossible. After all, Sidney had escaped in much the same manner himself.

He lowered his sword. "Were you followed?"

"No, Señor." The relief was evident upon Enrique's face when the weapon was no longer pointed at him. "This is why I took so long to find you, I wanted to be sure."

Sidney nodded, though he doubted this extravagantly dressed man with his white skin and flaccid muscles had the training to be certain of anything of the sort.

"Señor, I can help you reach Tarifa." Enrique's gaze moved over Jim and the two women. "It is far safer for me to travel with others, and I know the best routes. Please, sir, allow me to accompany you."

Though he hated to admit it, Sidney knew there was wisdom in Enrique's words. He still didn't like the idea of a stranger joining their party, but he had two women and an injured soldier to transport through the Spanish mountains. Another able-bodied man, especially one who knew the area, would be more than beneficial. He held out a hand to help Enrique to his feet.

Enrique bowed elegantly as he was introduced to the women. Sidney shot him a look, and the Spaniard stepped away and studied the dirt beneath his nails. Sidney set about distributing the gear, making sure to watch the newcomer closely. He did not like how Enrique looked at the women, and Spanish men were notorious for their flirting.

He was grateful that Doctor Sharpe had been so quick to procure some basic supplies from his regiment, mostly cooking elements and some food. Sidney kept the Brown Bess musket, along with the sword since he didn't trust Enrique with a weapon and Jim was too ill to use it. Sidney gave Jim a short blade that the colonel strapped in its scabbard upon his belt. He loaded the majority of the equipment into the knapsack, which he hefted onto his back, and gave Serena and Enrique each a haversack containing some salt pork and hard tack biscuits.

Sidney handed Emma a small sack. She followed Serena's example and slung it over her head and under one arm. Serena helped her stuff the boots with pieces of cloth since they were too large for Emma's feet. The sight of her soft, airy dress hanging over a dirty pair of boots must have caused her some anxiety, as she repeatedly moved her skirts to hide them. It was on the tip of Sidney's tongue to tell her that it did not matter—her dress was already quite ruined—but he thought better of it.

Emma seemed to be resigned to the situation. In fact, her face showed hardly any emotion at all, which concerned Sidney more than if she'd thrown a tantrum or wept.

Once the group was ready, Sidney led them through the forest, away from the battle in the direction Jim instructed. Sidney and Enrique took turns supporting the colonel, even though he protested, claiming that he could walk on his own.

When they reached the edge of the trees, Sidney conferred with Jim. The doctor had assured him that the French troops were not encamped so far east, but there was still the danger of being spotted by scouts.

"We could wait until nightfall," Sidney said. "It would give you a chance to rest."

"Every minute we are not moving away from the fort increases the probability of recapture," Jim answered, leaning against a tree. "I will not rest easy until we have put miles behind us."

Sidney nodded. He studied the terrain outside of the forest. Wide-open plains dotted with loose rock stretched toward steep mountains in the distance. He knew that Jim intended to make it as far as the foothills before dark, but the route would not be easily negotiated.

Sidney wished for his spy glass as he squinted toward the horizon, searching the hills for any sight of enemy lookouts. French soldiers or thieves could be hiding anywhere, even in the same shadows at the edge of the woods, and would shoot without provocation. He could not be too careful leading the group from the safety of the trees. Finally, loading his musket and holding it at the ready, he moved to step out of the cover of the forest.

The sound of Emma's voice stopped him.

"Wait. Can we not stay in the forest until dark?" She turned purposely to avoid Jim's line of sight. "Please? What if French soldiers are just waiting to fire at us?"

Sidney stepped toward her. "There are none close enough that we have to worry about their aim. The battle is behind us, and we will be safer the farther we are from it." He reached out to lift her chin with his crooked finger. "I need you to be a soldier, Emma. Will you do that?"

She nodded, wrapping her arms around herself and drawing her eyebrows together.

Sidney led them from the forest slowly. They walked silently, watching the hills. But, though Sidney and Jim remained alert, scanning for any threat, the rest of the party allowed their caution to wane and finally vanish as those first tense minutes stretched into hours of trudging over the hard ground. At first, they stayed close in a small clump, but as time passed, they stretched into an irregular line. Sidney led the way, supporting Jim, and for a while, the women walked together, but eventually, boredom led to a change in positions. When Sidney stopped next to a boulder to allow Jim to rest, he saw Serena walking alone and Enrique escorting Emma.

Emma stumbled slightly, and Enrique reached out to steady her, holding on to her elbow. She rewarded him with a smile, and Sidney's gut clenched. What did he really know about this man? Enrique was not a soldier. That much was obvious by the way he walked—*pranced* was more like it. His manners were refined and his gestures grandiose. A Spanish dandy, Sidney decided. No doubt women swooned over his handsome looks with his long, straight hair, and thin mustache. What was a gentleman such as Enrique doing imprisoned in a French fort? Sidney resolved to find out as soon as possible. He needed to protect not only the women but *all* of them from Enrique, should he prove to be planning some sort of deceit.

In William's absence, Sidney was Emma's guardian, and he did not like the way Enrique walked so close to her or managed to find reasons to touch her.

Enrique held one of Emma's hands as she used the other to lift her skirts high enough to step over a pile of rocks.

"A woman doesn't fancy a man like him for long." Jim lifted his chin toward Emma and Enrique.

"Pardon me?" Sidney said.

"Look at how he pampers her, treats her like a child. Lady Emma no doubt has her share of people who coddle her. What she needs is someone to challenge her, allows her to accomplish difficult things. There's a woman who needs to feel strong."

"What makes you think she's the sort of person who needs to prove herself? Perhaps she enjoys being taken care of." Sidney looked back at Emma. All he could see was a delicate young woman in a setting completely unsuited to her. She should be somewhere comfortable and beautiful, not in a perilous war zone.

Jim turned to look at him. "She's here, isn't she? I'd say that is precisely the type of woman she wants to be. Though it will take some hard experiences for her to become so."

Sidney watched Enrique and Emma as they drew closer. "And how is it that you know so much about women, Colonel?"

"Not merely women, sir. In my military career, it has been useful to understand the inner workings of people's minds. Such a thing is particularly advantageous in . . . obtaining information. All people have a need. They often do not know what it is themselves, but once you discover it, you can either use it to your advantage or theirs."

Sidney's stomach churned as he listened to Jim. He knew firsthand the psychology that went into interrogations, and he was glad that he and the colonel were on the same side. He had no doubt that Jim could be ruthless, and combined with his intuition when it came to understanding the human psyche, he would be a formidable enemy.

Jim took a drink from the canteen. "Señorita Alvarez was much the same a few months ago. I predict Lady Emma will take a similar course."

Serena, Enrique, and Emma joined them, and the group took the opportunity to rest for a moment.

Emma moved toward one of the large boulders. Enrique hurriedly brushed the surface off and laid his coat on it for her to sit upon. Emma thanked him and scooted to the side, smoothing the coat next to her. Enrique moved as if to sit beside her, but Emma, apparently unaware, called instead for Serena to join her. Enrique pursed his lips, standing awkwardly to one side as the women talked.

Sidney smiled. As he watched the interchange, he thought about what Jim had said. He knew Emma had been sheltered by her family, especially her mother, no doubt as a consequence of her father's cruelty. He wondered how she managed to endure years of fear and abuse. He had heard from

William that their father had mistreated Emma and Lady Charlotte dreadfully, though William had not told him any specifics. How had she managed to remain so gentle and sweet-tempered when merely two months of ill-treatment had left Sidney feeling irreparably damaged? He didn't know if he would ever be restored to his former self. Would he always be mistrustful and paranoid? He was constantly on alert, scanning the people and area around him. Just the thought of finding himself trapped or being caught off guard set his heart racing, caused labored breathing, and sent him spiraling into a complete panic.

His mind wandered back to Emma. Perhaps Jim was right. It was possible that accomplishing things without assistance gave her the strength she needed to combat the pain of her past and to defeat the feelings of worthlessness that such maltreatment caused. Maybe that was the reason she had come to Spain in the first place.

Sidney watched as Emma chatted with Serena. She seemed to be putting on a brave face, trying to make the best of things. When Jim offered the women the canteen, she took a sip and then wrinkled her nose in an expression that reminded Sidney of a petulant child as she tasted the stale water. But the moment she replaced the cap and stood, turning her head to the side and smiling at him, the realization that she was no longer William's little sister but a grown woman hit him with a force that surprised him.

"This next stretch will be particularly difficult," Jim said, interrupting Sidney's thoughts. "The salt marshes. But just a few more hours will put us at a good location to make camp."

At his words, Emma closed her eyes and took a deep breath.

Sidney hid a smile and moved past the women to assist Jim.

"I'm not crippled," Jim grumbled when Sidney offered his hand. "It's only a headache." But he allowed Sidney to help him stand and did not complain when he walked close enough that Jim could hold on to his arm.

Their path led through a wet plain. Vegetation grew sparser. The salt water had killed the flora in the region. The dark mud was streaked with white veins of dried salt. Broken sticks and dead plants stuck out of the ground in various spots. The marshland was mosquito infested, sweltering, and the odor was terrible. Beads of sweat trickled down Sidney's back; his legs burned as he slogged his way through the smelly marsh. As they walked, the mud became increasingly sticky and difficult to maneuver through. He assumed the others were equally miserable.

Sidney turned his head to evaluate the group's progress just as Emma's boot became trapped in the mud, and her foot slipped out. She lost her balance and swayed for a moment, crying out, and then plopping hard in the mud.

Sidney, Serena, and Enrique all started toward her.

"Emma, are you hurt?" Sidney called from where he stood with Jim.

Emma shook her head. She looked stunned but unharmed. A moment later, however, her face crumpled, and her shoulders began to shake.

"It's remarkable she held out so long," Jim said, dryly. "I expected this hours ago."

Sidney ignored his sarcasm, handed the colonel his musket, and made his way through the sticky mud toward Emma.

She bent her head to wipe her eyes with the backs of her gloved hands. Her shoulders shook, and the sight of her trying not to weep tore at Sidney's heart.

"Enrique, help Colonel Stackhouse and Señorita Alvarez. Continue toward the river. Lady Emma and I will join you shortly," Sidney said and then squatted down to Emma's eye level. He pulled her hands from her face and retrieved a handkerchief from his jacket pocket, grimacing as he looked at it. Lieutenant Trenchard was obviously not fastidious about cleanliness.

When he offered it to her, she held up her palms and saw the mud covering the palms of her gloves where they'd landed on the ground. The sight was apparently too much, and she began to weep in earnest, sobs wracking her body.

Sidney lifted her chin and found the cleanest corner of the handkerchief to wipe her cheeks. "Emma, do not cry."

His admonition only served to make her weep harder.

"You did not injure your . . . um . . ." Sidney glanced down to where she sat in the mud. "Your . . . *self*, did you?" he asked.

Emma shook her head.

"Then, we can overcome whatever is distressing you. Tell me what is wrong."

"Nothing has happened the way it was supposed to." Emma choked on her sobs, and Sidney knew enough to remain silent and simply listen.

"I have disappointed my brother, first by sneaking aboard his ship, then by sneaking away from Cádiz. And it is because of me that Colonel Stackhouse was injured. I cannot walk to Tarifa in these ghastly boots. It is impossible. I am not a soldier."

She had stowed away on William's ship?

Her sobs were building in momentum, and Sidney found her increasingly difficult to understand with the keening cries distorting her words. He dabbed the corner of the handkerchief over her cheeks again, searching his brain for anything he might say to comfort her.

She continued speaking, and he strained to listen. "Images in my mind . . . men broken . . . and . . . dying. And horses . . . and . . . the screams and cries and explosions . . ."

Sidney empathized completely. He had violent images of his own—some twenty years old—that refused to leave his mind. His chest ached as he realized she would carry these memories with her always. "I am sorry, Emma. War is more horrific than anyone who has not witnessed it could possibly imagine. How I wish I could take such things from you."

"And I ran away . . . I should have helped the soldier in the forest, but I was afraid, and . . . I am so ashamed."

Sidney planted one knee in the mud next to her and put his arm around her, pulling her close to cry on his shoulder. He wondered what she had seen. It must have been shocking to leave such an impression upon her.

"Shh. Nothing could have prepared you for such a thing."

"I should not have run away. I deserted him—another human being—in his most desperate hour. I am a terrible person."

He pulled away and lifted her chin, forcing her gaze to his. "You are not a terrible person. You are a wonderful person who was in a terrible situation. There are times when the most seasoned soldier cannot endure what war does to him. Do you understand?"

Emma nodded and laid her head back upon his shoulder. "I will not do it again," she said softly. "I will not neglect a person I can help."

"Of course you will not," Sidney said.

They remained quiet for a time, with only Emma's sniffles breaking the silence.

Although they needed to make haste, Sidney found that he wasn't at all annoyed by the interruption. It was surprisingly comfortable to pass the time in such a way. Even though it was humid and they were in the mud of a stinky bog, Emma still managed to smell wonderful. She was soft and warm, and he decided that comforting her was perhaps the most pleasant thing he had done in years.

However, as much as he didn't want to put an end to the moment, he knew the others were waiting for them. "Are you ready to continue, now?"

She took a deep shuddering breath and lifted her head. She nodded, and Sidney stood, reaching for her hands to assist her.

Emma looked at her soiled gloves and then moved her eyes to her stockinged foot that had sunk partway into the mud. She twisted slightly to examine her dress; the entire back of the skirts was stained.

Her lip began to tremble once more, but before she could start to weep again, Sidney flung himself down, sitting in the mud next to her.

Emma made a sound somewhere between a shriek and a giggle. "Sidney! Your . . . trousers are filthy."

"I thought we might attempt to begin our own trend. I predict it will soon be the height of fashion upon the Spanish plain to have mud covering one's backside."

Emma's face turned crimson, and a laugh burst forth. She bumped into his shoulder with hers. "And will it also be a la mode to travel with no bonnet or parasol and develop a face full of freckles?"

"Undoubtedly." He tapped his finger against her nose. "The more freckles the better." He rose and turned to help Emma stand and balance while she slid her muddy foot into her salt-and-mud encrusted boot and pulled it up beneath her skirts. "And now, my dear, if you will accompany me on a stroll about this delightful bog . . ."

Emma laughed again, and the sound penetrated into a part of Sidney's heart he hadn't remembered existed. It was strange that he had not realized how much he'd missed the sound of her laughter until now. And stranger still how quickly he pledged to himself that he would move heaven and earth to hear it again.

Chapter 11

As Emma walked next to Sidney, she was overcome by a myriad of emotions: she was embarrassed by her outburst, bolstered by Sidney's faith in her, but mostly, just exhausted. She had never walked so far in her life. She tried to adjust her floor-length shawl over her shoulders, but it was hopeless—the wet silk merely stuck to her skirts. She held her soiled gloves between her fingers. The boots she wore rose over her knees, making it impossible to completely bend her legs. One boot was filled with mud and made a wet, squishing sound with every step. The other continued to slide off her heel as it stuck to the ground, and she had to twist her foot to lift it.

When she pondered the hours she had spent in deportment training where she'd practiced moving across the floor as though she were gliding, a smile twisted her lips.

"What are you thinking of that amuses you so?" asked Sidney.

Emma glanced up at him, not realizing he had been watching her. "I was remembering my finishing school instructors. They believed me to be prepared to behave with decorum in any possible situation. Certainly they did not foresee such an eventuality as this." She pulled her boot out of the mud with a loud squelching sound to prove her point.

Sidney chuckled. "I imagine that all your gentlemen suitors would still consider you every bit as desirable, should they see you at this moment. If not, then they are completely unworthy of your affection."

She kept her eyes on the muddy ground in front of her. Sidney had spoken lightly, having no idea what his words did to her. She wished that *he* found her desirable. She imagined how differently he would look at her if she were in London wearing a ball gown—perhaps something with gossamer netting—feathers in her hair, and lace at her neckline. If only she were in her element, she would know the perfect thing to say, the exact tilt of her head and curl of her lips that would captivate him.

"Clearly you have not spent much time among the *ton*," she said. "I cannot think of one gentleman of my association in London who would not be repelled by such a sight as this." Emma made a waving motion, encompassing her dirty gown and the stinking bog surrounding them.

"Ah, yes. Those soft-fingered fops who prefer servants waiting on them as they lounge around a drawing room in an embroidered waistcoat instead of getting their boots dirty doing an honest day's work." His voice had lost all trace of humor. "Avoid that type at all cost, Emma, unless you aspire to a life of boredom. Surely you can find someone with more substance."

Emma didn't think she had ever heard such bitterness in Sidney's voice. She felt her hackles rise in defense of her friends and her brother. "Not every gentleman is lazy, sir. William attends Parliament and sees to the needs of his tenants, and even now is establishing an import business to bring sugar from Amelia's plantation in Jamaica. He works extremely hard, I assure you." She had begun to breathe heavily, whether from the effort of walking or the lump that was growing in her throat, she did not know.

Sidney stopped. "Emma, I apologize. I certainly did not refer to William when I spoke. I am afraid I allowed a few particular examples to color my opinion. It was not my intention to pass judgment upon an entire class when my own experiences are with a select number. I should have thought before I spoke." His eyebrows raised as his gaze met hers. "Please forgive my words."

Emma nodded. "Of course. I understand."

Sidney resumed walking, patting her hand where it rested in the crook of his elbow and sending tingles up her arm. "And now, I believe it is time to change the topic. Why don't you decide upon a subject, as I made such a blunder with the last?"

Emma glanced ahead. They were nearing the others, who had sat down beneath a dead tree to wait for them. She estimated that she would have Sidney's undivided attention for a few minutes more and did not want him hurrying off to join the others.

"I do have something I would ask you . . ." she said, "about the prison."

She felt Sidney stiffen. "What would you like to know?"

Emma pressed on, not wanting to back down now that she'd broached the subject. She could tell he was uncomfortable, but truthfully, she was feeling a bit vindicated as he'd not seemed to mind touching on topics sensitive to her. "When I arrived and asked to see you, the guard told me that there was no prisoner with your name, which was the same report given to Lieutenant Wellard. However, another guard began to argue with him, stating that you were, in fact, a prisoner, and the first attempted to quiet him and send me away."

"And being an accomplished lady, you understood them." Sidney's mouth quirked in an expression that warmed Emma down to her toes.

"It seems that the French army has underestimated Miss Carlisle's insistence that her finishing school's graduates be proficient in French and German. I did not ever imagine that conjugating verbs and memorizing vocabulary sheets would be useful." Emma lowered her head to hide her blush, wishing she had a bonnet to conceal her face. She was rather pleased by the fact that she had outsmarted those fools at the gate, but she did not want Sidney to think her proud.

"Yes, well," she continued, "once I learned you were indeed inside the fort, I demanded to see you, and when I was shown to the . . . Oh, Sidney, how did you ever endure that place? And why the deceit? William told me that the typical practice in the capture of an officer—especially a captain—would be the issue of a ransom demand. If you had given your parole, you should have been treated more like a guest than a common prisoner. Why was your imprisonment concealed?"

Sidney stopped walking. "What is the date, Emma?"

"The fifteenth of June."

"Nearly two months then," he muttered. He glanced toward the tree where the other members of their party rested; then he withdrew an object from his trouser pocket and offered it to Emma. "I retrieved this from Lieutenant Trenchard's coat."

She looked up at his face as she took the object and then turned her attention down to study it. It was a misshapen, flattish piece of tarnished metal with jagged edges. When she moved it to catch the light, she noticed symbols pressed into the faces—most notably, a large cross.

"I am afraid I do not understand," she said. "Is this a coin?"

"Not just any coin. A 'piece of eight,' a *real*, minted in Peru by the Spanish conquistadors 250 years ago," Sidney said, sweeping his hand in a flourish.

"Is it from a pirate chest?" Emma looked back at the coin. "Did you find a buried treasure?"

The corners of Sidney's mouth lifted in a tired smile. He shook his head. "If only it were so exciting. No, I merely found the coin shortly after coming ashore. I saw it on the ground and, thinking it looked interesting, put it in my pocket. That action has proven to be the greatest regret of my life. The warden, Lieutenant Trenchard—lovely gentleman—you remember?"

Emma shuddered at the memory and nodded.

Sidney continued, "He considers himself quite the numismatist—an expert in coins. When he found the *real* upon my person, he was convinced that it came from the lost treasure of de la Cruz, rumored to be hidden by smugglers centuries ago near the coast of Tarifa."

"And do you remember where you found it?" Emma asked. "Why did you not tell him?"

"Well, aside from the fact that the information compromises the confidentiality of troop movement, I am convinced that the last thing Napoleon and the Republic need is a fortune in conquistador silver."

"Such a thing could win the war for them," Emma mused.

"It certainly would not hurt their cause," he said, scowling.

"And Lieutenant Trenchard concealed your capture because he did not want the navy to pay your ransom and take you away before he could discover where you found the coin."

"Exactly correct. He was convinced that given the right . . . encouragement, I would lead him to the treasure."

Emma's stomach clenched as she realized what type of encouragement Sidney meant. "And that is why you were in the dungeon, and why your face . . ." She took a breath and spoke softly. "He tortured you. Oh, Sidney, I am so sorry." She handed the coin back to him, wishing she could kiss away each cut and bruise and the look of anguish upon his face.

Sidney held the coin between two fingers, staring at it as he spoke. "I do not know if I shall ever be the same man, Emma. I lost two months of my life. I may have surrendered a piece of my soul for this chunk of metal." He clenched the coin in his fist and pulled back his arm as if to throw it.

Emma laid a hand upon his shoulder, stopping him, and he turned his head toward her with brows raised in question.

"If you indeed paid such a high price for it, I do not think you should cast it away."

Sidney studied her for a moment. The typical playfulness in his eyes was replaced by a dark sorrow that caused Emma's heart to ache. His eyes never left hers as he reached for her hand and pressed the coin into it. "Nobody has a better claim on my soul. If it were not for you, I would still be in that—" He swallowed and closed his hand around hers. "You keep this."

They stood a moment longer, and Emma thought her heart would explode from her chest as Sidney held her hand and looked into her face.

A noise nearby startled them, and Sidney whipped around, drawing his sword and thrusting Emma behind him.

"Señor! Captain Fletcher, it is only I."

Emma peered around Sidney's shoulder and saw Enrique standing in much the same stance as the first time they had seen him. He held his hands up, and his eyes were wide and frightened. Enrique began backing away, and when Sidney did not immediately lower his weapon, Emma placed her hand upon his arm.

"Sidney . . ."

He was breathing heavily, and his arm shook beneath her hand.

Emma stepped around until she was facing him. Beads of sweat stood out across his forehead.

He looked at her strangely for a moment before his eyes seemed to widen in recognition. He lowered his sword and resheathed it, taking a few unsteady breaths. "I beg your pardon, Señor. I'm afraid it is unwise to startle me."

Enrique cocked his head to the side and pursed his lips. "I apologize for taking you by surprise, Captain. I simply wanted to ensure that Lady Emma is well?"

"I am quite recovered, Señor. Thank you." Emma said. Her eyes flicked briefly to him but returned immediately to Sidney. Though his breathing had reverted to normal, his muscles still seemed tense, and the lines around his mouth indicated that he felt a great deal of strain.

"And perhaps you will walk with me to the river?" Enrique said to Emma. His gaze darted to her clenched fist that held the coin.

"I thank you, Señor, but I would prefer to walk alone for a bit." Emma looked back at Sidney, whose eyes had narrowed as he watched Enrique. She wondered if he had seen Enrique's errant glance as well. The more time she spent with Enrique, the more uncomfortable she had become with his flirting and his "innocent" touches.

Taking her leave, she hurried ahead of the men, walking as quickly as she could through the mud. She wanted some time to herself to process the things Sidney had told her.

He had not given details of his mistreatment, but she had seen the expression on his face when Enrique had startled him. His eyes had bulged, darting in terror, his nostrils flared, and his breathing was ragged. And he did not seem to recognize her until his panic had subsided. She had seen nearly the same thing in her mother after her father had been particularly brutal. And Emma had even felt it to a much lesser extent when he had mistreated her. The worst part had been the horrible shame that followed—the feeling that it could have been prevented if only she had behaved or tried harder to please her father.

She was nearly to the river when she glanced behind to see that Sidney and Enrique had stopped walking and were engaged in conversation. Sidney unconsciously shook a lock of hair off his forehead, and the sight caused her heart to flutter.

The uneven edges of the coin pressed into her palm, and Emma tucked the bit of metal into a pocket hidden in the folds of her gown, resolving to find a way to help Sidney recover. Whatever it took, she would find a way to bring the laughter back into his eyes.

Chapter 12

SIDNEY STUDIED ENRIQUE FROM THE corner of his eye as they followed Emma toward the river. It hadn't escaped his notice that Enrique had glanced at Emma's hand when he spoke to her. Had he heard any of their conversation? Had he seen the coin? If so, he knew that it was in Emma's possession. And Señor Trevino's interest in Emma, whether innocent or not, brought out a protective side of Sidney. It must have been his elder brother feelings resurfacing.

When Sidney thought Emma was far enough ahead of them, he turned to the other man. "Señor Trevino, if I might have a word?"

Enrique stopped and gave a slight bow. "But of course."

Sidney held Enrique's gaze, allowing his expression to become cold. His voice took on the commanding tone he used during the discipline aboard his ship. "Let us dispense with the deceit. I have no patience for half-truths, so I will give you one chance to answer my questions." He laid his hand upon the hilt of his sword to give Enrique no doubt that he was serious.

Enrique's eyes widened and then darted toward the remainder of the group before returning to Sidney.

"If you are afraid that none of the party can reach you in time, should I decide to fillet you like a herring, you are quite correct. However, if you answer honestly, we will have no need for something that would be unpleasant—and actually rather messy—for both of us."

Enrique crossed himself, and Sidney felt the satisfaction of knowing he had the upper hand. The man had already seen the sharp end of his sword twice in one day and was apparently not eager to repeat the experience.

"Why were you at Matagorda?"

"I told you, Captain. I was a prisoner like yourself."

Sidney's hand tightened on the sword's hilt, and he slowly began to remove it from its sheath.

The soft screech of steel caused Enrique to jump. He held his hands up, moving them as if to push Sidney away. "*Por favor.* I do not lie. I was captured by the French near Chiclana."

"But you claim to be from Tarifa."

"Sí. It is the truth. Tarifa is my home. I was inspecting my family's holdings in Chiclana."

"Why were you arrested? You are no soldier, and I do not believe you have the constitution for guerilla strikes." Sidney attempted to imagine Señor Trevino as part of a rebel band using farming tools to savagely attack French troops. He found he could not do it.

"There are other ways to resist the French invaders, Captain. We do not all fight with weapons."

Sidney narrowed his eyes. "You are a spy?"

"Sí," Enrique said with a small shrug of his shoulders.

"For whom? The Cortes of Cádiz?"

"No. For the Spanish people still loyal to *el Deseado*, King Fernando."

"If this is indeed the truth, you would have been executed the moment you were discovered, not imprisoned in a garrison."

"Sí, but my family is very influential." Enrique lifted his chin, and the haughtiness that had vanished began to seep back into his countenance. "When Lieutenant Trenchard learned who they are—"

"He kept you while awaiting your ransom." Sidney slid the sword back but kept his hand upon the hilt. Whether he liked it or not, the man's story made sense.

Enrique nodded and tipped his head, brushing an imaginary bit of lint off his sleeve. Sidney had nearly had enough of his arrogance.

"Like Señorita Alvarez," Enrique said. He stepped closer, apparently confident that Sidney had accepted his story. He tipped his head and furrowed his brow. Sidney found the man's exaggerated facial expressions to be immensely irritating. "I wonder if the señorita is who she claims to be. Her speech tells me she is from Madrid, but I do not recognize her family name, and I am quite familiar with the elite of—"

"Do not attempt to change the subject," Sidney barked, furious that Enrique would try to turn him against a member of his party. The man was devious. He played mind games, and Sidney's main weapon against him was, well, his weapon. He shifted his hold on the hilt, drawing Enrique's attention to the sword once again. "I trust Señorita Alvarez implicitly. I take seriously my duty to the people in my charge, and I will not have you sullying Señorita Alvarez's or Lady Emma's reputation with your words or actions.

"And do you think Lady Emma is in danger of sullying her reputation with me?" Enrique asked, raising and lowering his eyebrows.

Hearing these words, Sidney completely forgot that he had a sword and drove his fist into Enrique's jaw so forcefully that the man collapsed into the mud. Sidney pulled him back up to his knees, holding onto the Spaniard's collar as he blinked his dazed eyes.

Sidney leaned close, speaking through clenched teeth. "Let me make myself clear. If I feel that you so much as look at Lady Emma in any manner that I deem inappropriate, I will not hesitate to run you through. Do we understand one another?" He shoved Enrique back, tamping down the surge of protectiveness that had again overcome him.

Enrique rubbed his jaw. He nodded. "There is no need for such action, Captain. I am sure we can settle any difficulties like gentlemen."

"That is where you mistake me, Señor. In such a case, I have no intention of acting like a gentleman."

Sidney left Enrique wallowing in the mud and walked quickly toward the riverbank, where the rest of the group waited. He did not think any of them had seen the altercation. Based on Emma's smile and wave as he approached, he felt reassured that she hadn't seen him lose his temper. He realized that ensuring Emma had no reason to fear anyone, especially him, had risen extremely high on his list of priorities. He attributed it to the absolute trust she had in him. He wouldn't want her to ever believe it was misplaced, although he knew he did not deserve the honor.

The women stood upon a small hill. Emma called to him, "Sidney, you simply must see this!" She pointed across the marsh. He walked closer until he crested the hill and saw an enormous flock of flamingos.

Emma's face shone. "Have you ever seen such birds? They are pink!"

Sidney smiled. "Yes, I admit I have. In the West Indies and Galapagos Islands. Lovely, aren't they?"

"Look how they stand on one leg and dip their long beaks into the water." Emma clapped her hands together as a number of the flock began to beat their wings and, as one, lifted to fly to another part of the salt marshes. "They are delightful. What was it that you called them, Serena?"

"*Los Flamencos.*" Serena smiled at Emma's enthusiasm.

Sidney thought of all the times he'd observed similar sights—amazing vistas, exotic animals. He'd always appreciated the fact that the navy had granted him an opportunity to see parts of the world that few others ever would. And the thought that sprang unbidden into his mind was that he wanted to show it all to Emma, to watch her delight as she experienced the wonders of an Indian palace or a South American jungle. He shook his head. It was becoming ridiculous how contented he was with her. Emma *had* a brother to dote on her, and Sidney would do well to remember that family life was not in the cards for him. He was obviously lonely from his months in prison and needed to be returned to his ship and shipmates. Perhaps even some time in Cheshire with his own family would cure him of these strange feelings that Emma was awakening.

Sidney left the ladies to admire the flamingos and turned his attention to Jim a short ways away. The colonel sat upon a white patch of dry ground with the musket across his lap. Jim kept his hand over his eyes, and Sidney could see that his color had not improved. He needed rest. Soon.

"Colonel, how much farther do you intend us to travel today?" Sidney asked. The group had kept a good pace. They had not stopped to eat and had rested only a handful of times. He estimated by the sun's position that only two hours of daylight remained and possibly less when they reached the hills across the river. The river was close to ninety yards across. Walking through waist-deep water would tax all their strength, but especially Jim's. And the women would be impeded by their skirts.

"The site is just across the river there." Jim squinted and shaded his eyes with one hand while he pointed with the other. "Easily defendable, sheltered from weather, and plenty of dry wood and fresh water."

"Are you sure you're—" Sidney began.

Jim interrupted him. "We can't very well camp here, so let's get on with it," he said harshly.

Both men glanced up as the women joined them.

"Everything is well, sí?" Serena was saying to Emma.

"Yes," Emma said. "I am quite all right now."

"A fit of feminine hysteria." Jim spoke without removing his hand from his eyes. "Avoiding that sort of thing is precisely why I joined the army in the first place."

Emma merely raised her brows. Apparently she was becoming used to Jim's rudeness and did not think his words warranted a response.

Sidney coughed to hide a smile as he watched her reaction.

Enrique joined them but maintained his distance, standing sullenly away from the rest of the group. Sidney made it a point to ignore the Spaniard. He needed the man's help, but it didn't mean he had to like him.

"Very well then. Let us get to it." Sidney began to unload the knapsack, spreading two blankets and a greatcoat upon the ground. He removed his own coat and took Jim's and Enrique's, laying them on the blankets; then he began sorting through the pack. He added two white shirts to the pile and wrapped the entire collection into a bundle. He then removed the musket balls and a bag containing gunpowder, handing those items to Serena, who placed them into her haversack. Taking the musket from Jim, he gave it to Serena as well. He wished he could carry it himself—it would be fairly heavy for the small woman—but Sidney knew that Jim needed more help than he was letting on, and should he need to be pulled from the water, the weapon would undoubtedly get wet. Entrusting their only musket to Enrique was simply not an option.

Once it was emptied of ammunition, the pack still contained the heavy cooking equipment and food the doctor had procured. Sidney thrust the knapsack at Enrique.

"Emma, I will need to assist Jim—" Sidney ignored Jim's protests. "I need you to carry the blankets and coats, and keep them dry."

"We will cross here?" Emma asked. Sidney could tell she was trying not to sound completely frightened at the idea of wading through the water. She glanced up and down the river.

"The blasted French have destroyed any bridge they are not keeping under guard," Jim said. "So don't waste your time searching for one."

"It is not very deep or . . . ah . . . *rápido*," Serena said, encouragingly to Emma. "And your skirts will be much cleaner when we reach the other bank."

Emma simply nodded and lifted the bundle, wavering a bit under the weight of the heavy woolen coats. She was apparently too tired, too hungry, or too resigned to form any sort of protest.

Sidney felt guilty, knowing how difficult the crossing would be after their tiring day, but Jim was right—they had no other choice. He put Jim's arm over his own shoulders and then led the way down the salt-crusted bank and into the water.

The cool water felt refreshing after the long, hot walk. The river bottom was sandy and soft, and each step required effort. Before long it was waist-deep, and a glance backward showed him that Enrique, Serena, and Emma had each lifted their equipment above their heads. He did not estimate that it would get much deeper, but if it did, they would have to return to the shore and find logs to help them float across.

Nobody spoke as they pushed their way through the water. Jim was practically dead weight. Sidney wasn't sure if he was even conscious. Luckily the water buoyed him enough that Sidney could hold him up.

Sidney slowed and allowed each member of the group to pass him. It would be easier to keep an eye on them if he didn't have to continually turn around.

Enrique's pack was certainly the heaviest, and he did not make an effort to conceal the fact. He huffed and groaned and repeatedly traded arms to rest one at a time.

Serena was able to do the same. With some difficulty, she shifted the musket and her haversack into one hand and shook out the other arm before repeating the same process on the opposite side.

Emma seemed to be having the most difficult time. Her wet skirts were heavy, and while her load was lightest, it was also large and awkwardly shaped. She tried holding her haversack by the strap and moving the large bundle onto her shoulder then lowering one arm to rest it, but the load didn't balance, and her arms were too short to hold it steady. The river was nearly as high as her chest, and Sidney saw her falter a few times as she encountered a particularly swift-flowing spot. But she carried on, and he felt immensely proud. Even though every instinct in him screamed to help her, he could not let go of Jim.

The water grew shallower as they neared the other side. Instead of helping, this made it more difficult to support their tired arms and heavy loads. Sidney had to hold up most of Jim's weight as the water was now only slightly past his knees. Serena and Enrique were nearly at the opposite bank, while Emma was at least thirty yards behind. She had lowered the bundle from over her head and held it in front of her chest. Her arms were trembling, and he was sure she could not see where she was going.

Sidney hurried ahead of her to get Jim safely to the opposite bank before returning to assist her. The bank was much steeper than it had appeared, and it took Sidney longer than he'd expected to pull Jim out of the water and help Serena and Enrique. He hurried back, sloshing through the water quickly without his burden. Sidney had nearly reached Emma when he saw her chin trembling.

Her face was pale, and she held the large bundle in front of her. She heard him approach and looked up. At that moment, she stepped on a submerged log that she obviously couldn't see over her bundle and fell to her knees, dropping the rolled blankets into the water.

Emma grabbed the bundle at the same instant that Sidney grabbed her.

He set her on her feet and moved to take the load from her, but she shook her head.

"It was my one duty. I will finish it." Her voice was exhausted, and she sounded near to tears.

Sidney felt a swell of pride in his chest. He put his arm around her, much the same way he had supported Jim, and together they slogged toward the riverbank.

"I am sorry." Emma's voice cracked, and she sniffed. "My arms are just so tired, and now everybody will be wet tonight."

"Emma, you are the only one I worry about. Being a bit damp on a warm Spanish plain will never compare to where the remainder of us spent last night."

"I have made a disaster of every task I have set out to do," she said. "And I can only imagine what Colonel Stackhouse will have to say when he sees that his coat is wet."

"If you delivered him a brand new coat, fashioned from unicorn hide, and hand sewn by the Prince Regent himself, the colonel would still find a reason to complain."

Emma's smile was halfhearted at best, and Sidney tightened his arm around her.

When they reached the bank, Serena and Enrique helped pull them up, and the group made their way to the base of a rocky cliff with Emma still holding the dripping bundle. Sidney found it hard to believe how different the landscape was on the other side of the river. Jim had been right about the spot. It was strategically perfect. It would be difficult for anyone to sneak up on them with the river on one side and the steep mountain on the other. Fresh water flowed from a mountain stream nearby, and trees and shrubs surrounded them.

They wrung out their dripping clothes as well as they could. Serena set about finding wood for a fire, and Emma began to lay out the coats and blankets to dry, hanging them from branches and spreading them over shrubs. Sidney found a comfortable spot for Jim, who immediately fell asleep. In just a matter of a half hour, the group's spirits had lifted considerably. It was amazing what a fire and the smell of dinner cooking could do for morale. Enrique, surprisingly enough, turned out to have some talent when it came to combining ingredients and soon had a stew of sorts with beans, spices, and some dried meat.

Serena woke Jim and urged him to eat.

It was not long before the shadows of the cliffs grew across the campsite, and the group began to move closer to the fire. Emma shivered and then rose to rearrange the drying blankets and coats.

When it was fully dark, Sidney bid everyone good night, admonishing them to all rest well, as they would have a full day of walking on the morrow.

Enrique did not need any more encouragement. He lay near Jim and was snoring within minutes.

Sidney took the musket, turning away to take up his post as sentinel.

Emma's voice stopped him. "Sidney, are you leaving?" He heard a nervous quiver in her tone.

He tried to sound reassuring. "Just moving a short distance away to keep watch."

"Oh." Emma rubbed her arms. "You will not stay awake all night, surely. You must be as tired as the rest of us."

"I'm afraid I must. Jim needs his sleep to recover from his injury, and Enrique . . . I do not know him well enough to entrust all of our lives to him."

"You will be cold. I am sorry about your coat."

"No more apologies, Emma. I have spent many nights much colder than this on watch. Mostly thanks to the kindness of my commanding officer, Captain Drake." He winked at her, and Emma smiled uncertainly. "Do not make yourself worried on my account. I plan to enjoy my first night of freedom watching the stars and listening to the sounds of the night.

Emma seemed to consider his words for a moment before she nodded. "Good night then." She dipped in a small curtsey and walked back to the fire to join Serena.

Sidney walked slowly away from the camp. Another thing he could thank the years of naval service for was his ability to keep himself awake even when his body cried out for sleep. He'd spent the past several weeks abused, malnourished, and isolated. His body was physically and emotionally exhausted, and the responsibility of his small company's safety weighed heavily on him. One injured colonel, one devious Spaniard, and two women. How would he possibly get this group through enemy territory and deliver them safely to Tarifa? He let out a heavy breath and, for a moment, allowed himself to feel the full burden of his anxiety. Then he pushed it aside as he had done so often commanding lives upon his ship. These people depended upon him, and he would do whatever was required to protect them.

He found a spot that afforded a good view of the camp but was far enough away that his eyes would adjust to the darkness and not be blinded by the firelight. He listened contentedly to the low murmur of women's voices then the sounds of the fire crackling. Noises that he would never take for granted again. Sidney sat back, admiring the moon as it rose above the river and smiled to himself as he tried to remember the last time anyone had bid him good night.

Chapter 13

EMMA LAY UPON THE HARD earth. She had tired of shifting her position. No amount of moving would make the ground comfortable. She felt cold and her underclothing was still damp. If only she were not wearing so many layers beneath her dress. What she wouldn't give to remove her corset, petticoats, chemise, and small clothes; slip into a dry nightgown; and crawl into a soft, warm bed.

On top of her physical discomfort, the nocturnal noises startled and frightened her. She even thought she heard a wolf howling. When she did finally begin to relax, scenes of the battle unfolded in her mind, jarring her out of any sort of restfulness.

Finally, Emma rose from where she lay next to Serena and walked around the campsite, checking and adjusting each wet blanket, shirt, and coat. She stood next to the fire, holding her thin shawl around her shoulders and shaking her skirts, hoping to dry them. She picked up one of the blankets and took it close to the fire, raising and lowering it and turning it around to repeat the process. She continued for some time until it was dry and then laid it over Serena, tucking it around her. Then Emma went back to the fire and placed some more wood over the flames. She repeated the process, this time with the soldier's great coat. The heavy wool took quite a bit longer than the blanket, and when she had finished, she stood for a moment, hesitating before walking toward Jim and spreading it over the sleeping colonel.

She picked up Sidney's coat from where it hung upon a low branch and began to dry it in the same way.

"You need to sleep, Emma." She was startled to hear Sidney's voice behind her, and she turned.

"I am nearly finished. I did not want everyone to be cold." She looked at him then lowered her lashes. "I have never slept outside before."

"I will be close by if you should need me."

Emma nodded but made no move to leave the fire. She pulled the sleeves inside out and held the jacket closer to the heat.

Sidney set the musket against a rock then picked up a blanket, bringing it to the fire. He followed her lead, raising it and lowering it, shaking it and turning it until he was apparently satisfied. He took his coat from Emma, put it on, then wrapped the warm blanket around her. "Now sleep. Tomorrow will be another long day, and"—there was a rustling in the branches above them as a bird moved in the trees.

Emma looked up and moved closer until Sidney held her in an embrace—"I will watch over you," he said, and she could feel his voice rumbling in his chest.

She wished she could remain in the circle of his arms forever. There was nowhere she felt safer. But all too soon, the moment ended, and he stepped back, his hands upon her shoulders.

She tipped her head back to look up at him. The fire cast moving shadows over his bruised face, but his eyes held warmth. "Remember, you are a brave soldier." He winked and picked up his weapon before leaving the circle of the firelight.

As Emma lay back down next to Serena, she sighed contentedly. *Who knew that something as simple as an embrace from Sidney Fletcher could banish my fears and turn the cold, hard ground into a warm, snug bed?*

***

When Emma awoke, she peered out of the cocoon of her blanket. Serena stirred something in a pot over the fire, talking to Enrique. Near them, Jim was sitting upon a rock sharpening his knife in long strokes. Emma stretched, wincing at the stiffness in her body and the soreness of her feet. She stood and folded her blanket then moved to where she had left her boots the night before, hoping they were dry. She lifted a boot, noticing it felt heavy. When something inside moved, she jumped back, dropping it. The boot landed on the ground and a snake slid out.

Emma's mind emptied of all rational thought, and she shrieked, scrambling up onto a rock. Her screams grew louder as the snake slithered across the ground toward her.

Emma heard a whistling sound followed by a *thunk* and saw the snake jerk then lay still. It took her a moment to realize Jim's quivering knife had speared the snake, fastening it to the ground.

She let loose with another scream that shook the hillside.

Sidney tore into the camp. His sword was brandished, and he looked around frantically, trying to figure out what was going on. He had obviously run from the stream. His hair was combed back and held with a cord. Wet strands hung over his forehead and ears. He wore a clean shirt that he'd apparently been in the middle of buttoning when he had heard the screaming.

"What the devil is going on?" Sidney demanded, looking around.

Emma didn't bother to pretend to be shocked by his language.

His gaze landed upon the snake and understanding registered in his eyes. He resheathed his sword, the corners of his mouth twitching. He was clean and freshly shaven, standing tall and handsome with a strong jaw and laughing eyes. A few bruises and scrapes still marked his face, but he was every bit the Sidney she remembered. Heat flooded over Emma's cheeks. She sucked in a breath and put her hand over her mouth, attempting to hold back the wave of emotion that had suddenly overtaken her at his appearance. He looked every bit the man who had stolen her heart all those years ago.

"Lady Emma's found breakfast." Jim walked across the campsite to pull his knife from the ground.

Emma had completely forgotten the snake. She avoided Sidney's eyes as he offered his hand to help her step down from the rock. Her head felt light, and her heart pounded. She hoped the group assumed that she was merely overcome by reptile terror. Her reaction to Sidney was simply ridiculous under such circumstances, she chided herself.

Sidney tilted his head to catch her gaze. "Do not be distressed. Jim has dispatched the snake; although if he had not, I am certain the screaming would have done the job. It nearly frightened the life out of me." He grinned.

"I was startled. I did not mean to react in such an absurd manner." Emma kept her head down, not wanting Sidney to see the color in her cheeks.

"Nonsense, I have heard many a weathered veteran shriek in a similar situation." He squeezed her hand and lifted his eyebrows, attempting to coax a smile, but Emma was too overwhelmed by her rush of emotions. She forced her lips to curl but knew it did not look natural.

Sidney continued in his attempt to cheer her up. "Perhaps you would like to ask your brother about the time we came ashore in Fiji. While the ship was being resupplied, some of the men slept on the beach. When they awoke and found themselves surrounded by hundreds of iguana lizards who had decided to bivouac among them, the squeals and cries could be heard all the way to the ship." He laid his other hand upon her shoulder. "You are not still troubled?"

"No. Although I am terribly embarrassed."

"There is no need—" Sidney was interrupted when Serena joined them.

"Perhaps, Emma, you will join me to freshen up this morning?"

In all the excitement, Emma hadn't even considered her appearance. She had slept without unpinning her tresses and had not given a thought to curling papers. Wincing, she imagined her hair sticking in all directions. Emma glanced around the camp. The sight of Jim slicing the skin off the snake was the last bit of encouragement she needed to follow Serena to the stream.

Emma withdrew her hand from Sidney's, eager to escape. Her reaction to Sidney had shaken her, and she wanted some time to compose herself.

The morning air had a slight chill as the women made their way through the shade of the trees, following the burbling sound of running water and emerging in an open, sunny field at the base of the high mountain.

The stream was cold, but it felt wonderful to wash her face and hands. Emma sat back on the rocky bank and, following Serena's example, pulled off her stockings to let the cold water wash over her sore feet. She hadn't realized how much damage one day of walking in ill-fitting boots could do.

Serena leaned her head back, resting on her hands. Her hair was nearly long enough to brush the rock she sat on. She closed her eyes, turning her face to the sun. "You have known Captain Fletcher for a long time?"

"Yes. Since I was a young girl. He is a close friend of my brother." Emma wondered again about Sidney and Serena's relationship.

"He is a good man." Serena did not open her eyes. "The first time we met him, Colonel Stackhouse told me we can trust him. He knew the captain will help us escape from the prison. And he was *correcto*." Serena allowed a smile to touch her face.

Emma remained quiet. It did not seem as if Serena sought a reply.

"And Captain Fletcher is very handsome, no?"

Emma had lifted her feet from the cold water to examine the blisters, and Serena's question caught her off guard. She glanced up, ready to give a casual answer, but the words lodged in her throat when she saw Serena's expression. The woman's dark eyes searched her face, but instead of scrutiny, they held compassion. Emma knew she could confide in her.

"He is handsome. I had forgotten until just now, how he looked . . . before."

"And you love him."

Emma returned her attention to her feet. "Is it so very obvious?"

"Only to another woman. The men, they notice nothing."

Emma looked up and gave her a half-hearted smile. "He does not know."

"I did not realize until today. But I should have seen this. I should have guessed this is why you came to España at such a time. And Captain Fletcher, he is very lucky to have one such as you."

Serena had brought a comb from the soldier's pack, and she moved to sit on the rock behind Emma, unpinning her hair, then pulling the comb through it.

Emma allowed herself to relax. The gentle tugs felt wonderful, and she was relieved to have Serena for a friend and not a rival.

"And why are you here?" Emma asked, feeling emboldened by Serena's lack of propriety and finding it easier to talk when they weren't facing one another. "I mean, why were you at the prison? Did you travel with the army?"

Serena was quiet for so long that Emma began to worry. Was it offensive to imply that someone was a camp follower? Serena twisted Emma's hair, holding it atop her head and replacing the pins. Finally, she laid a hand upon Emma's shoulder, turning her partly around to look her in the eye, their knees nearly touching.

"I travel to England with Colonel Stackhouse. My brother awaits me there. We were part of a larger party, captured three weeks ago, and . . ." Serena's eyes were wet. She swallowed, blinking hard.

Emma's chest suddenly felt heavy. "The rest of your company was killed?"

Serena nodded.

"I am sorry. Was one of the soldiers your husband?"

"No. The dispatch were *guardas*."

"Guards? What were they guarding?"

Serena leaned close; her hand was still on Emma's shoulder. Her eyes darted toward the camp once before she said softly, "My father, he is very *importante* to the Spanish government. *Un grandee*—a nobleman. The army thought the French would use me to hurt him if I was captured. It was the plan to have the group escort me from España to safety."

Emma looked at Serena. She certainly had the mannerisms and poise of nobility. "And you travel incognito, dressed as a . . ."

"*Una maja.* A peasant."

Emma remained quiet, guilt churning in her stomach. Serena had worn peasant clothing for weeks, possibly longer, as she marched with soldiers. No wonder she had been irritated when Emma had refused to wear the old boots.

"Colonel Stackhouse is an officer," Emma said, piecing together the things she had learned from William's shipmates about prisons and ransom. "The warden no doubt kept him for an exchange." She tilted her head, hoping she did not speak offensively. "Why were you afforded such comfortable living quarters if your identity was unknown?"

"It was the colonel's idea. When we were captured, he told them the truth. It saved my life. But he did not tell them the true name of *mi familia.*" Serena's eyes narrowed slightly, and she raised her chin. "The French soldiers in the fort, they do not know the noble houses of España."

Emma took the comb from Serena and motioned for her to turn around. She ran the comb through the other woman's hair. If it was all true, Serena was every bit the gentlewoman Emma was. And she had traveled much longer, slept in a prison, and watched a troop of men die in her defense. How did she maintain such calm when Emma couldn't manage a few hours without either screaming or breaking down in tears?

Serena kept talking. "Mi familia, we are loyal to *el Deseado*, King Fernando. But many of our friends support France, *afrancesados.*" She said the word as if it left a sour taste in her mouth. "My parents, they were taken to France as prisoners. I fled to the home of our family friends in a small village near Sevilla. When the French army came, they storm through the village, burning and killing and stealing everything in sight. I hid in the small chapel behind the house. I do not know what happened to my friends. Colonel Stackhouse, he found me. He protects me ever since." Serena spoke like she had forgotten Emma was there. The words tumbled out as if she'd held them in too long and needed to unburden herself.

Emma continued to draw the comb through Serena's hair as she listened, hoping the action was soothing.

Serena's shoulders drooped. "Sometimes I smell the smoke and hear the screams in my sleep. Colonel Stackhouse's men, I remember the face of each of them. I see them when I close my eyes. They died because of me. I do not know whether I will see mi familia again. I do not know which of my friends are alive or whether my home is gone. These French, they have taken everything from me." Her voice had dropped to a whisper, followed by a sob.

Without even realizing it, Emma had pulled Serena into her arms and was holding her while she shook and cried.

How did one comfort someone who had seen the things Serena had? Emma thought back to the times she had been held by her mother in this same way when her father had berated her or struck her. It hadn't been her mother's words that had made a difference. Emma had simply wanted to feel as though someone loved her.

When Serena's breathing began to return to normal, Emma spoke. "They have not taken everything. You still have the ability to love, you still have hope, and you have not become like them. Inside, you are still Serena, and nobody can take that away unless you allow it." Emma repeated the words her mother had told her so often.

Serena remained quiet for a long moment. Finally, she shook the hair from her face and wiped her eyes with her fingers. "Emma, I thought to comfort you this morning, but you have brought me comfort instead."

"It is what friends do. Sometimes they cheer each other, and sometimes they break a pot over an ugly Frenchman's head."

Serena smiled weakly.

Emma realized that she could possibly do more than stumble along blindly behind the group. Each of the people in their small company had been imprisoned. They had been part of a war and had seen and experienced horrible things to varying degrees. Though they had endured different hardships than she, the years of comforting her mother, of finding comfort of her own, gave her a capability that she had not thought of before as an asset. Obviously, she didn't have much to offer as far as physical strength, but providing encouragement and understanding had always been something she did well. Her support had made a world of difference to her mother through years of mistreatment. Emma could use this skill to ease the burdens of the small band. Perhaps then, she would not be simply a burden herself.

Chapter 14

SIDNEY HELD HIS MUSKET IN the crook of his elbow, listening to Serena and Emma. He was not close enough to hear their words, but the sound of their voices assured him of their safety. He had followed the women from the camp, remaining out of sight to give them privacy yet close enough to be available should they need him. He didn't dare let them wander off on their own. Not when there could be French soldiers, Spanish thieves, or any number of situations in which they could come to harm. They were leagues behind enemy lines, and such a place was dangerous for anyone, especially women.

Serena had been lucky that Colonel Stackhouse and his company had discovered her when they did. During his campaign through Spain, Sidney had seen a number of women who had not been so fortunate: women whose ears bled from having earrings ripped from the lobes, women with torn clothes and the empty eyes that attested to wounds that would not heal with time, women and children with injuries so brutal that Sidney had been sickened as he imagined the men who had inflicted them.

He shifted the musket to his other elbow. Battles upon the sea, firing cannons at ships full of faceless enemies were infinitely different. He didn't have to see the widows and orphans, ruined lives, and the decimated lands that were the result of foreign armies clashing in the places where people had previously felt safe. War had been his business for nearly twenty years, and recently, he had found himself wishing he had established another way to support his family. The burden of his responsibility for their welfare sometimes felt tangible, like his chest was being compressed.

The women became silent, and Sidney moved closer to the stream. When he still heard nothing over the flowing water, he called out, "Emma? Serena?"

"We are here," Emma responded.

Sidney found them sitting upon the rocks, Emma's arm around Serena's shoulders. Serena was wiping her cheeks, and Sidney could tell she had been weeping. He glanced at Emma, and seeing the slight shake of her head, he knew not to inquire.

"I thought to check on you," he said lamely.

"We are quite all right," Emma said. "Thank you." She reached for her stockings but, seeming to realize that Sidney was watching, hurriedly swung her feet to the other side of the rock, out of view.

Sidney cleared his throat and turned away. He did not want Emma to think he was being indecent, but he couldn't help but notice the deep, bleeding blisters on her feet. He winced. She must have been in a great deal of pain yesterday, walking in boots that didn't fit properly. Today's march would likely make her injuries worse. He wished there was some sort of salve among their supplies. Sidney also could not help but notice the curve of Emma's delicate ankles, and instantly reprimanded himself. He needed to discard these kinds of thoughts. He was her guardian after all. He cast about for something much less pleasant to look at. Fate must have decided to support him in his endeavor as his eyes landed upon Enrique, who approached from the campsite.

Sidney's eyes narrowed. What was he doing here? And more importantly, had he seen Emma's ankles too? Did this pompous Spaniard have no respect for the women's privacy? Sidney ignored the little voice reminding him that Enrique was not the only one intruding.

"*El coronel* is anxious to travel as soon as possible today. The food is prepared, and I think you will quite enjoy it."

"Ah, yes. I find that a side of fried serpent improves any meal, don't you, Serena?" Emma said brightly.

Serena smiled, looking up at Emma gratefully through her lashes.

Sidney felt his heart warm at Emma's attempt to cheer Serena. He had no doubt that the thought of eating a snake was anything but appealing to her. And he couldn't help but be pleased that she did not once look at Enrique as she spoke.

"If you gentlemen will please allow us a few more minutes, we are not quite ready." Emma indicated their discarded boots and stockings.

Sidney stood aside for Enrique and then followed him away from the stream. A few moments later, the women joined them for a hurried breakfast of rice and snake, which somehow, miraculously, Enrique had made palatable. They packed their supplies and began to make their way in the direction that Jim indicated. Which just happened to be up.

***

The group began their ascent of the mountain. At first glance, the slope didn't seem extremely steep, but as they fought their way through dense scrub, around trees, and over loose stones, the incline began to be more of an issue. One particular spot where they would be forced to climb single-file between two large slabs of rock looked particularly daunting. Sidney climbed up first. Not only was it extremely steep, but where the large boulders met, the ground was covered with loose rock, causing him to slip. The only way he managed to navigate over the unstable ground was by pressing against the walls to take as much weight from his feet as possible. As one hand held a musket, he was forced to use his forearm. The pain in his ribs flared up with each stretch and pull, but there was no other choice.

Sidney emerged onto a ridge that ran like a backbone among the green hills. Trees and rocks covered the landscape. The mountain air felt crisp, and the sun was warm. Though not quite the summit, the area was high enough to afford good visibility of the surrounding area.

He was covered with sweat, and his muscles shook. He gently rubbed his side. It was true that he wasn't in prime physical condition after two months in prison, but he was surely the strongest of the party. He had no idea how the remainder of the group would manage.

Where was some rope when he needed it? A sardonic grin touched his mouth. He'd never had that thought before. Aboard a ship, rope was everywhere. He'd spent hours coiling; uncoiling; pulling; climbing; and as a young boy, unraveling rope to make oakum. He'd learned to tie knots, memorized the proper position of every line, and replaced them countless times. He'd had rope burns so deep his hands hadn't healed for weeks. A staple of his life at sea, he'd taken it for granted, and now he would have given anything for a simple length of the stuff.

Sidney searched for a moment and finally found a broken tree branch. It wasn't smooth or even straight, but it was long enough that the others would only need to climb about fifteen feet before they could grab hold. He propped his musket against a rock then planted his feet against the sides of the opening and reached the branch down.

Jim sent Serena first, then Enrique. Sidney recognized that the sequence was by design. Jim was the likely choice to follow Sidney, as he was injured, and Enrique should have been last. But obviously Jim shared Sidney's reservations about leaving Enrique alone with the women.

Luckily Jim seemed to be much improved after a good night's sleep, although the red streaks spreading across his skin underneath the bandage still caused Sidney some worry. Aboard ship, the surgeon would have placed Jim's name on the binnacle list, sparing him from his duties and giving him a chance to recover his strength. However, in this circumstance, taking time for recuperation was not an option.

Jim seemed to be giving Emma some instruction, demonstrating with his hands against the rocks.

Sidney moved the musket closer to his leg, even though Enrique sat a few yards away in the shade of a tree. He wouldn't chance the man taking it while Sidney's attention was diverted.

With Jim's help, Emma pushed her hands against the walls and began to climb, holding herself up with first her arms, then legs, and finally, pressing both feet against one side of the crevice and her back against the other. Sidney let out a breath he hadn't realized he was holding. She was nearly close enough to grab on to the branch. He assumed she was resting her arms, preparing for the next segment, so he was surprised when she turned awkwardly to look behind, and leaning, reached her hand down to assist Jim.

Sidney felt a tingling in his chest that spread warmth through his body. Emma was by far the weakest and smallest of the party, and yet she would assist another, even though she likely did not have the strength to actually be of any use to the colonel.

Jim shook his head, motioning for her to continue, and Emma shifted around and resumed her ascent. Sidney's pulse pounded in his throat as he watched each strain of her muscles and every grimace she made as she struggled closer. He tapped his fingers nervously on the rock. Finally, she was close enough to grasp the branch. Sidney held it with both hands and pulled until he could reach her arm. She let go of the branch, clinging to him instead, and he lifted her the remainder of the way through the gap. Once she was on firm ground, he relaxed and allowed the tension to leave him. He hadn't realized how worried he'd been.

Emma's arms were shaking, and she breathed heavily; however, she immediately turned around and knelt, pulling the branch through the crevice to reach for Jim.

Sidney crouched next to her and took the branch from her hands. "Emma, I will assist Jim. Sit with Serena and regain your strength. "

She looked toward him and then back down between the large slabs where Jim was climbing. "Jim is not well," she said, quietly enough that the colonel would not overhear. "His skin is burning with fever."

"I know he needs rest, but he will not allow us to stop and care for him."

"He will if he thinks it is his idea." Emma pursed her lips. She seemed to be forming a plan. She looked at Sidney for a moment with her eyes squinting, and he would have given a mountain of Spanish silver to know what she was thinking.

A smile of amusement tugged at the corners of his mouth. "Lady Emma, I do believe you are plotting a scheme of some type."

"Perhaps." Emma raised one eyebrow, tilting her head with a teasing smile.

Sidney was caught off guard by her expression. Undoubtedly, she had used the same charms as she flirted with gentlemen among the *ton*. It was, in a word, irresistible. Was she aware of the power her smile had? He shook his head. He was merely a friend, her guardian, and she was certainly not flirting with *him*. In fact, such a concept should not have come to his head.

He turned his attention downward, and Emma followed suit. Jim neared the branch and grasped on to it. Sidney pulled. When Jim was close, Sidney and Emma both reached for one of his arms, hauling him out of the crevice.

Jim sat, leaning against a rock.

Emma offered the canteen, which he gratefully accepted. "Captain Fletcher, I believe the remainder of our party might be thirsty. If you don't mind . . ." Emma raised her eyebrow ever so slightly, signaling that she wanted a moment to talk to Jim.

As he reached for the canteen, he realized that Emma had somehow taken over his command. She had given him an order and effectively dismissed him to carry it out. He was surprised to realize that he didn't mind in the least. It was a relief to have a partner, someone to ease the burden of responsibility, someone to depend on as Jim's condition worsened. The concept was a new one. He'd risen through the ranks of the navy, making decisions as befitted his station. And none of those serving under him questioned him. Life as an officer was lonely.

Perhaps it was her familiarity or the way she calmed and comforted those around her. Maybe it was the solitary months he'd spent in prison. Or knowing she was the closest thing he had to a younger sister. Whatever the reason, Emma's presence and friendship filled him with a joy he was completely unprepared for. And it was as if a heavy weight sunk in his stomach when he considered how fleeting their time together was to be.

Chapter 15

EMMA SAT UPON THE GROUND next to Jim, frowning as she arranged her dirty and torn skirts over her legs. "Colonel, are you certain we are traveling in the right direction? This hardly seems like a path." She indicated the crevice behind them.

"Perhaps you think I am merely torturing you, choosing the most difficult route?" Jim growled.

Emma studied the colonel's face for a moment. His brows were pulled together, his eyes squinted in a scowl. But there was something else—a challenge?

"I would not put it past you, sir. You did, after all, consider a *serpent* to be a suitable breakfast food." Emma tipped her head and gave her most teasing smile. "I wonder what other designs you might have up your sleeve."

Jim lifted his eyebrows, the corners of his mouth turning down in a calculating expression. "Not intimidated by me anymore, I take it, my lady. Seems like a few days as a soldier has given ya a backbone." He nodded. "And about time too."

Emma was relieved. She knew the colonel would listen to her now that she had figured out how to get through his gruff exterior. "Colonel, I am worried about Captain Fletcher."

The man's eyes darted toward the group and then back at her, widening slightly. "And why is that?"

Emma glanced toward the others too before leaning closer to the colonel and lowering her voice. "He was on watch the entire night, and then he pulled each of us through the rocks. I believe it has quite worn him out. I am certain he has some pain in his ribs as well. He will be too exhausted to march another day and stay awake all night without a few hours rest.

However, I know that he will not consider stopping unless he believes that it is for the benefit of the entire group. Perhaps if you should suggest it?"

Jim studied Emma for a long moment, chewing on the inside of his cheek. Finally he seemed to come to a conclusion. "I believe you are correct, my lady. We'll walk a bit farther, and when we reach a suitable spot, I will recommend a halt."

Emma smiled, relieved. One lesson she had learned during her time among the *ton* was how to cater to a man's pride. And it turned out that military men possessed the same attributes as gentlemen in that respect.

The colonel stood, and Emma pretended she did not see his wince as the movement undoubtedly intensified the pain in his head. He offered his hand, and she took it, nearly gasping as she felt the fever on his skin.

Jim called out to the rest of the party. "We'll march a bit farther and then halt for a few hours. Señor Trevino mentioned that he'd like to try and snare some rabbits, and we can avoid the heat of the day if we find some shade and a good, easily defendable position." He offered his arm to Emma, and she took it, noticing the surprise on everyone's face that the colonel would perform such an action. They began to walk along the ridge of the hills.

"Why did you choose this path, Colonel?" Emma asked, feeling as though she should think of something to fill the silence. "There must be easier routes."

"We are nearly twenty miles behind enemy lines. Here, the terrain is difficult, but we have a chance to defend ourselves. Cavalry can't follow us, and the infantry patrols the valleys, but those Frenchies won't venture far because of the militia bands in the hills."

"And the French army is no match for these bands?"

"It is an interesting strategy, my lady. The guerillas, or irregulars, strike small groups of the Frenchies. And they are ruthless. I have seen men nailed to a tree or cut into so many pieces that they were unrecognizable. These bands are no match for the trained army, but their impact on the soldiers' morale is what makes them formidable. Because of the fear inflicted by these irregulars, the French rarely patrol in small groups. Which is another reason we are safer in the hills. We'd see a large company a long way off."

Emma could not believe the colonel was speaking so genially or so bluntly. There was no trace of sarcasm or exasperation in his tone. She wondered if the pain from his injury had become so unbearable that he couldn't maintain his bad-tempered disposition, or if he simply needed someone to listen. "And are we in danger from these guerillas?" she asked, testing the unfamiliar word in her mouth.

The colonel shook his head. "I've no doubt they know of our presence. They could be watching us this very moment, but my red coat is a signal to them that we fight the same enemy. We'll likely be safe."

Emma didn't like the lack of a guarantee. The idea of ruthless warriors watching them caused the hair upon the back of her neck to rise, and she looked around the hills nervously. "How long have you been in Spain, Colonel?" she asked, hoping to distract herself.

"This is my third campaign upon the peninsula."

"And before that?"

Jim sighed and touched his fingers to his temple, and Emma wondered how much longer he could maintain their pace. "Before that, it was much of the same. My father purchased my commission nearly twenty-five years ago, and I began my military service as an ensign. I've fought the same blasted French on three continents—through Egypt, Italy, France, the colonies. Always marching, fighting, searching for food, and preparing for the next battle."

"And do you grow weary of such a life?" Emma could not imagine how anyone could endure the business of war for so long.

"It is what I do." Jim raised his shoulders in a small shrug. "It is the life I have, and at times, it does grow weary. I have seen indescribable horrors."

They stepped over an uprooted tree that lay in their path, and the colonel continued talking. "One freezing winter in Portugal, we occupied a small town. The inhabitants had long since fled or been slaughtered by the French—likely both. The men were so cold that we burned everything we could find. Furniture, shutters, floor boards, rafters. Finally, they began to dig up the churchyard, tossing the corpses aside to use the coffin wood.

"Another time as we marched through Spain, we came upon a river so choked with bodies that we could have walked across without a bridge. I shall never forget these sights."

Emma felt her insides clenching at these images, but she did not protest or comment. The colonel seemed almost to be speaking to himself, and she felt as though anything she might say would simply remind him that she was merely a "screaming debutante."

"But I have also seen remarkable things," Jim continued. "I saw a man, so injured that he could hardly stand, drag his fallen comrade to safety before collapsing and dying. Men, sacrificing themselves so that the rest of the company would have a chance, giving their last morsel to a starving orphan, even as their own stomachs were cramped with hunger. There are few bonds as close as soldiers fighting together, risking their lives for each other. Soldiers become family. And war has a way of proving men's merit."

Jim was silent for a long while and finally turned to look at her. "I'd not meant to wax nostalgic. I hope I have not caused you distress with my ramblings."

"Not at all, Colonel. I feel fortunate that you would share such things with me."

Something that looked almost like a smile touched Jim's lips, but it was gone so quickly that Emma wondered if she imagined it.

He made a sound that was a mix between a sigh and a growl. "Trying to make me soft. That's enough of this genteel talk." He withdrew his arm and reassumed his surly composure before turning to the others. "We'll halt here."

Emma looked around the bluff where they stood. Large boulders were scattered about, and there was a cluster of tall trees next to a mountain stream. The green hills spread as far as she could see. Bright yellow flowers completely covered an entire hillside, and groves of olive trees climbed up another. The prospect was stunning.

Serena filled the canteen at the stream and handed it to Jim.

Jim took a drink and then continued to bark orders. "Señor Trevino, set your snares; see if you can catch us a few coneys for supper. Captain Fletcher, you maintained the watch last night. Bivouac there among the trees. I'll join you in the shade before my blasted head explodes. Lady Emma and Señorita Alvarez will patrol." Without waiting for any acknowledgement, he turned and stomped toward the trees.

Sidney stared after Jim for a moment and then turned to Emma and Serena. "I think the colonel and I have been shanghaied by one lovely young sentry. Be careful around her, Serena, or you will find yourself doing something of which you had no intention, all the while convinced it was your idea."

"I'm afraid I do not know what you mean, sir." Emma replied with every ounce of innocence she could muster; however, she couldn't help but allow a small lift of her brow.

Sidney continued to study her, a smile playing over his face. "And which of you sentries will carry the musket?"

Emma looked at Serena, who shrugged, and then back to Sidney. "We shall take turns, Captain."

Sidney handed her the musket, and she had to rebalance herself. It was much heavier than she had expected. Sidney leaned closer, all traces of teasing gone from his expression. "Do not allow the musket out of your sight." His eyes flickered toward where Enrique had disappeared into the brush farther down the hill. "If anything makes you uncomfortable, wake me immediately."

"You do not trust him." It wasn't a question.

"No."

She tucked the musket into her elbow the way she'd seen Sidney hold it. "Very well. Now, please allow us to do our duty." She began to turn but was stopped by Sidney's hand on her arm.

"I am serious, Emma, anything at all."

Emma nodded, feeling a chill creep up her spine. The warm sun and beautiful surroundings suddenly did not seem as comforting. But she didn't allow her uneasiness to show. She did not want Sidney to change his mind about resting.

She shifted the musket in her arms and touched her forehead in a crisp salute. "Now if you will excuse us, Captain, you are keeping us from our patrol."

Sidney returned her salute, his expression solemn, but a gleam shone in his eyes. "Very well, soldiers. As you were." Giving one last glance around, he turned and walked toward the shade.

Emma and Serena found a flat spot upon a large boulder that afforded a good view of the surrounding landscape. Emma thought how lovely it would be to lie down upon the warm rock, but she contented herself with scooting back and arranging her skirts over her legs. She laid the musket on her lap and sighed. If it weren't for the threat of surrounding enemy armies and the equally disturbing threat of freckles that were certainly sprouting upon her face this very moment, the setting would be exactly perfect.

The two women sat for a long time in a companionable silence, and Emma felt herself becoming drowsy. She shook her head, reprimanding herself. She would not fail in this assignment.

Serena lifted her heavy hair from her neck, and Emma felt a twinge of jealousy at the shine that moved over her dark curls.

"España, she is lovely, no?" Serena said wistfully.

"Yes," Emma replied. "My brother told me that, before the war, it was one of the most beautiful places he had ever seen."

Serena smiled sadly. "It is true. The war has destroyed much in my country, but still, I shall miss her."

"You shall love England," Emma said, attempting to cheer her. "The countryside is lush and green. If you will come visit me, we can walk into town or attend dances at the assembly hall. And we shall not have to worry about the French even once."

"I would like that, Emma. I hope it is something my brother will allow."

"Of course, he will be welcome as well. When we return to London, I will speak to my brother William and have him extend an invitation."

"I will love very much to have a friend in England," Serena said, looking at Emma through her lashes.

Emma linked her arm through Serena's and opened her mouth to reply when Enrique's voice startled her.

"If I might join you ladies?" he said, bowing formally with his toe pointed. He walked around the large rock and sat next to Emma.

She shifted the musket, laying it between herself and Serena. She did not like how close Enrique sat to her or how uneasy he made her feel.

"How delightful to spend time in the presence of you two ladies. The captain, he wishes always to keep you to himself." He lifted Emma's hand to his lips, and she was glad she wore her gloves. As filthy as they were, they still provided a barrier.

She pulled her hand away. "Did you find any rabbits, Señor?"

Enrique placed his hand upon the rock behind them, shifting to rest his weight on it but leaning close to Emma. His breath was warm against her cheek as he spoke. "We must be patient. When the trap is set, it becomes a matter of waiting for the right moment and hoping the other predators are not nearby to steal our prize. *Los conejos.* They are soft and delicate. Many creatures desire them." He brushed his lips against her cheek.

Emma bolted to her feet.

Serena clutched the musket.

"I think we should patrol the other side of the bluff now. Please excuse us, Señor." Emma pulled Serena from the rock, and they walked quickly away, finding a spot closer to Sidney and Jim. Emma glanced back to make sure Enrique had not followed them. He still sat upon the rock, his face twisted in a self-satisfied sneer. Emma had the distinct feeling that the man enjoyed making her feel uncomfortable.

While she dwelled upon these thoughts, her eyes swept the hills and valleys below, and from the corner of her eye, she saw what looked like a flash. She grabbed on to Serena's arm and pointed, waiting to see if she would glimpse it again. A few moments later, it reappeared between the trees on the valley floor. Emma realized several things all at once: the flash was caused by the sun reflecting off a shiny part of a French soldier's gear, there was a road winding its way through the valley toward them, and if she could see them, there was a real chance they could see her too.

Emma dropped, pulling Serena down to crouch behind a patch of shrubbery. Her stomach felt rock hard. She turned and motioned for Enrique to join them but to stay down.

He crept closer, all signs of his offensive flirtation replaced by paleness and wide eyes.

They watched as the four soldiers followed the road. They did not appear to have seen the group upon the bluff.

Emma's hands trembled as she reached for the musket. She crouched, preparing to run to the trees, and whispered to Serena and Enrique, "Wait here. I will fetch the others."

Chapter 16

SIDNEY REFLEXIVELY CLENCHED HIS MUSCLES when he felt someone shake his shoulder. He was instantly awake, pushing past the flare of terror before remembering that he was no longer a prisoner. Something was tickling his cheek, and upon opening his eyes, he found Emma crouched over him. Her hair was beginning to fall from its pins, and strands brushed against his face. *Not the most unpleasant way to awaken*, he thought.

"French soldiers," she whispered.

Sidney's heart slammed against his ribs. He sat up quickly, reaching for the musket that Emma placed into his hands. She pointed, and he saw Serena and Enrique crouched behind a clump of bushes.

"Wake Jim," Sidney said, and Emma nodded. Staying low, he crept toward the others, praying that they weren't about to be discovered. He pressed behind the bushes. From there he could clearly see the group of soldiers moving along a road a few hundred meters away.

Jim and Emma joined them.

"What do you make of this, Colonel?" Sidney asked in a low voice.

"I don't like it. It's unusual to see such a small band. And this close to the hills? They could be scouts."

"Or deserters," Sidney said.

Jim chewed on his lip, watching the French soldiers with his a crease in his brow. "Either way, we'll not want to be seen. And if a larger army is following behind, we're in for trouble."

Sidney felt as though his insides were tying themselves into knots. How would he defend this band against an army? Their best course of action was to remain out of sight.

They all remained crouched behind the bushes as the soldiers passed below them at the base of the bluff and continued along the road. If Sidney were to guess, he would not have thought them on duty. They talked and laughed and didn't seem to pay attention to their surroundings at all. He even thought they might be drunk. But there was no telling with the way the French army trained their troops.

When the soldiers were out of sight, Jim spoke again. "One of us should keep watch at all times. If a larger body is to follow, they will use the same road." He pointed to a group of boulders and trees. "There is the best location for our sentry. Clear view and easily concealed. We'll have plenty of warning against a surprise attack."

Jim studied the view and the bluff for a moment. "Captain, if I might have a word?" Jim tipped his head, indicating for Sidney to accompany him a short way off. Sidney did not take offense to this. Technically, the two of them were equal in rank; however, the colonel was the more experienced in military tactics upon land, and Sidney was grateful for the man's insight.

Once they were out of hearing from the rest of the party, Jim said, "We've about three hours until nightfall. We'll need a more secure location to bivouac tonight. I am of the mind that you are the most equipped to reconnoiter and find a new site."

"I am inclined to agree with you." Sidney felt a measure of relief to be actually doing something. Watching the progress of the soldiers and worrying that they were merely the precursor to a larger party had him feeling anxious to secure the group somewhere safe.

Jim chewed on his lip for a moment, a sign, Sidney was learning, that meant the colonel was deep in thought. "I think Lady Emma should join you."

Sidney could not have been more surprised by the colonel's suggestion. "I hardly think Lady Emma is . . . physically equipped to . . ."

Jim held up his hand, stopping Sidney's words. "It is true. She is obviously the least prepared for a mission such as this. But I have given it some thought." He raked his fingers through his graying hair. "It is no secret that my injury is not healing. I can feel the infection spreading, and at this very moment, it is taking all my strength to prevent myself from falling to the ground." Sidney reached for the colonel's arm, but the man batted his hand away impatiently.

"I would do little good if I were to assist you. The most likely choice is that Spaniard, but I don't trust him or believe his story. I'd rather keep him away from Lady Emma if at all possible. He seems to watch her more closely than the rest of us. Perhaps because she is the weakest of the party.

Or he may have a partiality for fair-haired ladies. Whatever the reason for his attentions, I do not know if I could protect her while you are gone."

Sidney nodded. Everything Jim said made sense. He'd noticed Enrique's interest in Emma, and his chest tightened at the thought of her being left defenseless anywhere near that man. "Do you think Serena is in danger as well?"

"Possibly, but I believe she would make it very difficult for him if he were to attempt anything improper. The fact is I am sworn to protect Señorita Alvarez. And I will do so until my dying breath—which likely will come sooner than later. But he could use one of the women against the other. I do not believe I am strong enough to defend both of them."

Sidney could tell this confession was difficult for the colonel. The man had undoubtedly been in a serious amount of pain the entire journey, and this was the first sign of weakness he had shown.

"And that little British gal might surprise you. She's much braver and quite a bit more resourceful than meets the eye. And I think she would be useful should you meet up with any irregulars. A woman will gain their trust more readily than a single soldier exploring the countryside."

Sidney could think of no argument, other than the potential damage to Emma's reputation by being alone with him. But a quick evaluation of their circumstances rendered that a paltry thought to say the least. London's rules of decorum were of no consequence when lives were in peril.

Jim had thought through the situation, and it seemed as if he had considered all angles. Sidney did not want to take Emma scouting through the rugged terrain, but what was the alternative? The mere thought of Enrique laying a hand on her sent a surge of rage through Sidney and made him want to pound the Spaniard's smirking face—again. And Emma had not complained once. He had seen her push herself to the point of exhaustion without faltering. Once she set her mind, she followed through. Sidney realized he could hardly think of a better man for the job. The thought made him smile.

Jim swayed a bit before he seemed to get control over himself. He turned to the others, speaking loudly. "Señor Trevino, take the first watch." He pointed toward the group of rocks he'd identified earlier. "We can forget about catching rabbits as we'll not be lighting a fire tonight."

Enrique scowled. Whether he was disappointed by the change of menu or the fact that he would be acting as sentry for a few hours, Sidney did not know or care in the least.

"And Lady Emma, you will accompany me?" Sidney said.

Emma blinked and hesitated for a moment, her brow furrowed. "Of course." She glanced to where Enrique was watching her and squared her shoulders. Her face took on a look of determination that Sidney was beginning to find utterly adorable.

Once Jim was settled again in the shade with Serena next to him and a cool cloth over his forehead, Sidney took one more look around the hills. He thought their most promising path would be away from the road, so he led Emma down the slope on the far side, following the stream.

The hill was rocky, and they both slipped on the loose stones, but neither fell. Sidney worried that he was moving too quickly, but Emma managed to keep pace with him.

They walked through a large meadow that was covered by sunflowers. The expression on Emma's face showed him that she was completely enraptured by their surroundings. He studied her from the corner of his eye and wondered how it was possible that such a woman as Emma was unattached. She was clever and pleasant—lovely, certainly. In Sidney's opinion, she was everything a man could want in a wife. It simply did not stand to reason that she had not been spoken for. The only explanations he could find were either William had chased away suitors with his sharp tongue—and where his sister was concerned, possibly his sharp sword—or, more likely, Emma had simply not accepted any offers.

Emma turned to him, smiling, and a warmth covered Sidney's heart. Despite their situation, it was very enjoyable to have her with him. If the circumstances were different, this would be a perfect country stroll. The setting was picturesque, the company amiable. But it was impossible to forget the threat looming over them.

"What exactly are we looking for?" Emma asked, shaking him from his thoughts.

"Primarily, shelter. It will rain during the night."

Emma looked at the sky and then at Sidney. "You are like William. He can predict a storm when there is not one cloud to be seen."

"It must be an old sailor trick."

"You are not an *old* sailor."

"But I will be someday, I fear."

Emma pursed her lips, and Sidney wondered what about his answer had bothered her.

Within a short time, the small mountain stream they had been following had grown much wider as a result of melting snow higher in the mountains. Sidney realized that following the stream would only continue to lead them down into the valleys. He spotted a fallen tree spanning the water like a bridge and decided it was the best place to cross. He pointed it out to Emma, and with sure feet accustomed to running across sail yards, he led the way. Upon reaching the other side, he turned back to help Emma.

She walked unsteadily in the oversized boots, and when she was nearly halfway across, she grabbed a branch that protruded from the side of the tree.

Sidney stepped up onto the trunk again, reaching out his hand, and she clung to it, nearly falling into him when she stepped down.

Emma let out a breath of relief, and Sidney realized she had been more nervous than she had let on. He brushed a strand of her light hair off her forehead, tucking it behind her ear. Her skin was impossibly soft, her hair like silk. And how had he never noticed that her eyes were the precise color of the sky over the sea in the moments before the sunrise?

What the devil has come over me? He shook his head, turned, and continued to follow the stream.

Emma walked alongside, her hands clasped behind her back.

Sidney cleared his throat. "Aside from shelter, we will want a position where we can remain concealed, as that will be our only form of defense should an enemy approach."

Emma glanced up at him for a moment before she must have realized that he was continuing their former conversation. "What is your opinion about the soldiers we saw? Were they scouts or deserters?"

"There is no way of knowing. This sort of thing is Jim's area of expertise, not mine."

"But they made the colonel quite uneasy."

Sidney nodded.

The two of them climbed the hillside silently.

Emma's breathing became heavier, but she didn't fall behind.

Near the top, they found themselves on a ledge covered with large stones. The ground between the stones was flat, and there were rocky overhangs protruding from the steep hillside that could provide a small degree of protection from the rain.

Sidney studied the area. They had walked for more than an hour, and he was convinced they were far enough from the road that the group would have a good chance of remaining concealed. There was even a space nestled among the large slabs where they might dare to light a fire.

He heard Emma calling to him and followed the sound of her voice. When he found her, she was crouched over, peering into a cavity in the hillside.

"I believe I have found the perfect spot," she said.

Before he could stop her, she took a few hunched steps into the small cave.

"It is quite large enough in here for our entire party, though I do wish we had a lantern." Her voice sounded a bit distorted as it echoed. "Come, see for yourself. You may have to turn to the side. Your shoulders are much broader than mine."

Sidney stopped at the entrance to the cave. His heart beat erratically, and sweat broke out over his body. He crouched down and peered inside. The smell of rock and stale water hit him, and he began to shake. Memories of his time in le creux crashed over him. He squeezed his eyes closed, his chest contracted, and he could not draw a breath. Sitting heavily on the ground, he pressed the palms of his hands against his eyes. The terror he felt was overwhelming and was only heightened by the fear that he was going mad.

"Sidney," Emma's voice sounded as if it came from a great distance. He felt her hands upon his wrists. "Sidney, you must breathe."

Emma pulled his hands from his eyes and placed her palms upon his cheeks. Her face gave him something to focus on instead of his terror. She shifted closer, kneeling upon the ground directly in front of him. "Breathe, in and out. It is all right."

Listening to the soothing sound of her voice, Sidney was able to calm his breathing and heartbeat. He allowed her nearness, the softness of her hands upon his cheeks, to comfort him, and finally, the episode began to ebb.

Sidney drew a ragged breath. "I am sorry, Emma." He realized that his hands were clasping her shoulders; he did not remember putting them there. He slid them down her sleeves to hold her hands, lowering them, but not releasing them. He continued to shake. "I am sorry you had to see me like this." He did not want to raise his eyes and see the look of disgust or, worse, pity that was sure to be upon her face. "It is the cave. During my incarceration, I developed an unnatural fear of tight places. It is ridiculous, I know."

Emma remained silent; he held on to her hands as if they were the only thing keeping him from falling back into the darkness that had overcome his mind. Perhaps they were.

"This is not the first time an attack has seized me," he continued, feeling the need to explain himself, to apologize. "I'm afraid I was quite unprepared for it." *What must she think?* He was her protector. The person responsible for keeping her safe from danger, both of man and beast that lurked in war-ravaged Spain. "I am sorry I caused you distress."

"Is that why you will not look at me?" Emma said. "Did you assume I would think less of you for such a thing?"

Sidney lifted his gaze and was astounded to find nothing of censure in her expression. Only compassion and a hint of sorrow.

"I understand far better than you know the effects left on the mind by ill treatment." Her voice was soft. She shifted to sit on the ground, her legs bent and her arms wrapped around her knees. "I do not know if William ever told you about our father."

Sidney cringed inwardly. He did not want to think of that horrible man who had hurt Emma. "Only a very little."

"I cannot blame him for avoiding the subject. The earl was a cruel man." Emma's gaze moved, focusing on a point over Sidney's shoulder, but she seemed to be looking into her mind's eye, remembering the past. "He was especially violent to my mother. And at times his mistreatment extended to me. My brothers were much older than I and rarely visited. William, of course, had no choice. He was sent to sea when he was ten years old—as the second son, my father had little use for him."

"Leaving you and your mother alone with your father."

Emma nodded. "When he drank, he became very angry. Mama and I would hide when he came home late, hoping he would fall asleep before he found us." Her eyes filled with an expression of pain that tore at his heart. "Sometimes he did. But others . . ." Taking a breath, she let it out slowly.

Sidney took her hands again. "You do not have to continue."

Emma shook her head. "I am not telling you this to elicit your pity. It is important for you to know that I do understand." He felt her steel herself and take another calming breath. "Father would scream insults at my mother, horrible things. His voice seemed to shake the entire house. As he yelled, he struck her, often until she fell into unconsciousness. And then, if he was still angry, he would turn his attention to me." As she said this last sentence, her chin began to tremble, but she did not break down.

How had these women survived? Sidney had suffered merely a few months of beating, but Emma and her mother had endured for years. The earl had died when she was fourteen.

Emma's hands grasped his more firmly, as if she were clinging to *him* to prevent herself from being overcome by memories. "I became very afraid of people. Particularly men. At times, when I unexpectedly heard the steward's or the butler's voice or even my brothers', I began to panic. I could not breathe; my heart raced. I felt as though I was looking down a long tunnel, and I lost feeling in my arms and legs. There were times I even fainted."

She had described it perfectly. The loss of control, the paralyzing fear. Relief poured over him like a warm liquid. She did know exactly how he'd felt. The knowledge that he was not alone lit a flame of hope inside him. "And how did you overcome it, Emma? What did you do when you had an attack like this?"

"My mother held me and spoke softly. She reminded me to breathe. And she soothed me until I regained control. But often I did not feel well for days after."

"And have the spells stopped?"

"They have decreased considerably, but no. They have not stopped completely." She adjusted her position, tucking her legs under her, and focused her gaze back on his face. "Telling someone, maybe understanding why you have these attacks might help. I think your fear comes from spending time in a small, cold cell, yes?"

Sidney shook his head. "It is much worse than that. Lieutenant Trenchard devised a torture called le creux. A pit covered with a grate, where I could not fully stand. I sat on the ground with my legs pulled up against my chest. There was no room to straighten them. Rain filled the pit, sometimes up to my chin, and the hot sun burned my skin until it blistered and bled. When I was released after a week, it took days for my legs to bear my weight. When the lieutenant was frustrated with my unwillingness to provide him with information about that blasted coin, he sent me back into le creux."

"How many times?" Emma asked. Her voice shook.

"Twice. Each time for a week."

"Sidney, I am so sorry." She brushed a lock of hair off his forehead. Her face was pale and her eyes wide. Why had he told her this? It was not the type of thing for a lady's ears. Sidney shifted his position to enfold her in his arms, resting her head against his chest. He hoped he provided as much reassurance to her as he drew from her warmth.

"I should not have told you." His chin brushed over her hair, catching the fine strands in his whiskers.

Emma shifted, pulling back to look at him. "Why? Because I am a woman and must be sheltered from the ugly truth of what happens outside of a civilized parlor?" Her lips twisted into a teasing smile, and just like that, the somber mood was broken. "It is too late for such a precaution, Captain."

Sidney allowed himself a smile as well. It was a relief to tell someone and even more to have her understand. It was as if he had been carrying a heavy stone upon his shoulders, and somehow this petite woman had been the one with the strength to lift it off.

He stood, pulling her up with him. "We have an hour's march back to the others, then another hour, at least, to bring them here. Are you up to it?"

"Absolutely," she said, smiling, but he noticed that her eyes were weary.

They walked back down the hillside in a comfortable silence, each lost in their own thoughts. Crossing the stream, they followed it back up the steep slope to the bluff where the others waited.

Sidney had been right. The march took much longer with Jim. The colonel didn't complain but leaned heavily upon Sidney or Enrique the entire journey. It was twilight when they arrived at the site.

Sidney directed Enrique to start a fire and set about preparing a meal. Serena filled the canteen at the stream, bringing it to Jim. Sidney eased the colonel onto the ground outside the cave. He rolled his shoulders and pressed his hands against his back to stretch, then turned to find Emma.

She sat upon the ground, leaning against a rock, her eyes closed. She must have fallen asleep where she'd collapsed after the long march. Sidney lifted off her pack and laid her head down gently upon the haversack. Her soft hair spilled over the pack, and he moved as much of her hair off the dirt as possible. He spread a blanket over her, and she pulled it closer, a soft sigh escaping her lips. For some reason, the small sound caused his heart to melt.

He wondered if he should remove her boots and gloves but thought it was a job more appropriately left to Serena. Her eyelashes rested upon her cheeks in soft brown crescents, and Sidney resisted the urge to find another excuse to touch her hair. On impulse, he leaned to press a kiss upon her forehead, and she shifted, exposing a tear in the palm of her glove. He drew it partially off her hand to check for any damage to her skin, relieved that there was none. When he folded the glove back, he felt something beneath her sleeve. Moving closer, he saw that it was the jade bracelet he had given her.

The sight of it elicited a feeling that he could not name. His pulse jumped, and a warm tingling spread from his chest throughout his body. The idea that she had thought of him during the long months while he was at sea—that, at least to Emma, he was not forgotten—filled him with contentedness, as if somebody had removed his insides and replaced them with sunshine.

He leaned back on his heels, studying her as she slept, wishing that she was not lying upon the hard ground with a ripped glove and her hair in the dirt. Another surge of protectiveness arose inside him stronger than any feelings of duty, self-preservation, or even the welfare of the other members of his party. He knew with a certainty he would do anything within his ability to ensure that nothing happened to Emma.

Chapter 17

EMMA WOKE TO THE SOUND of rain and hushed voices. She looked around the small cave and vaguely remembered Serena helping her stumble inside sometime the night before. With her fingers, she attempted to tame her hair into some semblance of its former style while her eyes adjusted to the muted light that shone through the clouds and spread through the narrow opening. She stretched and wrapped her blanket around her then joined Serena at the cave entrance.

Serena was talking to Sidney, who had not entered but sat close enough beneath the rocks that he remained dry.

Serena's cheeks were wet, and she wiped at them with her fingers.

Emma's heart plummeted. What had happened? She glanced at the other side of the cave and saw the shadowed forms of Enrique and Jim still sleeping.

Emma put her arm around Serena's shoulders, directing a questioning look at Sidney.

"Jim will not wake," Sidney told her.

Serena's shoulders shook.

Dread settled heavily into Emma's stomach. "What do we do?"

Sidney furrowed his fingers through his hair, and Emma did her best not to allow herself to be distracted by the wayward lock that fell upon his forehead. It was not the time to dwell upon Sidney's appearance. His rumpled clothing and day's growth of whiskers made him look like a dashing, swashbuckling rogue.

"Our options are rather limited," he said. "We could wander around these hills in a southerly direction and hope to reach Tarifa eventually, but the chances that we would not be discovered by the enemy are slim." Sidney breathed out heavily. His jaw was tense, and there were lines around his eyes and on the sides of his mouth. "Our food supply will not last longer than a few more days, and without some sort of medicine or a skilled doctor's treatment, I do not think Jim will survive."

"What about the *guerillas* in the hills?" Emma asked. "Would they not help us?"

Sidney seemed to consider the question for a moment then shrugged. "I hope that would be the case, but their camps are hidden, they do not answer to any authority, and I have no idea how to contact them."

Serena moved away, presumably to check on Jim.

Emma scooted closer to Sidney. The mist of rain carried on the air was cool upon her face, and she pulled the blanket tighter around her. "What are your thoughts?" She reached out of the blanket and took hold of his cold hand. His long fingers tightened around hers. She hadn't realized her gloves were missing until she felt his skin sending a tingle over her palm and a blush over her cheeks.

Sidney rubbed the thumbnail of his other hand over his bottom lip, thinking. "We cannot leave Jim here, and if we do not find him help, he will certainly die. If I did not have you and Serena to worry about, I would consider appealing to the first company of French soldiers that we could find."

"You would risk recapture?"

"As I said, our options are limited. The French have typically acted honorably toward British officers. Lieutenant Trenchard was an unfortunate exception." Sidney squinted his eyes. "But, I cannot guarantee that you women would be treated well. And I'll not wager upon your safety."

Emma pondered his words. Would Sidney really risk Jim's life to keep them from mistreatment in a French camp?

"There must be another option," Emma said. "Can we not find a village and appeal to the residents?"

Sidney studied her before answering. "That may be our only recourse. However, the road we saw yesterday is the only one Enrique knows of, and it could at this very moment be overrun with an army."

"Or, it could be empty. And it must lead somewhere." Emma raised her brows. "But how will we get Jim there?"

***

The rain continued to fall as Emma and Serena divided up the men's gear. The women were determined to lighten the loads as Sidney and Enrique would be carrying Jim. Sidney found two long, relatively straight poles, and using the greatcoat and his own jacket, he began to fashion a litter.

Emma convinced Serena and Enrique to help her move Jim to the entrance of the cave. The three of them slid him quite easily across the floor using the blanket, and Emma was grateful Sidney would not have to come inside to fetch him.

They ate a quick breakfast of oatcakes and salt pork, and since the weather seemed no closer to clearing, the group set off in the rain, each carrying a heavier load than they'd arrived with.

In only a matter of minutes, they were completely drenched. Emma and Serena took turns carrying the musket and wiping the rain off Jim's face. They walked slowly, slipping on the mud and wet rocks as they made their way down the hill. Their vision was limited, and they were forced to stop often to rest.

Emma could not think of a time when she had been more miserable. Her clothes were heavy and stuck to her. Water dripped down her face and back and into her boots. The haversack she carried was impossibly heavy, and the musket was awkward. She had slipped and fallen in the mud more times than she could count, tearing her skirts and bruising her elbows as she tried to hold up the musket. The only thing that kept her from collapsing in defeat was the knowledge that Sidney was counting on her and that he had faith in her. She wouldn't let him down.

When they reached the spot where they'd crossed the day before, they saw that the stream had swollen and the tree was underwater. Sidney did not bother to use the bridge at all, marching straight through the water, holding his end of the litter above his head, which forced Enrique to do the same. The rest of the group followed. Emma did not even balk at the idea of walking through the water. Had it been only two days ago that the mere suggestion filled her with such terror?

He led them around the base of the hill instead of up toward the bluff. It was nearly three hours from when they'd set off that Sidney called a halt. He laid Jim down next to a large tree that afforded a bit of protection from the rain and told the group to wait while he and Enrique scouted ahead.

Emma did her best not to crumple to the ground. She held on to the musket—which Sidney had not bothered to take with him, as it was wet—and sat next to Serena, who was tending to Jim.

"How is he?" Emma asked.

"Very hot," Serena replied.

"Do not worry. Sidney will find someone to care for him." Emma twisted her hair to squeeze the water from it, knowing that she must look like a drowned rat.

When Sidney and Enrique returned declaring that the way was clear, they took up their loads and continued their march, finding and following the muddy road in the direction from which the soldiers had come the day before.

Finally, Sidney stopped, and Emma peered ahead through the sheets of rain to see what he was looking at.

In the mist, Emma could only just make out a small farm nestled in the hills. Relief poured over her. Certainly someone inside would assist them. Sidney led them closer, and the rest of the farm became clear. A barn stood next to the house, built from the same whitewashed stone and topped with a red tile roof. The buildings both opened into a square court-yard. The other two sides were surrounded by a low white wall, broken only by an arch above the entrance gate.

Sidney and Enrique set Jim carefully beneath a cluster of trees and sank down next to him. Emma and Serena followed their lead. Sidney cleaned the musket, using a dry cloth from his pack. He loaded the weapon as they watched the farm. The wooden doors of the gates were open, and there was no sign of movement in the courtyard or any of the buildings. This did not seem surprising to Emma because of the pouring rain.

Sidney seemed to draw the same conclusion. He rose and looked first at Jim, then Serena, and then Emma. His eyes darted to Enrique for a moment before returning to Emma.

He motioned with his head for her to join him. "If anyone is inside, they will be more sympathetic if you accompany me."

The idea that she could be inside a warm, dry house prevailed over any nervousness Emma felt at whether the inhabitants would be friendly.

Sidney, however, clenched his jaw and covered the steel of the musket with his cloth to keep it as dry as possible.

Emma stayed behind him as he pushed the gate open and called to the house loudly in Spanish. When there was no answer, he and Emma crossed the courtyard and stepped up to the wooden door. The door was ajar, and Sidney knocked on it, announcing them again, and then pushed it open, cocked his weapon, and stepped inside.

Emma entered closely behind him, her eyes adjusting to the dim light. At first, her mind couldn't understand what she was seeing. The entire house was in disarray, furniture broken and overturned. Pools of dark blood dotted the wooden floor and splattered upon the white walls. Emma froze as she stared into a face. A man with bloody eye sockets lay upon the floor, his body ripped apart. Emma's gaze moved from him to another: a woman, her face like wax, half-dressed with torn clothes and bloody wounds lay next to the man, her body arranged in a vulgar pose.

Sidney turned quickly. "Emma, do not come in here!"

But it was too late. Although she had only glimpsed the scene for an instant, her legs weakened, and her head felt light. She stumbled out the door, falling to her knees in the mud next to the house, and her stomach heaved its contents. Sidney placed his hand upon her shoulder, but she shook her head, pulling away. She did not want comfort; all she could think of was getting away from this place, away from the images that were burned into her mind.

She staggered to her feet and ran through the courtyard to the barn. Tripping across the floor, she didn't even see where she was going. She collapsed in a dark corner, pulling her legs against her chest and sobbing.

Sidney's voice carried from the doorway. "Emma . . ." She heard his footsteps and felt his hand on her shoulder. "Emma, I am so sorry." But she shook her head, unable to articulate her thoughts. She only wanted to be alone. And apparently Sidney understood and squeezed her shoulder gently before he left her to her tears.

It was just too much to bear. On the battlefield, she had been terrified and heartbroken at the ferocious way men harmed one another. Seeing soldiers die had been difficult enough, but this was a family. She imagined that they were kind people, going about their day, perhaps preparing for dinner when . . . She jolted, trying to shake the thoughts from her head. How could she possibly endure another moment in this country? What kind of people murdered innocent families in their home? Her sobs were accompanied by keening cries that hurt her throat, but she didn't care.

When Serena had told her story, Emma had compassion for her. She thought she understood the depths of the horror her friend had felt when the army had attacked. But truly, Emma could not begin to understand what Serena had endured or what all the people of the country had suffered. She had comforted Serena, telling her everything would be all right, and she had thought it was true. But how could anything ever be all right again?

All she had wanted to do was find Sidney. But she didn't think she would survive one more moment in Spain. Not when such depravity and cruelty were around every corner.

As she continued to weep, she felt a hand upon her arm. *Sidney must have sent Serena*, she thought and lifted her eyes, but instead of Serena, the face before her belonged to a child. He spoke to her in Spanish, and though she did not understand what he said, she realized he was trying to comfort her.

The boy was very small. Emma had little experience with children and could not guess his age. Who was he? Was this his house? His parents? Emma bit back another wave of tears.

He asked her a question, and his large brown eyes looked into her face, waiting for an answer.

Emma took a deep breath, knowing she needed to calm herself before talking, or she would frighten him. "I am sorry. I do not understand." She placed her palm upon her chest. "My name is Emma."

The boy looked at her, his eyes squinting in confusion.

"Emma," she said again.

His face lit up, and he placed his hand upon his own chest. "Nico."

"Hola, Nico."

"Hola, Emma." His dark eyes looked at her with an innocence that touched her heart.

She reached into her haversack and handed Nico an oatcake, which he immediately began to devour. He must be hungry. How long had he been in this barn? When he finished, she gave him her last piece of salt pork. The two of them looked up as a shadow crossed the barn entrance. Nico scooted closer, and she put an arm around him as Serena entered the room.

"Do not be afraid," Emma said, though she knew he could not understand her. "Serena, will you talk to Nico? I do not know if this is his house or how long he has been here. Will you tell him that he is safe?"

Serena's eyebrows rose. She sat next to them and spoke with Nico. She listened, occasionally asking a question. "Nico asked if the bad soldiers are gone. I told him yes. He said his mother told him to hide in the barn and not to come out until she came for him. He wants to know where his parents are and if he can go to his house now." Serena's voice cracked, as she spoke. Her eyes shone with unshed tears.

Emma knew that her friend was remembering the horror she'd felt as she hid in a small chapel, not knowing what was happening outside. Her throat constricted. "Will you tell him that we are going to stay in the barn?" Emma put both arms around Nico. "And I think we need to tell him about his parents."

Serena nodded. She spoke softly to Nico, and Emma felt his shoulders begin to shake. She lifted him into her lap, and even though she was soaked, he buried his face against her as he cried for his parents.

Emma wept with him, her heart aching for this small boy who had lost everything. She stroked his dark hair, speaking to him in a comforting voice, knowing her words didn't mean anything to him, but hopefully her tone conveyed reassurance.

As she held him and rocked back and forth, Emma felt all of the despair that had threatened to overwhelm her replaced by a determination to keep Nico safe. He needed her, he seemed to trust her, and he had no one else. A renewed sense of purpose helped to center her mind, and she began to think about what she would need to do to care for him.

Eventually, he sagged against her and slept. Now and then, a small sob would escape his lips.

Serena had left for a moment and returned with a dry blanket. Emma laid Nico on it, tucking it around him.

"Serena, will you stay with Nico for a little while? I do not want him to awaken alone."

"Sí," Serena replied and took Emma's place against the wall, leaning back and closing her eyes.

Emma rose and made her way across the barn to the tools. She lifted a shovel and walked to the door just as Sidney stepped inside.

"Emma, what on earth are you doing?"

"I intend to bury Nico's parents before he wakes. I do not want him to see them like . . . that."

Sidney looked to where Serena sat next to the small boy asleep on the ground. "Nico?"

Emma nodded.

"Serena told me you found a friend." Sidney looked at her and stepped back. His lips began to curl into a shadow of a smile. Emma imagined how she must look. Wet, muddy clothing, her hair a partially dried mess, wielding a farm tool that she truly had no idea how to use. But thanks to her father, if there was something she knew well, it was how to clean up a mess—emotional or literal.

He reached for the shovel. "Enrique and I will do the job much quicker. Will you decide on a burial location?"

"Very well," she said, relieved. She allowed him to take the shovel and place it against the doorframe and then accompanied him out of the barn.

The rain had slowed to a drizzle, but Sidney still protected the steel of the musket. "How is Jim?" she asked.

"He is asleep in the house. Serena found some herbs, and she believes willow bark will help with his fever."

"Serena did not see—"

"No. I covered the remains before she came inside."

Emma felt some of the tension leave her shoulders. She was grateful to Sidney. She did not want Serena to have the horrible images in her mind. She undoubtedly had enough of her own.

"And you?" She motioned to his side. "I imagine willow bark would help your pain as well."

Sidney's eyebrows rose. "I'll admit, I did not even think of it."

"But you will when we return?"

He smiled. "I can hardly remember a time when anyone showed such concern for my well-being. I believe I could become accustomed to it quite easily."

Sidney took Emma's hand as they walked. She felt her heart trip at how easily he performed the action. The possibility that he would grow to care for her more than as a friend or sister bloomed once again in her chest. He led her through the gate and to the fields beyond. "There is a beautiful view from the hill above this field. It would make a lovely burial place."

"Thank you. It will be important for Nico to know that his family was buried properly." She stood in the area he had indicated and turned slowly to take in the view. The rain had stopped and bits of sunlight began to break through the clouds. Mist covered the green mountains above them like pieces of cotton. Sidney was right. It was beautiful. "What about over there?" She pointed to the other side of the farm. "Perhaps near those large trees?"

Sidney shook his head, looking decidedly uncomfortable. "We found the farm animals on that side of the fields. They were . . . slaughtered. I do not think we should allow Nico to see that."

Emma noticed birds gathering in the area and felt a surge of conflicting emotion. The idea that she and Sidney both had a common interest in the boy's welfare caused her heart to feel light, but the sensation was tempered by the repulsion she felt. "Who did such a thing, Sidney?" She turned to face him, holding tighter to his hand. "Do you think it was the soldiers we saw yesterday?"

"I do."

"Why?" she asked.

"I wish I could answer you. I do not know what drives men to such depravity. Perhaps it is in their nature, or it develops as a way to cope with the horrors they witness during battle. When a particular circumstance and a particular group combine, some people perform the most debased acts, while others the most heroic. Men's true characters are revealed at such times." He stroked his thumb over her hand, sending small waves of heat skittering up her arm. "I truly wish I could have stopped you before you witnessed such a scene."

Emma nodded. "I wish nobody had to witness such a thing. I do not know if I feel more pity for the people killed or those they left behind. Poor Nico. What will he do?"

Sidney's expression was tired. "As long as there is war, I am afraid there will be lives ruined." He gave her hand a small tug, and they turned back toward the buildings.

"And there will continue to be heroes. Like you and Jim." She squeezed his fingers, and he stopped outside the barn door.

When Emma looked up at Sidney, the confidence had slipped from his face, leaving him unguarded and his expression vulnerable. She had never seen him looking so exposed. Not even when he had confessed his anxiety to her the day before. "Am I a hero, Emma? Is that how you see me?"

She took a step closer to him, her boots sticking slightly in the mud. "Of course. Why would you ask such a thing?" Standing upon tiptoe, her heart thundering in her chest, she kissed his cheek. "I have always considered you the very best of heroes," she said before turning and going into the barn.

Chapter 18

SIDNEY STOOD STOCK STILL OUTSIDE the barn entrance, his fingers on his cheek. Emma's words still rang in his ears. Her simple declaration meant more than she could know. He did not think any words spoken to him in his entire life had touched his heart in such a way. Certainly not from his own family. He was a means to their lifestyle, and they had little interest in how he obtained the funds they consumed. He had been presented with commendations and even a medal for his bravery at the battle of Copenhagen, but he considered those actions merely his duty, and the words of the admiral rang hollow when Sidney compared them to Emma's.

She considered him a hero? A hero was supposed to be fearless, and Emma knew his dark fears. She had seen him attacked by a fit of panic, paralyzed with terror, and thinking he might die just from a memory. A hero did not falter, doubt himself, or make poor decisions. Sidney did all of these things, and yet Emma still looked at him with her wide eyes full of admiration. He allowed himself to savor the feeling. It washed over him, filling the dark places inside him with brightness. The person who married Lady Emma Drake would count himself the most fortunate of men, and an uncomfortable sick feeling churned in Sidney's stomach at the thought. He would miss her. He'd grown quite dependent upon the way she lifted his spirits. Emma was the closest friend he had known since William left the navy.

Enrique approached, and Sidney put his thoughts away to ponder upon later. "You and I will bury the man and woman upon that hill," Sidney said.

"Dig in the mud to bury strangers? You are mad." Enrique's eyes flashed with annoyance.

"They are your countrymen. Or have you forgotten your declaration of loyalty to the Spanish people?"

Enrique's eyes narrowed. "I have not forgotten." He pressed his lips together so tightly that they nearly disappeared.

"There are shovels in the barn." Sidney said. "We will need to hurry and complete the task before the boy wakes."

"Boy?" Enrique stepped into the barn and looked to where Emma and Serena sat next to the sleeping child.

Sidney stepped inside as well.

Emma was arranging the blanket over him and brushing back his curly hair. The peaceful sight in the midst of the turmoil surrounding them caused the tenderness Sidney had felt earlier to return full-force.

"This is ridiculous," Enrique said.

His voice echoed through the stone building, and Nico stirred. Emma spoke quietly, gently stroking his face to soothe him back to sleep.

"Nevertheless"—Sidney pushed a shovel to Enrique's chest—"I suggest you start digging before the rain returns."

"The dying colonel already slows our progress. We will never reach Tarifa if we gather every orphan along the way."

"We cannot leave Nico alone," Emma said, joining them. "He has just lost his family. He will not survive without us." Her eyes, already swollen from weeping began to fill with more tears, and Sidney knew he could not bear to see her cry again.

"Of course we will not leave him alone. Señor Trevino, you travel under my protection, and you will obey my orders." Sidney shifted the musket, and Enrique took a step back, though his lip remained curled in a sneer.

Sidney ignored him and led the way to the site he and Emma had chosen. With the benefit of the wet ground and Enrique's reluctant assistance, it took only an hour to dig the graves. The men wrapped the bodies in sheets and carry them back across the field. After they had been properly interred, Sidney returned to the house, hoping the willow bark could ease the pain in his ribs.

Jim seemed to be breathing much deeper, and his skin felt quite a bit cooler, although he still had not awakened. Serena had laid out blankets and coats in front of the fireplace, and when Sidney asked, she told him that Emma remained in the barn.

He crossed the courtyard to the other building and found Emma sitting beside a circle drawn in the dirt, playing a game of marbles with Nico.

A marble rolled past his boot, and he stopped it, then he sat on the other side of the circle, reaching out his hand to offer it to Nico.

Nico shrank back, scooting closer to Emma.

"It is all right, Nico. This is Captain Fletcher. He is a good soldier." She wrapped her arm around the boy's shoulders, smiling and turning her attention toward Sidney. "How do I say 'good soldier' in Spanish?"

"That depends. Do you want to tell him that I follow orders well? Or that I will not hurt him?"

"I should have said a *kind* soldier."

Sidney's chest lightened at her simple words. He was going to develop an overinflated ego if she continued in such a way. "*Soldado benévolo.*"

Emma turned Nico to face her. "Nico. Captain Fletcher is soldado benévolo." She raised her eyebrows and smiled at Sidney to get across her point.

Nico looked at Sidney for a moment and then turned his attention back to the game, shooting a marble.

Emma clapped her hands. "*Muy bien!*" she said, although his shot was terrible.

"I have no idea how the game is played," she confessed to Sidney, shrugging her shoulders.

Sidney leaned down and shot the marble, knocking one more out of the ring. Nico rolled the large shooter toward him for another turn. Sidney scored again.

Nico looked at him for a moment, his head tilted as if appraising Sidney. He pointed toward the shooter.

Sidney moved to a better position, aiming and knocking the last marble from the circle.

Nico pumped his little fist in the air, his face breaking into a grin. He gathered all the marbles and arranged them in an x-formation in the center of the ring. Apparently he wanted a rematch.

Sidney smiled. He had not played marbles since he was a child at his father's estate.

"Emma"—he knuckled down and took aim—"your clothes are still wet. There is a fire inside the house."

She shook her head, trying to disguise a shiver. Her hair was not completely dry, and she was obviously chilled. "I do not want Nico to see his house like that. It would replace his good memories to see his furniture broken and blood upon the floor."

Sidney congratulated Nico on his play and then, as he aimed again, said, "We need to decide what to do about him."

Even though he did not look up, he felt Emma bristle. "I will not leave him alone."

Sidney worried that Emma was becoming too attached to the boy and did not see that there were other options.

He sat back, watching Nico. "Perhaps he has family nearby."

"Will you ask him?"

Sidney asked the boy whether he had any grandparents, aunts, uncles, anyone that the boy could think of that he knew aside from his mother and father.

Nico answered each question in the negative. He did not know any relatives. He did like some of the children from the village, but the family hadn't seen them for a long time. He had heard his father say that many families left when the soldiers got close to the village. Sidney wondered why his parents had not fled. Were they *afrancesados*, who felt safe as long as their allegiance was to the French? Not that it mattered now.

Emma watched the exchange closely. She looked at Sidney with eyebrows raised.

He shook his head.

"Sidney, he will not slow us down. I promise. I will help him. I just cannot leave him."

"We will not leave him."

Emma's shoulders lowered, relief evident upon her face.

Sidney bent toward Nico, speaking quietly to him in Spanish. "Nico, I must ask you a favor. Emma is very cold. Her dress is wet and torn. Would you permit her to wear some clothing of your mother's?"

Nico looked at Sidney for a long time. He turned toward Emma, who was watching them with her brows knitted in confusion. She must have heard her name and known they were talking about her. He lifted his gaze to Sidney's. "Sí," he said solemnly.

Sidney's throat was tight. He ruffled Nico's hair. Clearing his throat, he turned to Emma. "Nico has given permission for you to wear his mother's clothes."

Emma's eyes widened, and she shook her head. "I couldn't. It would be too difficult for him."

"Emma, your gown, though lovely, is destroyed. We are climbing higher into the mountains, and you must remain warm. It is a matter of survival." He held her gaze to make sure she understood that he was serious.

Conflicting emotions swam across Emma's face before she finally said, "*Gracias*, Nico." Then, turning to him, "Gracias, soldado benévolo."

Sidney's breath caught in his throat. He attempted to cover his reaction with humor, bowing with exaggerated elegance from his position upon the floor. It seemed that the effect Emma's kind words had on him did not lessen with the frequency with which they were spoken.

He pushed his feelings away, becoming decidedly uncomfortable with their reoccurrence—or even more disturbing, he was becoming tremendously comfortable.

He looked around the barn in an attempt to distract himself, and his eyes lit on some scraps of wood in the corner. "Nico, I wonder how well you can hammer a nail?" he asked in Spanish.

"I hammer very well," he said, raising his chin. "My *papá* taught me."

Sidney pretended to consider him. "I think you might be just the man I need for a particular job." He turned to Emma. "Nico and I have some work to do out here. If you want to go change your clothing, we will be finished when you return. And then we can take Nico up to the hill for a funeral service."

Emma stood and brushed off her dress before she seemed to realize that the fabric was still wet, and it was a hopeless task. She gave Nico a quick hug and left.

Sidney searched through the wood until he found four boards, two longer and two shorter. At his request, Nico had shown him where to find nails and a hammer, and he laid the shorter boards over the longer, forming two crosses.

He allowed Nico to drive the nails into the wood, securing them together.

Nico's face twisted in concentration as his chubby fingers struggled to hold the hammer steady. He repeatedly missed the nail, but he did not become discouraged, only more determined.

Sidney was impressed at the boy's stubbornness. He had to be a strong person to obey his mother and not leave the barn, even though he must have been terrified at the noises he heard coming from his home. And he had undoubtedly been hungry. But he stayed the course. He would make a fine sailor, Sidney thought, with a swell of satisfaction that matched the expression on Nico's face when he had successfully pounded in the nails.

Sidney lifted the two crosses in one hand and held Nico's hand with the other, stepping to the barn door to wait for Emma.

Enrique sat sullenly in the courtyard. The women must have shooed him out of the house while Emma dressed. Sidney asked him to attend to sentry duty.

Serena emerged from the house carrying a basket of wildflowers. When Emma walked through the door, Sidney's pulse jumped, and his stomach did a slow roll. He could not take his eyes from her.

She wore a full skirt, with colorful petticoats beneath it, tied at her small waist with a bright green sash. Her cotton shirt was loose, exposing her soft neck and collarbones. The sleeves did not reach her elbows. She must have found a brush inside the house, as her long, shining hair hung straight, nearly to her waist, held away from her face by a piece of string. The British style of high-waisted gowns was terribly inadequate when it came to displaying the curves of the female figure to its full potential, Sidney decided.

Emma looked exquisite, and the emotions she stirred in him were completely improper for a guardian, elder brother, *or* a man on his way to a funeral. He chided himself and forced his eyes away from the curve of her neck, concentrating on her face, which did nothing to deter his wayward thoughts.

When Nico saw Emma, he rushed to her, and she crouched down to embrace him. Her gaze moved to the hammer he still carried and then to the crosses in Sidney's hand. Her expression softened, and she looked at Sidney gratefully as she took Nico's hand.

"I found a Bible." She pulled the book from a pouch she held. The fact that Sidney had not noticed the large bag full of what appeared to be mementos of Nico's family attested to how distracted he'd been by her change of wardrobe. "Perhaps you or Serena could read a verse in Spanish?"

"Yes, of course. Excellent suggestion." Sidney took the book from her hands, glad he had something to divert his eyes. He led the way across the field with Emma, Serena, and Nico following.

When they arrived, he held the grave markers while the boy pounded them into the soft ground. As the captain of his ship, a funeral was something with which he had far too much experience; however, performing the ceremony with a member of the family present was a new experience. His eyes prickled, and he cleared his throat repeatedly as he watched Nico place flowers upon the graves.

Sidney crouched down to eye level with the boy. "Nico, what are your parents' names?"

"*Mamá y Papá.*"

"Perhaps in *la biblia*," Serena said, taking the book from him and turning to the front. She showed him a list of family names, births, christenings, marriages, and deaths that spanned generations. "Alfredo *y* Maria Siguenza." She pointed to the bottom of the list.

"Will you say a prayer, Serena?"

"Sí, of course."

Serena took a breath. "*Subvención descanso eterno a ellos, oh Señor, y dejar que la luz perpetua brille sobre ellos. Que descansen en paz.*" She made the sign of the cross, and Nico imitated her.

"*Que descansen en paz,*" Sidney repeated.

Tears rolled down Emma's cheeks as she watched Nico. The boy did not cry, but he held tightly to her hand.

The sun was beginning to set, and the dispersing clouds were bathed in reds and oranges. The air around them was especially clear after the rain. Drops of water still clung to grass and leaves, sparkling in the golden light. Serena and Emma seemed to be appreciating the beauty of the evening as well. It seemed they had chosen an ideal location.

Finally, Sidney asked Nico if he was ready to leave, and the boy nodded. The group made their way back to the farmhouse, and Emma returned the Bible to the bag she carried. Sidney wondered what else she had gathered from the house. He accompanied Emma and Nico into the barn and lit a lantern for them.

Serena continued to the house to check on Jim.

Sidney walked to the road and found Enrique, who was more than happy to leave his duty and return to the farmhouse to prepare supper. Sidney accompanied him.

Serena reported that Jim had woken for a few moments and had spoken coherently. His fever seemed to be gone, though red streaks still spread from his wound.

It was decided that Enrique would remain in the farmhouse with Jim, and Serena would join Emma and Nico in the barn for the night. Sidney would stand watch.

While Serena gave Enrique instructions for Jim's care, Sidney took a cup of the soup Enrique had prepared out of onions from the garden and some of the salted pork. When he arrived at the barn door, he peered inside.

Emma had made a bed with some straw and blankets and was singing softly to Nico as the boy fell asleep. When she shifted position, leaning back on one arm, her hair spilled over her shoulder. Sidney thought he could watch such a scene every day for the rest of his life.

Emma looked up, and when she saw him, she stood, pulled the warm shawl closer around her, and tiptoed to the doorway. "How is Jim?" she asked.

"Better. His fever is gone, but the infection remains. Serena said he spoke to her."

"I am glad."

"And Nico?" Sidney motioned with his chin toward the sleeping boy.

Emma sighed. "I do not know how to comfort him. Sidney, could you teach me some things to say?"

"What do you want to tell him?"

"Reassuring things: You are not alone. I care about you. I will keep you safe."

Sidney took Emma's hand as was becoming his habit. Her fingers were so soft, her bones fragile and delicate. The firelight from the lantern shone in her eyes as she looked up at him. He lifted her hand to brush her cheek with his knuckles. Holding her gaze, he spoke softly. "*No eres solo. Me preocupo por ti. Voy a mantenerte a salvo.*"

Emma's breath hitched, and her cheeks flushed.

Sidney pressed the cup of lukewarm soup into her hand. "Good night, Emma." He took a step back, picked up the musket from where it leaned against the side of the barn, and hurried away to keep watch. It was becoming more and more difficult to remember that Emma was his *charge*. He glanced back to where she still stood, silhouetted in the rectangle of light from the barn door. He pulled his eyes away from the sight and forced his mind back to sentry duty. The sooner he got to his ship and returned Emma to her family, the better.

Chapter 19

EMMA LAY IN THE DARK long after Serena and Nico had fallen asleep. The words Sidney had said burned inside her heart. She repeated them over and over in her mind until she was sure she would not forget them.

No eres solo. Me preocupo por ti. Voy a mantenerte a salvo.

She sighed. Something between them had shifted that day. For the first time, when Sidney looked at her, there was more in his eyes than comfortable friendship. It was something that she couldn't name, but the mere thought of it sent butterflies fluttering in her chest and warmed her down to her toes. Her feelings for Sidney were stronger than ever, and she allowed herself to hope that he was beginning to have some of those same feelings for her too.

Nico shifted, and Emma scooted closer to him. She repeated the words once more in her mind, wrapping herself in the blissful memory of Sidney's voice, and fell asleep.

***

When she awoke, sunlight streamed through the door of the barn. Serena and Nico were sitting on his blanket, eating a watery porridge. Nico saw her sit up and stretch, and he hurried to crawl onto her lap.

Emma wrapped her arms around him and pressed a kiss on his curls. When she inquired about Jim, Serena told her he was awake and sitting in a chair, though he became too dizzy to remain standing for very long. Emma closed her eyes for an instant, relieved they would not have to bury Jim as well and that they would finally be able to continue their journey.

After they had all finished eating, Serena offered to comb Emma's hair. She had barely begun pulling the comb through the tangles when Sidney ran into the barn.

Emma's heart jolted when she saw his expression. His eyes were wild, his face pale.

"French soldiers!" He ran to them and grabbed Emma's arm, pulling her to her feet and nearly dragging her toward the door. She held tightly to Nico's hand and was followed closely by Serena. "They have cavalry. You must run. Hide in the hills." He pointed across the fields to the tree line and the rocky cliffs beyond.

Emma's mouth went dry.

Serena turned toward the house. "Colonel Stackhouse!"

Sidney stopped her, and Emma grabbed on to her arm. He pushed both women forcefully toward the opening in the wall. "I will retrieve Jim. Do not hesitate. Go now!"

He locked gazes with Emma for a breathless second then ran to the house without looking back.

Emma made sure Serena was moving away from the house then lifted Nico onto her hip, gathered her skirts, and ran as fast as she could through the courtyard and across the field. Her eyes darted once to the road, and horror coursed through her when she saw a company of soldiers, some on horseback. Though they were still hundreds of meters away, she knew they could most definitely see her.

The plowed furrows of the field were uneven, and she stumbled but did not allow herself to slow. Nico held tightly around her neck and buried his face against her shoulder. He grew heavier while she ran, but she forced herself on, following Serena.

They splashed through a creek and climbed between the rails of a fence, not stopping. Emma did not allow herself to look back but concentrated on the tree line ahead of her. She prayed that they'd find a place to hide and that the others would escape before the soldiers arrived at the farmhouse. She estimated that she had seen around thirty men. There was no possible way Sidney would be able to defend them from such a large company with only one musket and one sword.

She pushed herself on, feeling as though the distance to the cliffs increased instead of lessened. Her legs burned, and she developed a painful stitch in her side. When they reached the trees, she shifted Nico to her other hip. Her arms were trembling from holding him. She struggled for air as her lungs labored and ached.

"Where do we go?" she asked Serena through rasping breaths.

Serena's eyes darted around, and she shook her head. "I do not know."

Emma turned her head, but the trees blocked her view of the field. Were Sidney and Jim and Enrique following them? Were the French soldiers?

Nico said something and pointed.

Serena replied quickly then moved in the direction he had indicated, calling back over her shoulder. "He says there are caves in the rocks."

Emma followed Serena between the trees. Her heart raced, and with every sound of the forest, she was certain the French soldiers would leap out at them. How would she protect Nico? And where was Sidney?

The ground became steeper, and she moved Nico to her back, leaning forward against the slope. They reached the base of the rocky hills, and before long they spotted an opening in the rocks ten feet above them that was only accessible by climbing.

Serena scrambled over the rocks first, clutching tree roots and finally pulling herself up and over the rocky lip that formed the floor of the cave.

Emma struggled, still carrying Nico. She pushed him up onto a large rock, climbing after him. When they were close, Serena reached down and lifted Nico onto the small ledge.

"Is the cave large enough for all of us?" Emma called from below.

"Sí."

Emma turned, straining her ears—afraid the soldiers would burst out of the trees, afraid Sidney would not. "I am going to find the others," she said, turning to sit upon the rock and sliding back down.

She froze when she heard the blast of a gunshot. It sounded as if it were only on the other side of the trees. She felt a scream welling up in her throat but stifled it.

"Emma!" Serena's voice carried a note of anxiety.

Emma grasped on to a partially uprooted tree to lower herself. "I will hurry. Take Nico and hide." She slid, and the bark pierced and scraped her palms, but she did not stop to examine her hands.

Reaching the base of the hills, she glanced up quickly, relieved to see that Serena and Nico were completely out of sight. Then she ran into the trees, trying to remain as silent as possible. The sound of horses' hooves caused her mouth to go dry. The cavalry soldiers were close.

Cautiously, she emerged into the field. Sidney and Enrique dragged Jim between them, each with one of his arms flung around their shoulders. They were nearly to the trees. Behind them, the mounted soldiers rode across the field, drawing nearer with every second. They were close enough that she could see some of their faces.

Sidney looked up at her with panic. "Emma, no! Get back!"

She stepped back a few paces and waited for them behind the tree line. "Hurry, we have a place to hide." Another shot sounded behind her, and she ran, leading them through the trees, up the incline, and to the cliffs.

She heard the men's footsteps and heavy breathing but did not stop to look back, reaching for the tree, ignoring the stinging in her hands and climbing up the rocks.

When Emma reached the ledge and crawled into the opening, cool air surrounded her. Nico clung to her, his body shaking.

Enrique pulled himself onto the ledge and knelt, leaning back over to grasp Jim beneath the arms and heave him up.

Sidney followed closely behind.

Emma pressed back against the cool wall of the cave as Enrique pulled Jim inside and past them. Serena helped lay him gently down upon the floor.

Emma turned to the entrance and saw Sidney hesitate for an instant. The flush drained from his face, replaced by pallor. With Nico still clinging to her skirts, she grasped Sidney's hand, ignoring the pain as she pressed her raw palm to his. When their eyes met, she saw that his bulged with terror. She leaned back, pulling him inside and away from the entrance.

He crouched down and followed, sitting next to her. Nico climbed into her lap.

"Sidney, breathe," she whispered in his ear quietly enough that none of the others could hear. She rubbed her thumb over the back of his hand.

He took a few deep breaths, and she could see that it was with some effort he looked over the rest of the company huddled in the small cave. They could hear the shouts of men outside.

"It is only a matter of time until we are discovered," Sidney said, still breathing raggedly. He shifted his position to pour powder into the pan and then into the barrel of the musket, following it with a musket ball and the ramming rod. He cocked the weapon, the noise echoing in the small space. He grasped Emma's hand again and leaned so close that his rough whiskers scratched her cheek. "When they find us, you must identify yourself as a noblewoman. It is the best protection you will have."

Sidney squeezed her hand again and then released it. The pain from the scrapes on her palm was forgotten as dread settled heavy in her chest. They would either be captured or killed.

Sidney shifted as if to move toward the entrance when they heard a shout followed by the blasts of muskets firing outside the cave. He flung his arm in front of Emma and Nico, pushing them behind him against the cold wall.

The sounds of battle grew louder, and Emma was confused—who was fighting? Shots, screams, yelling in both Spanish and French. Emma held tightly to Nico.

"What is happening?" Emma asked Sidney.

"I think it must be a band of irregulars," he said. Sidney's eyes moved over the members of his company. Finally, his gaze landed upon Emma.

"Remain here, Emma. You must watch over the others."

It took only an instant for her to understand what he was saying. He intended to join the battle. A surge of fear shot through her. She wanted to grab on to Sidney and beg him to remain with them. She searched her mind desperately for something to say that would keep him from this course.

Sidney must have seen the turmoil behind her expression. He twisted around, cupping her face and brushing his thumb over her cheekbone.

She leaned against his hand for a moment, warmth from his touch chasing away the chills of fear that spiked through her veins.

"They need you, Emma." And with that, he was gone.

Emma scooted closer to Serena, clinging to her hand and pressing her cheek against Nico's hair. *But I need* you, *Sidney.* The itch of tears began behind her eyes, but she squelched them. She would not sit in this cave and weep when Sidney expected her to be brave.

The sounds continued outside the cave, distorting and echoing as they reached the small group hidden within. Occasionally a musket ball hit a rock nearby, sending pebbles and dirt skittering onto the ledge, and a now and then, a shadow passed in front of the entrance. Emma's jaw began to hurt, and she realized she was clenching her teeth. She had no inkling of how much time had passed or what was happening outside.

Which side was prevailing? Was Sidney injured . . . or worse? In an effort to push away these thoughts and keep her panic at bay, she turned her attention to her companions, taking stock of their situation. Serena's fists were pressed against her mouth. Her eyes were wide and shining. Jim was unconscious upon the floor, and Enrique huddled in the very farthest corner of the cave with his hands over his ears. Nico's face was pressed against Emma's shoulder.

She wanted to say something inspiring that would ease their fears but could think of nothing. None of them knew what would happen when the battle ended. Would they be killed? Returned to a French prison? Taken by the irregulars? And what of Sidney?

Emma wondered if she was merely imagining it, or were the shots becoming less frequent? The noise seemed to die down, and suddenly it ceased altogether, followed by a loud cheer. She glanced once again at her companions, hoping her smile looked encouraging while it felt like a stretched grimace. It was the moment they all dreaded. What would happen to them?

A scraping sounded outside the cave, and a shadow moved closer. Emma swallowed against the dryness in her throat, thinking she would be ill. She held on to Nico even tighter as she waited.

Chapter 20

"You can come out now. It is safe."

When Emma heard Sidney's voice, tears sprung to her eyes. She placed Nico on the ground and darted through the opening, barreling into Sidney and nearly flinging both of them from the ledge. Sidney's arms wrapped around her, and the tension she had not realized she held in her shoulders relaxed.

"There is no need to fear now. It is over."

"I was not afraid for myself, Captain," Emma said. She stepped back and examined him for injury. There was blood on his clothing, but he assured her it was not his. Emma didn't allow herself to dwell on the implications of his words. Aside from appearing completely exhausted and disheveled, Sidney looked to be unharmed. "Thank goodness you are well."

Sidney's eyes softened, and he looked as if he were about to say something when a voice interrupted him.

"*Capitán* Fletcher, if we had known such beauty was hidden among the rocks, my men would have fought much more fiercely."

Emma looked up and saw a man standing on a boulder above them. A Spaniard, according to his accent. He was young and quite handsome. He wore mismatched, patched clothing with straps and buckles crossing his chest, and his belt bristled with weapons. Emma's first impression was that of a storybook hero. Or perhaps a pirate.

"Marcos de Costales, Señorita," he said. When he smiled, white teeth flashed against his tanned skin.

"Lady Emma Drake."

"Señor de Costales is the *comandante* of the 'Tarifa Volunteers,'" Sidney said. "He has offered to lead us as far as Sierra del Niño."

"I am sorry I cannot take you all the way to Tarifa, Señorita," Marcos said. "But for the safety of my band, we must remain in the hills. Tarifa is less than a day's journey from Sierra del Niño. We will travel by way of Alcalá."

"Alcalá de los Gazules?" Serena asked. She had scooted to the opening and stopped, as there was not sufficient space for her to emerge while Emma and Sidney still stood upon the ledge. Serena's eyebrows were pulled together, and her lips tight with worry. Emma wondered why her friend was concerned.

Marcos's gaze rested upon her. His eyes widened, and he was silent for a moment, then he bowed graciously and spoke to her in Spanish.

Serena nodded, although she did not look convinced.

"Is your injured comrade still inside the cave?" Marcos asked in English.

"Yes," Sidney answered.

Marcos called out orders, and the hillside came to life. Men and some women dressed in the same haphazard manner as their leader scurried around. Some tended to the injured. A group at the base held the reins of the French horses. Emma allowed her gaze to travel around the slope. Bodies were scattered about beneath the cliffs. She turned quickly, not wanting Nico to see what lay below them. The boy was still inside the cave.

"Come," Marcos reached his hand to Emma. "We will treat your companion at our camp. It is not far, but we would like to arrive before dark."

Emma looked up at Sidney. They had left the barn without any of their supplies. "Nico's bag . . ."

Sidney nodded and turned back to Marcos. "I must return to the farmhouse, Comandante. We were forced to abandon our equipment when we fled."

"Of course, Capitán." Marcos called out to a man who waved in response. "José will accompany you. You will travel much faster upon one of my new horses."

Sidney hesitated for a moment, his lips pursed tightly together. Emma could not believe their luck. Marcos was accommodating and would help them reach Tarifa. He said they would even help Jim, yet for some reason, Sidney still seemed edgy.

"You fear to leave your women alone with strangers," Marcos said.

A slight raise of Sidney's brow was his only answer.

"Be assured, Capitán, that I am a man of honor, especially when it comes to protecting a lady. I give you my word that they will come to no harm under my care."

Sidney nodded, but his face did not soften.

"I will return as quickly as possible," he said to Emma. "Help the others." His eyes darted back to Marcos before he climbed down the cliff and ran to the horses.

Nico emerged from the cave, and Emma lifted him, making sure to shield his eyes from the bodies below. She handed him up to Marcos, who passed him higher up the cliff to another volunteer. Marcos took Emma's hand, and she winced at the pain. He cupped her elbow and helped her climb up. Once she stood on the boulder next to him, he looked closer at her palms, holding them near enough that she could feel his breath on her skin. His scrutiny caused her cheeks to burn.

"We must get this treated when we arrive at camp," Marcos said.

"Thank you." Emma withdrew her hands and looked up to check on Nico.

Marcos flashed his white smile again and called to somebody above, who threw down the end of a rope. He offered it to her. "Shall I carry you? Or do you prefer to climb alone?"

"I can do it alone," Emma said, though she knew it was far from the truth. Until the last two days, the only climbing she had ever done was in and out of carriages.

He tied a series of loops and helped secure the rope around her waist and beneath her bottom like a swing. When she grasped the rope, he called back to the cliffs above them, and with a jerk, Emma began to rise. The ride was uncomfortable, and Emma knew she was completely at the mercy of whoever was pulling her up. The thought that she had no control of her situation caused a few moments of panic, but by the time she had gotten her fear under control and figured out how to use her feet to keep from crashing into the rocks, she had reached the top and strong hands had reached to pull her over the edge.

She had not realized how tall the cliffs were until she stood at the top of them with Nico, watching as the rest of her group was pulled up along with the injured members of the irregular band. It seemed that most of the volunteers did not need the rope, they simply scrambled up the steep rocks like spiders.

Emma and Nico sat on the ground next to Serena and Jim. Marcos brought them water and fresh oranges to eat. It was not long after the last members of the party had been pulled to the top that Sidney joined them. He gratefully accepted the food and water Emma gave him and handed her the bag from Nico's house and a shawl for both of the women.

The group continued to care for their wounded, wrapping limbs and building litters and stretchers to transport the injured.

When Marcos was certain they were ready to travel, he gave the order for the group to move out. Jim was placed on a stretcher and lifted by two of the volunteers.

For the next several hours, they marched over the tops of the rocky hills. For most of the journey, Emma and Serena each held on to one of Nico's hands and Sidney walked behind them, but as the boy became more tired, Emma lifted him.

Sidney quickly took him from her, swinging Nico up onto his shoulders.

Emma's heart warmed to see Sidney talking to Nico, pointing out different sights to keep his interest. The pain in her palms became more pronounced, and she tried to work the larger pieces of wood out of her skin with her fingernails.

Emma slowed her steps to keep pace with Serena. "Why do you fear to travel to Alcalá?" she asked the Spanish woman.

"I do not fear it. It is a sad place. Nearly a year ago, the French general, Manbourg, took revenge on the town for an attack upon his company. Every person in the village, including the children, was murdered. Their throats cut. And the castle was blasted to bits."

Emma's skin tightened. She did not know how she still managed to be surprised after the things she had seen, but Serena's story was so terrible. How many more innocent people had suffered—would suffer—in this war?

"The comandante assured me that we will not go into the town, just the lands near it."

"We are getting close." Sidney stepped between the women and nodded toward the sentries in the rocks on either side of the path. They walked a bit farther, between large boulders and trees, and finally emerged in a valley hidden high in the mountains. Tents and campfires were spread across the rocky ground.

As the group snaked their way down the path into the valley, Marcos joined them. "How are your hands, Señorita?" he asked.

Sidney stopped and looked at Emma's hands, his head tilted slightly.

"Muy bien, Señor," she said.

Marcos's brow raised, and his face flashed a dashing smile. "My native tongue is beautiful upon your lips."

Emma lowered her head as heat seared her cheeks.

"I will bring someone promptly to see to your injuries." He turned to Sidney. "Capitán, your wounded man has been taken to the medical tent." He pointed to a large white tent in the middle of the valley. "José will show you where your company will bivouac, and he will arrange for food and water and anything else you might require. I have some matters to attend to, but I hope to meet with you and Señorita Alvarez as soon as possible."

"Of course. Thank you, Comandante," Sidney said curtly. His gaze was still upon Emma's hands. "Your hospitality is more than generous."

Marcos inclined his head and left them.

As Emma watched, Marcos walked slowly to a waiting group of women. His shoulders drooped. She could not hear his words, but she could tell that he spoke gently, embracing a few of the women as they began to weep. She realized that he must be informing them of the losses from the battle.

After José led the group to a comfortable campsite on the edge of the valley beneath a cluster of trees, Sidney and Serena left to meet with the comandante.

Enrique gathered some firewood, and Emma settled a drowsy Nico upon his blanket, making sure he ate some of the stew that José brought.

It was not long after that Marcos joined her, informing her that Sidney and Serena had gone to the medical tent to check on Jim. Marcos brought with him a woman who he introduced as Isabella. She quietly took Emma's hands and, using surgical tools, began to extract the splinters of wood. Emma inhaled sharply as one of the woman's tugs was particularly forceful.

She turned her attention to the comandante, who sat casually upon a log nearby, his legs crossed at the ankles. "I must thank you, Señor, for rescuing us and for the generosity you have shown."

"It is my pleasure. In España, hospitality is an obligation we do not take lightly. It is *muy importante* to us. I am sorry you have to see my country at such a time as this."

"I am sorry as well," Emma said, wincing as Isabella spread some sort of salve upon her palms.

"I do wonder how a young British lady, clearly a noblewoman, comes to be hiding from enemy soldiers in the Spanish hills."

Marcos's question seemed pleasant enough, but Emma thought there was something beneath his polite curiosity. Of course he would wonder what sort of people he had allowed into his camp and whether or not he could trust them. She did not know how much information to give him and so settled for the bare minimum. "My brother came to Cádiz to see to the release of Captain Fletcher from Matagorda prison. The ambassador thought I might have more success negotiating a prisoner's release, so I went alone. While I was there, the army attacked, and the five of us managed to escape. We found Nico at the farmhouse near the cave. His parents had been murdered there." Emma looked up to find Marcos studying her through half-lidded eyes. "I suppose one is never fully prepared for the surprises life has in store for us."

"I agree wholeheartedly. If it weren't for this war, I would have certainly made your acquaintance under more pleasant circumstances. It may surprise you to know that not long ago my life was quite similar to yours."

"It does not surprise me at all, Comandante. You possess the mannerisms of nobility and speak as though you are well educated. Your English is perfect."

Marcos inclined his head, acknowledging her compliment. "My father was the *conte* of Alcalá de los Gazules."

Emma's breath caught, and her stomach clenched as she remembered what Serena had told her of the fate of that city. "I am so sorry. Your family?"

"My family, friends, virtually everyone I ever knew was killed while I was having the time of my life traveling abroad." Marcos let out a slow breath. A muscle worked in his jaw, and the skin around his eyes had compressed ever so slightly, but that was all the emotion he showed. "I have found that I am of more service to my country hiding in the hills and planning attacks than I ever was dancing around a ballroom or attending dull assemblies. It is good to have a purpose, and this one has suited me."

Emma remained silent, contemplating, wishing she could take away the pain that he undoubtedly felt. How did he endure such a terrible tragedy? At the same time, she wondered how he could possibly prefer hiding in the hills and attacking Frenchmen to the life of a gentleman? She remembered Sidney's appraisal of the idle life of the gentry. After the life he had lived, could Sidney ever be content with a peaceful existence on an estate somewhere, commanding servants and attending parties? Could *she*?

Her attention was recaptured when Isabella stood. She had wrapped cloth strips around Emma's hands. Emma thanked her, and the woman left. Not wanting to wake Nico with their talking, Emma moved closer to Marcos, but still an appropriate distance away from him upon another log near the fire pit.

Sidney and Serena returned, and Sidney's eyes narrowed when he looked at Marcos.

Enrique entered the camp and dropped a load of firewood in his haphazard pile.

Marcos rose, and Emma wondered if he had been offended by Sidney's expression. She wondered what caused Sidney to act so unfriendly toward the comandante. Marcos bent forward in a bow. "I did not mean to occupy so much of your time tonight. You must be exhausted, and we have a long journey if we are to reach Alcalá tomorrow." He bowed to the rest of the group and then turned back to Emma, who had also stood. "I hope your injuries heal quickly."

"Thank you again. Good night, Comandante." Emma dipped in a curtsey.

When Marcos had gone, Emma sat back next to Nico.

Serena arranged her bedroll on the other side of the boy.

Sidney watched Marcos walk across the valley. His jaw was set, and his expression pulled into a scowl. When he saw Emma looking at him, he stepped toward her. He folded his arms across his chest, looking down at her. His expression seemed stern. "Stay close tonight."

"Are you angry with me, Captain?" Emma said, feeling small as she sat upon her bedroll with Sidney towering over her.

Sidney's expression softened slightly. "No. Of course not. I am only trying to keep you safe."

Emma lay down, pulling the blanket over her. She felt as though she'd been reprimanded but had done nothing wrong. For the first night since she'd found Sidney, she felt cold and lonely as she fell asleep.

Chapter 21

THE NEXT DAY, SIDNEY AND his company were awake, fed, and marching within an hour of sunrise. The irregular militia's knowledge of the mountain was evident as they guided the group up and down hills, over peaks, through narrow ravines, and across mountain streams. Sidney knew there was no way he'd have been able to lead his small party so smoothly through the rugged terrain.

Jim rode a burro and remained conscious much of the time.

As they marched, Sidney was again overwhelmed by the beauty of Andalucía—the rugged cliffs, the lush valleys, the fields covered with wildflowers, and groves of olive trees. It seemed that every time they crested another hill, a prospect more breathtaking than the last greeted them.

He remained behind his group, not quite understanding why he was wound as tightly as a spring. He could trace the onset of his unease back to the moment Marcos had laid eyes upon Emma and commented on her beauty. The fact that Sidney had not been able to protect her, and they'd instead been rescued by Marcos and his band grated at him. A sound much like a growl had rumbled deep in his throat at the sight of Emma's once soft and constantly gloved hands wrapped in bandages. *He* was her guardian. Not the blasted Spaniard.

Sidney's feelings were bewildering to him. Marcos was typically the sort of person with whom he would feel a camaraderie. He was well-spoken, brave, and honorable, but Sidney could not help but feel the deepest loathing for the man.

The presence of the band of irregulars apparently had the opposite effect on his companions. The comfort of traveling in a larger group had raised their spirits considerably. Emma, Serena, and Nico took turns choosing songs and teaching words to the others. Nico burst out in giggles when Emma attempted to pronounce the Spanish words. Even through his tension, Sidney was relieved to see a smile upon the boy's face.

Marcos slowed to walk with them and joined in singing the Spanish folk song. When they finished, Nico ran ahead to find Jim and the burro, and Serena went after him.

"Señorita," Marcos said, offering Emma his arm, "since we shall be traveling companions for a short while, might I ask you a personal question?"

Sidney's hands clenched into fists from his position a few steps behind them.

"Of course, though I cannot guarantee that I will answer." Emma slipped her hand into the crook of his elbow and smiled up at him.

"How is it possible that you are yet *una señorita* and not married to the happiest man in England?"

Even without seeing her face, Sidney could tell the question made her uncomfortable. What was the blasted Spaniard thinking, asking a lady such a thing? Perhaps it was time he had a lesson in basic propriety.

"I . . . Unfortunately, I have yet to receive an offer I am willing to accept," Emma said.

"Ah. It makes sense to me that you have rejected many suitors."

"Not *many*. But some."

Sidney walked closer, unable to take the man's obvious flirting any longer.

Emma glanced behind her at Sidney. "It is a decision I do not take lightly."

Marcos's glance followed hers. "I see," he said, pinching his lower lip with his thumb and finger.

Sidney tapped her upon the shoulder. "Lady Emma, if I might speak to you for a moment?"

"Of course." She turned back to Marcos, who was looking between the two of them with an odd expression. "Please excuse me."

Marcos halted the group for food and rest, and Sidney led Emma a short distance from the company.

"Emma, what happened to your hands?" he asked when he turned to face her. He lifted her arms and examined her palms that were still wrapped with bandages.

"I slipped and scraped them on a tree, but it was nothing. Certainly such a minor injury should not warrant so much attention."

"The severity of your wounds is not the point. As your guardian, *I* am the one who should be taking care of your injuries."

"My guardian? I do not remember you being appointed as such, and I hardly think it is your fault I have a few splinters."

Sidney swiped at the lock of hair that had fallen onto his forehead, and his eyes darted to Marcos. He was slightly surprised that the sight of Marcos talking to Serena did not bother him in the least. He turned back to Emma. "Whether you realize it or not, in your brother's absence, I am responsible for you. And I feel it is my duty to warn you that the comandante's intentions toward you may not be entirely pure." Even as he said it, he knew he sounded like a ridiculous old woman.

Emma frowned. "And what do you mean by that?"

"I simply mean to warn you, Emma, that you are possibly too trusting of those who may do you harm."

Emma's eyes darkened. Sidney should have recognized the warning of a coming storm. He knew he was acting foolishly, but blast it all, he didn't want the man around Emma.

"Do you mean to say, Captain, that you do not trust Señor de Costales? The man who risked his own life and those of his men, many of whom he was forced to bury in the Spanish mountains, to save us? The same Señor de Costales who cared for Jim and who is even now escorting us through the mountains to safety? Is that the case, Sidney Fletcher? Or is the truth that you do not trust *me*?"

"Emma, I simply wish to put you on your guard. You are a lovely young lady . . ." Sidney swallowed as he tried to think of something to say to her that did not sound completely prudish and condescending.

Spots of red rose in Emma's cheeks. "Thank you, Captain. But I assure you I am quite capable of handling myself around a gentleman. You and my brother, as my *guardians* would both do well to realize I am not a child any longer, and I would consider it a personal favor if you did not treat me as such." Emma turned on her heel and walked back toward Serena.

Sidney watched her go, wondering when their relationship had changed from one of comfortable companionship to something that caused him teeth-grinding frustration.

The remainder of the day did not improve Sidney's temperament as Emma seemed to be avoiding his company.

As they climbed yet another hill, Marcos began to make his way back through the group. He reached Sidney and fell into step next to him. "We are nearly to Alcalá. There is a clearing near the town where we can halt for the night."

Sidney nodded. "Thank you, Comandante."

The scorched ruins of the castle appeared first, high above the valley. As they got closer, they could see the white stone buildings of the town set against the lush green of the Sierra Cádiz Mountains.

Emma and Serena joined Marcos where he stood gazing across his family lands. Dotting the far side of the valley, mounds and crosses indicated the extent of his loss.

Emma wished she could think of something to say. Instead, she laid her hand upon his arm, deciding that comforting her friend was more important than the breach of etiquette.

"It is so beautiful, no?" he said.

"Yes. I am so sorry, Señor de Costales."

As they walked around the outskirts of Alcalá de los Gazules, the mood was somber. The group circled the town, giving it a wide berth, and climbed the hill on the far side. They made camp next to a burned orchard near the edge of the forest. Marcos sent a detachment into the town to draw water from the well, and within an hour, they had prepared and eaten a hearty meal of stew and bread.

Shadows from the surrounding hills spread over the valley, plunging it into premature darkness. Emma arranged a bed for Nico, and Serena told him stories until he fell asleep.

Marcos made his rounds, admonishing the group to rest. They would be well guarded. They had a full day of marching before they reached Sierra del Niño, and the terrain would be difficult.

"Emma, if I might speak with you for a moment?" Sidney said, not missing the look of trepidation in her eyes. She must be concerned that he meant to chide her again. He smiled, hoping to reassure her.

Sidney took her bandaged hand carefully, and they walked away from the group. The setting sun combined with the shadows cast strange light through the charred branches. Emma shivered and pulled her shawl closer around her shoulders. They found a rusted wrought-iron bench near a crumbling wall, the view of the destroyed town spread out beneath them. *Not the most charming prospect.*

He turned toward her, pressing her bandaged hand gently between both of his. "Emma, do you mind very much if we sit for a moment?" he said, gesturing to the bench. "There is something I should like to ask you."

Emma stilled, perhaps realizing the importance of the conversation, and he continued, "I have very much come to depend upon you these last few days. You have constantly surprised me with your bravery and determination. Your ability to act under the most desperate of circumstances, not to mention your compassion, has led me to believe that you are the very person . . ." He leaned close to her, lowering his voice. "Emma, would you—"

"Yes, Sidney," she burst out. "Of course I will."

He blinked, slightly taken aback by her enthusiasm. "Perhaps you should hear what I am asking before you agree to it." He had made a good decision; Emma was dependable like no other. Her eyes shone in the light of the sunset, and at the sight of her, heat spread through his chest. "I do not know what will happen between here and Tarifa. Jim is still ill, and he has entrusted me with Serena's care should anything befall him. If I am unable to perform my duty and conduct her safely from Spain, will you do so?"

Emma pulled back. Her face paled and then flooded with color. "Serena?"

He did not know to what he might attribute her strange reaction, but he continued on. "Yes, Serena is not who she claims to be. She is, in actuality, *Princesa* Serena de Talavera, niece to King Fernando. You can, of course, see how crucial it is to keep this information from our enemies."

"You want me to ensure that Serena arrives safely in England." Emma's voice sounded strangely dull, and she kept her gaze fixed upon the ground. "Of course I will."

"I knew I could depend upon you, Emma," Sidney said. Only a slight sense that something was wrong niggled into his feeling of relief at discharging the assignment.

Emma stood abruptly. "Please excuse me. I have left Nico too long." She didn't wait for an answer but rushed away through the orchard.

Sidney moved to follow her, puzzled, but the sound of a snapping twig drew his attention. He cautiously approached the wall, looking as far up and down both sides as he could in the dwindling light. He saw nothing. Returning to the bench, he sat, studying his hands. He would never understand women. How had Emma progressed through so many emotions in one day? It had only been fifteen minutes earlier that she'd seemed delighted to assist him, even before she knew what he'd intended to ask of her. What had changed? What had she thought he would say? He pondered on every possibility, and his confusion only increased—until he thought back to Marcos's conversation with Emma earlier that day in regard to the suitors she had dismissed.

Sidney's head jerked up, and his heart thumped in his chest so hard he was afraid it had stopped.

Could Emma have mistaken his intentions for a proposal of marriage? He drove his fingers through his hair. And more astonishingly, she had said yes. Not simply yes. He thought of her precise words. *Yes, Sidney. Of course I will.* She would marry him? After turning down others, she would agree to marry a man with no title and limited family holdings, who was literally afraid of the dark?

He stood and, clasping his hands behind his back, began to pace as if he were upon the quarterdeck of the HMS *Venture*. How could he have been so blind? The truth of the situation settled around his heart like a warm blanket. Lady Emma Drake loved him. She had stowed away aboard William's clipper, snuck away to an enemy prison, escaped through a battlefield, marched across rugged terrain on blistered feet wearing a dead man's boots, all the time witnessing atrocities no person should have to see. And all for *him*.

He continued pacing. Forcing himself to be honest, admitting to himself something he'd known all along. He had fallen in love with Emma. He'd stupidly attempted to explain his feelings away as nostalgia or friendship or even brotherly affection. The warmth that had begun in his chest spread throughout his body, and he allowed himself to experience the sensation for a moment until it was doused by the cold waters of reality.

He couldn't permit himself to love Emma. He had promised to take care of his family, and the only avenue available to him was that of a sea captain. He'd made up his mind long ago not to marry. Emma deserved more than a husband who merely visited every year or so.

The moon had risen above the mountains and illuminated his path as he walked back to the campsite. He pondered what to say to Emma. If he told her his true feelings and his inability to act upon them, it would undoubtedly hurt her. But if she believed her own feelings were not returned, would it be even more painful?

Still turning these thoughts over in his mind, he glanced over his small group. Jim slept deeply. Enrique's bedroll was empty. He must be in the woods, attending to personal business. Nico slept between Emma and Serena. Stepping closer, he saw a strand of hair stuck to Emma's cheek. He bent to brush it away and found that it was wet. She had been weeping. His throat constricted as he crossed the campsite to his bed roll. Enrique still had not returned, and just as well. He was quite high on the list of people Sidney wished to avoid.

Sidney wrapped himself in his blanket, but it didn't take long to realize that his mind was too occupied for sleep. Stepping quietly across the camp, he sat against a tree and began to clean his weapon.

Emma shifted in her sleep, pulling her blanket over her shoulder and resting her knuckles against her lips.

Sidney spent the next hour debating whether he would rather possess the fingers that touched her soft lips or the lips that kissed her delicate fingers. Either prospect seemed immensely appealing.

Chapter 22

THE NEXT DAY, EMMA HARDLY noticed the steep slopes she climbed or the gravelly paths she slid down. She found it difficult to rally her smile when Marcos walked next to her, and she couldn't focus on any conversation for longer than a few moments. Enrique had not returned, and a search was inconclusive. Had he left on his own, anxious to reach Tarifa? Or had he met with some misfortune? She knew she should be worried about him, but Enrique's absence somehow decreased some of the tension in their group. Especially in regards to Sidney.

Emma's chest ached, and her cheeks burned as she remembered their conversation the night before, the moment her elation at her fondest desire finally being realized was dashed. She lifted Nico, finding some measure of comfort in his small arms wrapping around her neck. She had made an utter fool of herself and didn't know if she would ever recover from the mortification. Hopefully tomorrow they would reach Tarifa, and she could sail away from Spain, from Sidney, and from everything.

She looked ahead to where Serena walked next to Jim. *Princesa de Talavera*, Emma reminded herself. It was not surprising. Serena's poise and grace made her the perfect candidate for the position. It did not take much for Emma to imagine her friend in a beautiful gown with her thick curls piled on her head, held with a jeweled diadem.

Holding Nico in front of her obstructed her view, and she stumbled over a rock.

Sidney caught her before she fell.

She hadn't even noticed his approach. She mumbled some sort of thanks and turned away, but he did not release her.

Nico wiggled out of her arms and climbed into Sidney's, freeing Emma from Sidney's grasp but leaving her feeling exposed. She pulled the shawl around her shoulders, hurrying after the group.

"Emma."

She fought down the rise of emotion brought on by his tone. Shaking her head, she did not turn but hurried forward, not trusting herself to speak.

Sidney easily matched her pace, catching her hand and stopping her. "Please, Emma. I cannot bear it if you will not speak to me." The softness of his voice stopped her. It was not his fault she had humiliated herself.

She kept her eyes downward. "I do not want to fall behind the group."

Sidney cupped her chin, lifting her face to meet his gaze. "Emma, I should have thought before I spoke. I am so sorry to have caused you any discomfort. Truly, such was not my intention."

Emma lowered her gaze and nodded. She pulled away and continued walking.

Sidney walked next to her, clasping her fingers to avoid the bandages on her palms. "I cannot marry," he said.

Emma's stomach dropped. She had thought it would be impossible to feel any more humiliated. "Please, Sidney, you do not have to—"

"But I would explain myself. My father's final admonition to me was to preserve my family's name. I am responsible for ensuring that they do not fall to ruin. My brothers—"

"I know your brothers," Emma said. She had been shocked when she'd found out that the Viscount of Stansbury and his arrogant family were Sidney's relatives. Surely there were none among the *ton* as well dressed or as loose with their purse strings. The idea that they were so free with the money Sidney risked his very life for made her want to scream.

Sidney nodded. "I imagine you do. Then you understand why I cannot leave this livelihood. The expenses required to ensure that my family's holdings don't fall into debt are substantial."

Emma remained quiet. It was not her place to criticize how the viscount and his family chose to expend their funds.

"I wish my circumstances were different. Truly, I do. In the last twenty years, I have spent only a few months in England. I would not condemn any woman to the fate of a sea captain's wife."

"You do not need to explain anything to me," Emma said. "Especially matters of such a private nature as your family's finances."

"It is important for you to understand, Emma."

Emma's embarrassment had begun to dissipate, and creeping in to take its place was anger. Anger at herself for betraying her feelings so openly, anger at Sidney's family for taking advantage of him in such a way, and anger at Sidney for allowing it. She stopped abruptly and turned to face him, pulling her hand from his grasp.

"Why is it important?" Emma said. "How can your family's personal business be any of my affair?"

Sidney's eyebrows shot up. "I only thought to explain myself. To set you at ease." He adjusted his hold upon Nico, repositioning the musket beneath his arm. The boy had fallen asleep. "I seem to have done the opposite. It was not my intention to make you angry."

"I am not angry. Why would I be angry?" Emma tried not to do anything as undignified as clench her fists or stomp her foot. "Because your brothers and their families have enormous estates and townhomes while you live in a small cabin aboard a warship with eight hundred men? Would I be angry that they attend parties and purchase expensive clothing while you dodge cannon fire and wear blood-stained uniforms?" Sidney's mouth dropped open, but now that the words had begun to flow, Emma could no more stop them than catch spilled water. "If I were to be angry, it might be because while you were tortured and beaten in an enemy prison, William and Amelia wept for you. *I* wept for you. Upon hearing there was a chance you might be alive, my brother—*we*—immediately boarded a ship and came for you. All the while, the very people you sacrifice your happiness and your very life for, threw a grand ball for the entire *ton*." Emma clapped her hand over her mouth as she realized the impropriety of her words. "I am sorry, Sidney. I should not have spoken so rashly." She did not wait for a reply but gathered her skirts and ran to join Serena.

She made it a point to avoid Sidney for the remainder of the day. The climbing up and down rocky cliffs had become exhausting, and none of the party had the energy for talking.

It was late afternoon when they spotted Sierra del Niño. As they approached, they came upon a small mountain village. The entire town was a burned-out shell. Houses had been looted and destroyed. Evidence that this had been an army encampment for some time was scattered around in the form of cast-off bits of equipment and broken wagon wheels. Scars of campfires and wheel ruts marred the landscape.

A monastery stood on a hill above the town. The overgrowth and disrepair, visible even at a distance, testified that it was deserted.

As they neared the village, they could see the white stone buildings set against the lush green of the Sierra Cádiz Mountains. A bell tower rose from the church set prominently in the middle of town. The scene was picturesque but eerily silent.

They followed the road that led through the village and up to the other side of the valley. The high rocky peaks rose in front of them, and Marcos explained that beyond was *la frontera,* the plains that led to Tarifa. "We will accompany you to the other side of the town," Marcos said.

The buildings were close together with narrow streets running haphazardly between them. Broken windows and absent doors created black holes in the white stone houses, reminding Emma of missing teeth. The plaza in front of the church seemed to be the only open space. A few rats scurrying through the shadows were the only sign of life in the quiet streets. Nico looked at the desolation with wide eyes, and Sidney lifted the boy onto his shoulders.

Emma hurried her pace and felt a wave of relief when they had left the empty buildings behind. Ahead, they had only one mountain peak. Tarifa was merely hours away.

Marcos stood silently, waiting for the remainder of the group. His lips were tight.

Emma thought how difficult it must be for him to see his beloved country in such turmoil. "I am sorry, Marcos. For Spain, for Acalá, your family . . ."

He gave her an appreciative smile. "If we do not feel pain, then we did not truly love, and for that knowledge, I am grateful."

Emma studied his expression for a moment, wondering if he intended more with his words. She was unable to read anything but sorrow in his face.

He was silent a moment longer before he seemed to shake off his somber mood.

"It is here that we must leave you," Marcos said. He lifted Emma's hand, pressing a kiss to her fingers. "Though we did not meet under the most ideal of circumstances, I consider it a great honor to have made your acquaintance, Lady Emma."

"Thank you. I do hope we meet again." She dipped in a curtsey, made more difficult by her high boots.

Marcos turned to Serena, speaking to her in Spanish. He bowed deeply and formally, and she pressed a kiss to both of his cheeks in a gesture that seemed to Emma to be very ceremonial. Señor de Costales must know Serena's true identity, Emma decided.

After ensuring they had adequate supplies to reach Tarifa and that Jim was recovered enough to walk, the irregulars departed the way they had come.

Emma and her small group of five looked at each other uncertainly for a moment before beginning their ascent of Sierra del Niño.

Serena linked her arm through Emma's. "It is springtime," she said sadly. "A village like this should be celebrating with flowers and Easter processionals."

Emma did not have any words of comfort. It was as if this forlorn place had cast a shadow over them. They continued to walk in silence until they were over the hill and could no longer see the town through the trees. In front of them spread a prospect of woods interspersed with grassy meadows and farmland. Relief washed over Emma as she realized they would not need to climb any more mountains.

She looked ahead to where Sidney still carried Nico and wondered what he was thinking. She feared she had crossed a line, fracturing their friendship in a way that would never be repaired. The thought caused such pain in her already-aching heart that she gasped.

"Are you unwell, Emma?" Serena said.

"No. I am quite well." She squeezed Serena's arm and smiled.

Sidney halted. "Can you smell the sea?" he said when the remainder of the group joined him. Nico awoke, and Sidney spoke to him in Spanish. The boy sniffed loudly, and Sidney laughed, setting him down and ruffling his hair.

Smiling, Nico ran to Emma. "*Huelo el mar!*" he said.

"*Qué bueno*," Emma responded, using a phrase that Serena had taught her. She glanced up to see Sidney's eyes on her. He opened his mouth to say something but stopped when they heard a noise in the trees.

Sidney cocked his musket and started in the direction of the sound, and Jim pulled the women back.

Emma's pulse sped up.

"There will be no need for such violence, Captain." Enrique stepped out of the trees, and Emma relaxed.

Sidney however leveled the weapon at him. "Would you care to explain your whereabouts for the last fifteen hours, Señor?"

A smug grin spread across Enrique's face that sent cold chills down Emma's spine.

"Captain Fletcher, I suggest you lower your weapon immediately, or you might find that you dislike what Lieutenant Trenchard devises for the members of your little company."

Emma's knees shook, and Sidney's face paled as the warden stepped from the trees, followed by three French soldiers.

"*Bonjour, mes amis.*"

Chapter 23

SIDNEY FOUGHT THE NAUSEATING WAVE of panic, knowing that it empowered the warden to see his fear. "Lieutenant," he said, resuming his sarcastic demeanor. He smiled as he was shoved to his knees and disarmed. "It has simply been too long. And I see we share a mutual acquaintance—not that I should be surprised to find Señor Trevino is an *afrancesado*. He is certainly too cowardly to be a patriot for his count—" A kick to the stomach stopped his dialogue, as he folded over. Another kick beneath his jaw sent him sprawling.

Nico cried out and tried to run to him, but Jim grabbed the boy, practically throwing him at Emma, who pressed his face against her shoulder, whispering to him and stroking his hair.

Sidney spoke to keep the warden's attention on himself. "Ah, Lieutenant, we have been through this countless times. There is no treas—"

After a few more blows, Lieutenant Trenchard left Sidney in the care of his soldiers, one pressed a musket to his head, and the other stepped a booted foot upon his chest.

The lieutenant turned his attention to the remainder of the party. He pushed Jim to the ground, pulling the knife and scabbard from his belt and thrusting them toward a soldier, who bound the colonel's hands.

Jim remained silent, his face defiant, but Sidney knew the man well enough to see the pain that hovered around his eyes.

The women cringed away from the warden when he stepped toward them. "Hola, Princesa," he sneered with a crude gesture.

To Serena's credit, she did no more than raise an eyebrow.

"Señor Trevino," the warden said, "you were correct in your theory about this prisoner. If I had only known, I would have sold her to Napoleon myself, but as I promised, she is your prize. *Madame le guillotine* is not concerned with how she obtains her victims."

"*Merci*, Lieutenant," Enrique said, walking toward Serena. Jim began to struggle, but Enrique struck him in the head as he stepped past.

Jim crumpled to the ground, and Serena moved toward him with a scream.

Enrique caught her arm, but she tore it from his grasp. His face twisted in an ugly expression, and a vein bulged in his neck. He struck Serena across the cheek and grabbed her arm again. "You will find, Princesa, that our time together will be much more agreeable if you will learn to obey."

Nico's terrified sobs were the only sound in the small clearing.

Lieutenant Trenchard stood for a moment, studying Emma and the boy before he spoke. "And here we have the weak link. The colonel and the noblewoman can be ransomed, the princesa sold to the republic, and Captain Fletcher possesses knowledge making him invaluable. But *ce garçon* . . ." He pulled Nico roughly away from Emma and held the kicking boy in the air by the yoke of his shirt.

"Nico!" Emma screamed reaching for him.

The lieutenant pushed Emma toward a soldier, who left the unconscious Jim and held her as she strained to get to the terrified child.

Sidney tried to rise but was pressed back to the ground. His breath burned in his throat as he seethed with helpless rage.

"*S'il vous plaît, Mousieur.*" Emma was shaking. "Please. Do not hurt him. My brother is Lord Lockwood, I promise he will—"

At the lieutenant's signal, a hand was clamped over Emma's mouth.

Serena began a tirade in Spanish but was silenced by another blow from Enrique.

"Mademoiselles, the last thing we need on our little expedition is a crying child." He began to draw his sword, and Emma strained harder. She elbowed the man in the chest and stomped on his foot, lunging toward Lieutenant Trenchard, but the soldier didn't release his grasp. Sidney could hear her screams and sobs, muffled by the soldier, and see the tears dripping from her face.

"Enough," Sidney said in the voice he used to command eight hundred men. Even from his position, prone upon his back with weapons held against him, his tone caused all activity to cease. He continued in a low voice. "I will take you to the treasure, Monsieur. But you will not harm one hair upon the boy's head, or our arrangement ends."

All eyes moved to the lieutenant. He lowered the boy slowly to the ground.

The soldier released Emma, and Nico raced to the comfort of her embrace. She sat on the ground, cradling him in her lap and rocking him back and forth while they both wept.

Sidney stood, holding himself straight despite the new pains in his body. He spoke calmly, though inside his heart raced. He had no doubt that the lieutenant would have murdered Nico. Seeing a child he had grown to love nearly butchered by his enemy—and the thought of what it would have done to Emma—was transforming his terror into blind rage. He struggled to control the fury he felt, turning it instead, as he had so often done, into single-minded clarity. He focused upon one objective. He must save his companions, at any cost.

"Lieutenant, it will be dark in less than one hour, and I suggest finding shelter as it will rain tonight. We have a long day of marching if we hope to reach Baelo Claudia tomorrow."

"Baelo Claudia?" The lieutenant looked toward Enrique.

"Roman ruins near Tarifa," Enrique told him.

"And this is where we will find the treasure?" Lieutenant Trenchard asked Sidney.

"Yes." Sidney felt the ugly clenching in his chest as he revealed the very information the lieutenant had tried to rip from him through months of torture. He was repulsed at having to disregard the promise he'd made to himself—never to break, never to tell. But he knew he'd do it again in a heartbeat to protect Nico.

Lieutenant Trenchard smiled. He and Enrique moved out of earshot to deliberate, and Sidney studied the three soldiers. By the lazy way they held their weapons, he could tell they were untrained, yet he could sense a ruthlessness in their demeanor, no doubt the reason Lieutenant Trenchard recruited them. The three of them stood casually about, apparently trusting that their weapons held enough sway over their prisoners that they did not need to stand at attention. None of them seemed to give any thought to sentry duty.

Serena knelt next to Jim, attempting to wake him. Emma and Nico moved to stand next to Sidney. Nico wrapped his arms around Sidney's leg, and though his hands were bound behind his back, Sidney did his best to comfort the boy with words.

Emma touched Sidney's face, which he just realized was bleeding.

"Thank you," she said, her voice catching.

Sidney's heart, which he had just managed to calm, began to race again, but this time, the sensation was not unpleasant. He had no regrets about giving up the treasure's location. He would do anything to keep her safe.

They turned at the sound of Jim's moan. Serena was helping him to sit up.

"Blast that Spaniard," Jim muttered.

When Enrique and the lieutenant returned, they informed the party that they would be traveling back to Sierra del Niño, the mountain village, to bivouac in the monastery. Sidney held back a smile. The men were doing precisely as he had hoped.

They marched back the way they'd come, through the green valley, which did not seem as beautiful when one was bound and being led at gunpoint. The soldiers seemed decidedly uneasy as they passed the deserted village, and more than once Sidney heard them mention the word *fantôme*. They were scared of ghosts.

The monastery was a maze of rooms and hallways which the soldiers gave only a cursory glance—checking for anything that could be used as a weapon or any windows low enough to climb through—before leaving the prisoners and adjourning to the entrance hall. Sidney was sure, as he'd seen the shoddy manner in which the prison was administrated, that the soldiers would not be overly vigilant in their guard duties once the perimeter was secured. It only took a moment for Emma and Serena to remove the bindings from the mens' wrists.

Jim lay down and was slumbering within minutes.

Emma lay out Nico's bed roll in a corner of the large dining hall and set about calming the child for sleep.

Serena lay down next to them.

Lieutenant Trenchard entered the room, and Nico sprung into Emma's arms. Serena sat up, scooting against the wall.

"I do not anticipate any trouble from you tonight," he said to the group, "but I shall keep the child with me to ensure that none of you attempt to escape." He reached for Nico, who began to wail, clinging to Emma's neck.

Sidney stepped toward them, prepared to intervene.

The lieutenant's lip curled in disgust. Apparently the idea of enduring a crying child all night was not something he looked forward to. "*D'accord*," he said, his gaze moving from the boy to the rest of them. "You know what is at stake."

Sidney waited until the lieutenant had left the room and then followed him, making sure he had indeed joined his companions. When Sidney came back into the dining hall, he sat next to Emma, who was rocking and whispering to Nico. He overheard her soft voice and recognized the words, "*No eres solo. Me preocupo por ti. Voy a mantenerte a salvo.*"

For a moment, he smiled and lost himself in the lightness that such a sight produced in his chest, but a shadow of worry crept into his mind. His plan would never work if Emma did not trust him implicitly. And after all that had happened the night before, he was no longer sure such a thing was possible.

Chapter 24

EMMA STARTED WHEN SHE FELT a hand on her shoulder, shaking her awake. "Nico," she muttered, automatically reaching for the boy lying next to her.

"Emma, come with me." She recognized Sidney's whisper but could only see the vaguest outline of his form in the dark.

He found her hand and led her silently through the halls and rooms and doorways. They stumbled down a dark staircase, and he finally stopped, releasing her hand. Emma's heart pounded. What was Sidney doing? It was certainly the very essence of impropriety for them to be alone together in the dark like this.

"Sidney, what are—?"

A scraping sound and a burst of cold, damp air were her only answer.

"Sidney?"

She felt his hands upon her shoulders. "There is a tunnel, most likely leading to the church in the town. We do not have much time."

Emma felt as if her insides had turned to ice. "Sidney, you cannot flee. Nico—"

"We will return before our absence is discovered, but we must hurry, Emma. It is our only chance."

"I cannot leave him. What if it is discovered that we have gone?" She swallowed against the lump forming in her throat.

"I have watched for hours, they do not maintain a patrol. None of them know there is a way out. You *must* trust me. Jim and Serena will delay the guards if necessary. Come."

"But Nico—"

"It is his only chance as well. I guarantee the lieutenant does not intend to split the treasure with a four-year-old child."

A pang shot through Emma's heart as she realized the truth in his words.

Sidney had begun to pull her forward into the passage as he spoke. Though she could see nothing, she felt the compression of the air and heard the echoes of their footsteps change, indicating they had entered a small space. The air smelled damp. He must have been feeling his way along the wall the same way as she and Serena had when they descended into the prison dungeon.

"And what is the plan when we reach the end of the tunnel?" she asked.

"We must find a way to signal the irregulars. They cannot have gone more than a few miles. If we could find something to burn, it is my hope that Marcos will return to the town to investigate the smoke."

His hand squeezed hers tightly, and it began to hurt her injured palm. She opened her mouth to tell him so when she heard his quick breathing. She had been so consumed by anxiety for Nico that she'd given no thought to how terrified Sydney must be in this underground space.

"I'd begun to worry that this particular monastery was not built with underground access until I found the stairs." He continued to speak, and she wondered if he was trying to distract himself. Though she could not see, she could feel that they were moving downhill at a rather steep angle.

"Sidney, why did you bring me with you? Would not Serena or Jim be a better choice?"

He was quiet for so long that Emma thought he would not answer. Finally, he said in a low voice, "I knew I could not enter this place if you were not with me."

Heat spread through Emma's body as she pondered on his words. Perhaps their relationship was not as damaged as she'd supposed. "I am sorry, Sidney. Earlier . . . the things I said, I should never have presumed to—"

"It seems we both have said things we wish we could retract." He squeezed her hand, and even though she knew it was a gesture of friendship, she still could not help but flinch at the sting on her damaged palm. "I will gladly forgive you if you will do the same for me."

"I will."

Sidney stopped abruptly, and Emma nearly collided with him.

"There must be a door somewhere." He let go of her hand, and Emma realized they had reached the end of the tunnel. She heard shuffling sounds as he apparently began to feel around the walls.

She ran her hands over the stone, searching for anything that might be an opening. She came upon what she thought must be a doorframe, but upon closer inspection she realized it was a ladder attached to the stone. "It is in the ceiling." Emma said.

Sidney joined her and climbed the ladder. "Here," he said a few moments later. She felt the waft of fresh air as he pushed open a trapdoor.

He climbed the rest of the ladder and then turned to assist her. They emerged into the darkened church, behind where Emma guessed the altar would have been, if the entire room wasn't completely empty. The sight gave her a chill of uneasiness as Sidney pulled her out into the night.

They ran through the town, searching house after house for anything they might burn, but any furniture, door frames, even the pews from the chapel were gone. Turning down another street, Emma glanced up at the sky lightening behind the church and felt panic burst from her chest and shoot down into her fingers and toes. They needed to return before their captors awoke.

Something tickled at the back of her mind as she looked toward the church. "Sidney, the bell."

He turned toward her, his eyes narrowed in confusion, but an instant later, understanding dawned on his face. "Brilliant, Emma!" They ran back to the church and stood beneath the bell tower. Even in the dim lighting, they could see that the rope had been cut twenty feet up.

Sidney didn't even hesitate. He grabbed on to the coarse stone and began to climb, swinging himself up over the rafters and wooden supports as she imagined he had climbed riggings aboard his ship.

Emma's hands were clenched into fists, her knuckles pressed against her mouth as she leaned back to watch his ascent.

Reaching a crossbeam, he scooted away from the wall toward the middle of the tower, holding on to the timber with his legs. "Cover your ears," he called down as he reached for the rope.

The wave of sound that hit Emma was enough to shake her off her feet. She crouched on the stone floor of the tower, with her eyes squeezed shut and her hands clamped over her ears until Sidney grabbed her arm, pulling her through the church and down the ladder into the tunnel. Her ears continued to ring.

They ran as fast as they could, Sidney pulling her so strongly up the slope of the tunnel that she felt as though she was not in control of her feet. Her legs ached from the effort of lifting the heavy boots with each step. In the darkness, she could feel the jarring as Sidney's shoulders banged into the walls, but he did not slow down.

Her chest heaved as she struggled to catch a breath. Only the thought of Nico drove her to push past the pain in her legs.

They stumbled up both flights of stairs and through the monastery's turning hallways. The early morning sun shone through the high windows of the rooms they passed.

When they arrived at the hallway outside the dining hall, Sidney pushed her back against the wall while they both tried to catch their breath. They could hear Lieutenant Trenchard's voice booming through the hall.

"Where are they?"

"Lieutenant, I do not presume to speculate as to my friends' private business, but if I were to guess, I suspect they might have slipped away for a midnight tryst."

Emma gasped. How could Jim possibly insinuate something as indecent as a *tryst*?

Sidney looked as if he were holding in a laugh at her horrified expression. He mussed her hair and tousled his own then pulled her beneath his shoulder, whispering, "Put your arms around my waist and act as if you are enamored with me. And for heaven's sake, have the decency to look embarrassed when we are discovered."

"Sidney!" She attempted to put a sufficient amount of indignation in her whisper as heat spread up her neck. Even though he was teasing, she was still mortified.

"Well done." His eyes twinkled. "The blush is a perfect touch."

They walked into the dining hall, Emma feeling like a strumpet draped all over Sidney. What on earth would her mother say if she could see this behavior?

"Lieutenant Trenchard, such a lovely morning, is it not?" asked Sidney brightly.

The lieutenant's eyes squinted as he looked between the two of them. "Where have you been, Captain?"

"Surely you do not expect me to divulge such a thing with the lady's reputation on the line. When it comes to questions about my personal liaisons, I am afraid I must demur."

Emma's ears burned. She cast her eyes upon the ground, knowing full well that the lieutenant was the only one who actually believed she had been involved in anything inappropriate, but even the implication left her feeling humiliated. Nico rushed toward Emma, and she let go of Sidney to lift the boy into her arms. Her eyes met Serena's, and her friend moved her hand back and forth in imitation of a bell ringing and winked.

Enrique rushed into the room, Sidney's sword dangling from his belt. "We have seen nobody leave the town, lieutenant. The soldiers are afraid, worried that it is haunted."

"They should worry less about ghosts and more about the savages in the mountains." The lieutenant turned to the prisoners. "We will depart immediately." He stormed out of the room with Enrique following behind.

The group let out a collective sigh of relief. They had done it. And now they had only to hope that Marcos had heard the bell and would return to investigate.

They gathered their supplies and ate a quick breakfast. Emma thought if she never saw another oatcake in her life, she would consider it the greatest of fortunes.

While she helped Nico with the canteen, Emma overheard Jim speaking quietly to Sidney. "Unusual signal."

"The bell was Emma's idea."

"I told you that gal would surprise you," Jim said, and Emma turned away so the men wouldn't know that she'd been listening. She felt an expansion in her lungs. The words of the two men and their faith in her made her feel strong, which she found she quite liked.

The sensation did not last long as the soldiers arrived to bind the men's hands and escort them to the entrance hall, weapons at the ready.

Enrique approached Emma, and she turned away, but the movement did not dissuade him as it had before. "Señorita, you are mistaken if you believe you are in a position to avoid me." He stepped toward her, crowding her until she backed against a wall. Her breathing accelerated, and her eyes darted past him to the other members of the company.

Sidney was being restrained by two soldiers, his skin flushed and nostrils flared.

Enrique moved to block her view. He slipped his fingers up her arm, resting his hand upon her shoulder, his fingers caressing her bare neck.

Emma's skin crawled at his touch. She tensed as he leaned his face close, brushing his lips on her cheek.

"You would be wise to join yourself with the winning side, Señorita."

Emma did not pull away; she would not allow him to see that he had power over her. "Señor, that is the craven's way." She spoke clearly, not allowing the fear she felt to enter into her voice. "I will not associate myself with cowards who betray their people."

Enrique's face flushed. His eyes narrowed into a glare, and his hand moved to clench around the front of her neck. "You make the mistake of believing you have a choice." He bent his face toward hers, and Emma was terrified that he would kiss her, but Lieutenant Trenchard inserted himself between them, pushing Enrique.

"Señor, we must march now. Soon enough, you will have time with the mademoiselles."

Enrique's intense stare burned into Emma as his mouth curled into a sneer. He released his hold upon her neck. "I will not forget how you treated me, and in the end, I will get what I want, Señorita."

Emma drew a deep breath when her throat was able to expand to full size. There was no disguising her fear now. She wrapped her arms around herself.

She lifted Nico from Serena's arms and retrieved her gear. She was afraid to look at Sidney. Though she knew his anger was not directed at her, she felt too humiliated by Enrique's words and familiar touches to meet his gaze.

When the group emerged from the monastery, the morning was silent and the valley empty.

"It did not rain, Captain," Lieutenant Trenchard said to Sidney.

"My mistake. I suppose one cannot always predict the weather," Sidney replied, shrugging his shoulders.

The soldiers were anxious to leave the valley, talking amongst themselves about the church bell that had chimed before sunrise. They hurried the prisoners along over the path they were treading for the third time. Emma fully expected to see Marcos and his band pop out of the trees, but the prisoners reached the location where they had been captured the day before without incident.

She began to wonder if they should delay. Marcos had told them his territory only extended through the mountains. Would he find them on the plains? Was he even searching for them? She wondered if she should stall or create a diversion, but looking down at the child whose hand she held, she knew she could not risk angering the lieutenant.

"My lady," Jim said, quickening his step to walk next to her. "For the life of me, I cannot remember the words to that ditty you and Nico sang a few days ago. If you would oblige me?" He nodded slightly, his eyes holding hers, trying to communicate something.

"Certainly, sir." Emma began to sing the folk song, nervously, at first, as she glanced around at the soldiers. But they didn't seem to mind. Nico joined in and then Serena.

Lieutenant Trenchard turned from where he marched at the head of the column, annoyed. "Silence! You will alert the guerillas to our position."

"Monsier, that is a very astute observation. Unusual for a Frenchman."

The lieutenant whipped his head around.

"Marcos!" Emma nearly swooned with relief as the man stepped onto the path with a group of his men, surrounding them and freeing Sidney and Jim from their bonds.

The commander of the militia brandished a sword and bowed. "I heard the church bells from the village calling me back. This was no doubt your doing, Captain Fletcher?" Marcos tossed him a sword, and Sidney raised his brows and smiled.

"We would never have found you if it were not for the sound of my favorite childhood tune floating upon the air." He inclined his head toward Emma. "How could I not join such a merry band?" His words were light, but his eyes intense as he stared at the men who had captured his friends.

Lieutenant Trenchard's face contorted with rage as he looked at Sidney. He drew his sword, and Marcos courteously stepped out of the way as Sidney lifted his own weapon.

Emma saw only the flash of the swords before a hand clamped roughly over her mouth, and she found herself being dragged into the trees. She heard the sounds of steel clanging and men yelling as she kicked her legs and scratched at the arms of her attacker. One of her boots flew off in the struggle, but whoever was accosting her continued to pull her away from the group. The sounds of fighting grew fainter. Desperate about the distance between her and the group, she sunk her teeth into his hand.

Enrique cried out and threw her to the ground, the impact forcing the air from her lungs. Emma struggled to draw a breath. Within seconds, he was upon her, his weight smashing her against the rocky earth. She dug her fingernails into his face, but he struck her so hard her vision blurred and her stomach heaved.

Terror laced through Emma's veins, as she realized that no amount of fighting would prevail against this man's strength. Her instinct was to surrender and retreat into herself as she had done so often when her father had hurt her, but she was no longer a frightened child, and she would continue to resist until she could not.

Enrique's face was nearly unrecognizable as the handsome Spanish gentleman she had known. Spittle accumulated in the corners of his mouth, and his eyes were bloodshot and crazed. Red streaks ran down his cheeks where she had scratched him.

As she continued to writhe and struggle, Enrique struck her again. Darkness tinged the edges of her vision, slowly closing in. She did her best to force it away, but her muscles were weakening, and her body hurt. Just as she started to give in to the shadows spreading over her consciousness, she heard Sidney yelling her name.

The weight was lifted from her, and she blinked, attempting to awaken her mind, but it was sluggish.

"I warned you, Señor," she heard Sidney mutter, as they seemed to draw away from her, and then it was silent.

Emma jerked, not certain whether she had slipped into unconsciousness or whether she had been left alone. Her vision was blurred, and she couldn't see anything but the trees surrounding her. She struggled to sit up, blinking against the pain and dizziness. Not knowing quite how it happened, she found herself in Sidney's arms.

He knelt next to her, tilting her head from side to side, as he examined her face then cupped her cheeks in his hands. "Emma." The look in his eyes threatened to melt her heart. "I thought I'd lost you."

Before she could think of something to reassure him that she was all right, Sidney pressed his lips to hers, and the world stopped.

Emma wrapped her arms around Sidney's neck and was flooded with heat that sent shivers over every nerve ending. Her heart pounded, and her skin tingled. Every terrible thing that had happened these last few days was suddenly pushed aside, and Emma felt as if nothing in her life could ever be as magical as the feel of Sidney's kiss. When their lips parted, she sighed and tried to convince her mind to work once again.

She opened her eyes, blinking against the fogginess in her brain. The pain in her head combined with the jumble of emotions made it difficult to focus. She struggled to pull her mind from the darkness.

Sidney brushed his thumbs along her jaw. "I love you, Emma," he said, his voice low and raspy.

"Truly?" she asked, hoping that the fogginess in her mind was not causing her to hallucinate.

Leaning close, he touched his lips softly against hers once again. "Truly."

Chapter 25

SIDNEY CARRIED EMMA THROUGH THE woods despite her insistence that she could walk on her own. Her eyes seemed unable to focus, and she swayed when she stood. Her body trembled, and he could tell she made an effort to stop herself from weeping. The sight of the ugly bruises and drying blood marring her delicate skin made his chest ache. She leaned her head against his neck, and he brushed a kiss on her hair.

Stepping out from the dim light of the forest, Sidney squinted as his eyes adjusted. He did not see the bodies of Lieutenant Trenchard and the French soldiers, and he was grateful to Marcos and his band for removing them and sparing Emma, Serena, and Nico from the sight.

Marcos and Jim stood to one side, and Serena sat upon the ground with Nico. When they caught sight of Sidney and Emma, the entire group rushed toward her.

Sidney set her down, laying her back carefully against his pack. Emma closed her eyes. Serena used a wet rag to wipe the blood and dirt from her face and arms while Nico stood close to supervise. Sidney smiled at the serious look on the boy's face. If Nico hadn't yelled to Sidney that Emma had been taken, he may never have found her. Nobody else had seen it happen. He glanced down at her feet, setting the boot upon the ground next to her. The boots she hated had likely saved her life when he'd found the one she lost and known in which direction to search.

Sidney stood and listened to Jim and Marcos's report about the skirmish. He was relieved to learn that his tormentor would no longer be a threat. He told them in low tones about Enrique, and the men shook hands, feeling the mixture of elation and soberness that a victory resulting in loss of life always produced.

He returned to Emma. She was awake and speaking to Serena and Nico. When she saw him, she smiled warmly.

Marcos knelt on one knee next to her. "How do you feel, Señorita?"

"Aside from a slight headache, I am well." She moved to stand, and Marcos took her hand, pulling her to her feet. She wobbled slightly but steadied herself.

"If you are well enough to travel, I am afraid I must bid you farewell once again," Marcos said.

Emma embraced Marcos, who glanced to Sidney before putting his arms around her. She kissed his cheek. "We knew you would come, Señor. Gracias."

"For such a payment, I would gladly do so again." He reached to assist Serena, bidding her and Nico farewell. He bowed to them all and signaled his men. The irregulars disappeared into the trees.

Emma rubbed her fingers on her forehead, and Sidney took her arm.

"If you are not well enough, we can travel to Tarifa tomorrow."

She began to shake her head but stopped quickly. It must have been painful. "I want to go home, Sidney." Her lip trembled as she glanced toward the forest where she had been dragged and assaulted. Hugging her arms around herself, she looked up at him; the troubled look in her eyes and bruises on her face made his stomach sink. "Enrique . . ."

"You need not fear him anymore," Sidney said quietly.

Emma nodded her head, and he was relieved she did not ask for details.

The group made relatively good time descending the stony ridge of Sierra del Niño and marching across the rolling hills of la frontera. They stopped often for Emma to rest, although she protested vehemently each time. Sidney could not have been prouder. She had become a true soldier. They walked through olive groves and across rolling hills. The smell of the ocean was becoming stronger, and the group quickened their steps.

When they reached a road, Sidney was hesitant to follow it, desiring the cover of trees, but almost immediately, they were surrounded by a company of British soldiers, and he practically sagged in relief. His company—Emma—was safe.

The sight of a naval captain and an injured colonel, to say nothing of the two lovely women who accompanied them, spurred the soldiers into action. A wagon was procured, and a detachment escorted them through the city to the Costa de la Luz, where a fleet of British ships floated in the harbor.

Nico's face lit up when he saw the vessels, and Sidney was delighted at the boy's interest.

Jim reported to the officers in charge of the city, and Sidney left Serena and Emma in the care of the general's wife while he took Nico to the harbor. It was only a matter of hours before he made his report to the admiral in command of the fleet. Admiral Stembridge offered the use of his cutter to convey the company up the coast to Cádiz, and then arranged transport for Sidney back to his ship in Portsmouth. Jim would accompany them and continue on to Portugal to join his regiment.

Once they were all aboard the small ship and Sidney's companions secured in their accommodations, it was well past midnight. He paced the deck, breathing in the sea air. The familiar sounds of water lapping against the hull, creaking wood, and the snapping of the sails soothed him. Had it only been this morning that he and Emma had crept through the dark tunnel to ring the bell? So much had happened in one day. His emotions had been tossed around like a dinghy in a storm—from the very depths of fear when he'd found Emma missing to burning fury as he discovered Enrique assaulting her to sublime tenderness when they had kissed. Just thinking of how soft her lips were, how she'd practically melted into his arms made his breath catch.

He allowed himself to absorb the contentment the memory produced and then forced his mind to think of something else. It would not do to dwell on what could never be. The idea of saying good-bye to Emma after the time they'd spent together caused such an ache in his chest that he looked around for a distraction. Leaning his back against the gunwale, he studied what he could see of the cutter by the glow of the starboard running lights. But for some reason, he did not feel the thrill that typically came with walking the deck of a ship. He shook his head. It was time to accept the facts. This was the career he had chosen. It was his duty to his family.

Unbidden, the memory of Emma's words came to mind. Were the things she had said about his relatives true? She wouldn't lie to him, he was certain, but was she mistaken?

The few times he had seen his brothers since his father died, they had complained about their lack of funds and worried that they would lose their family lands. Had it all been an act? His family finances were something that definitely needed investigating.

He stepped down onto the companionway, headed for the quarters the admiral had assigned to him. He was physically and emotionally exhausted and fell asleep the moment he lay in the berth.

Sidney awoke and came on deck at four bells—only a few hours after he'd fallen asleep. It seemed his old habits hadn't been completely erased. He watched the sunrise and admired the maneuverability of the cutter. He paced the deck, supervising the crew that did not require supervision, and was relieved a few hours later when a sailor approached with Nico in tow.

"Found this scallywag in the companionway lookin' fer the cap'n."

"Thank you, sir."

Sidney and Nico ate breakfast in the stern galleries, and afterwards, he took the boy on deck, showing him everything from the long bowsprit—that gave the ship excellent maneuverability—to the cannonades that armed the small vessel. Nico took everything in excitedly, and Sidney could not help the immense pride he felt in the boy.

Sidney lifted Nico to peer into the binnacle box at the compass. Sidney was completely unprepared for the swell of affection he felt when the boy wrapped his arms around Sidney's neck. It would be nearly as difficult to bid farewell to him as to Emma.

Some time later, Jim stumbled up onto the deck, his face green. "Blasted unnatural way to travel," he complained before leaning over the gunwale and heaving.

Sidney clapped a hand on his friend's shoulder. "We are nearly there," he said, pointing to the opening that led to the Bay of Cádiz. "Nico, we need to wake Emma."

When they arrived at the door to Emma's quarters, Sidney raised his hand to knock, but Nico opened the door and walked in, stepping over his small pallet on the floor to where Emma slept on her berth.

Sidney drew a deep breath. Emma's hair spread out over the pillow, and her cheek rested in her palm. He had half a mind to continue watching her sleep, knowing this was the last opportunity he would have to view the sight, but Nico had other ideas. He climbed into the berth and began patting Emma's face, urging her to wake.

She sat up and wrapped her arms around the boy, burying her face in his curls before she looked up with sleepy eyes. Sidney watched the two of them, feeling a tightness in his chest. He hoped the image would imprint in his mind so he would remember the feeling in the long, lonely years ahead. He blinked and stepped back.

"Emma, we are at Cádiz," he said and had the pleasure of seeing her face light up. Even with purple bruises marring her light skin and her hair tousled from sleep, she looked stunning.

Their eyes met. It seemed as if there was so much to say, but now was not the time, and Sidney did not know if he would be able to say the things he needed to and so, instead, said nothing.

He closed the door, muttering something about leaving her to get ready, and turned to knock on Serena's door.

Chapter 26

IT WAS NOT DIFFICULT TO locate William's ship among the commissioned vessels and tattered merchant ships in the bay. The *Lady Jamaica* sat at anchor, her sails reefed, and Sidney took a moment to admire her, taking in the shining wood and immaculately maintained riggings. *William certainly knows his boats*, Sidney thought with a smile.

The cutter dropped anchor, and the company climbed into a dinghy. Sidney thanked the lieutenant who commanded the vessel, and they set off toward William's ship. Emma fidgeted, and Sidney could only imagine the eagerness and anxiety that must be at war inside her as she prepared to face her brother.

When they neared, Sidney hailed the ship. The five of them climbed aboard while the captain was summoned. Sidney was overwhelmed by the welcome he received from his shipmates.

Young Riley's chin trembled as he shook his hand. "I knew you were alive, Cap'n Fletcher," he said, and Sidney thought it was high time the young gentleman was promoted to midshipman.

The greetings and well-wishes were cut short as William stepped onto the deck. The earl looked terrible. Dark smudges stretched beneath his eyes, and there were lines on his face that were definitely the result of strain. Sidney had only seen the look of extreme tension on his friend's face a few times before, most often following a battle and once when they were captured by the French. William's gaze fell upon Emma, and Sidney could have sworn there were tears in his eyes, but he knew better than to mention it.

Emma hesitated, apparently unsure whether she would be reprimanded. But William held his arms out to her, and she fell into them sobbing. "I am so sorry, William," she said, her voice muffled against him.

When she had calmed, William placed a hand upon her shoulder. "Emma . . ." He brushed his fingers over the bruises on her face and cleared his throat a few times before pulling her back against him. He kissed the top of her head and turned toward the others, keeping his arm around her.

Sidney stepped forward, and William clasped his hand. "Welcome back, Captain. I cannot thank you enough for returning my sister to me." The sincerity that radiated from William's eyes was nearly disconcerting as Sidney had been prepared for one of his friend's signature insults. The fact that he spoke so courteously attested to the strain he'd been under for the past week.

"Of course, your Lordship," Sidney said. "But actually, it is Lady Emma who deserves the thanks, as she rescued me from prison."

William and the entire crew turned to look at Emma, disbelief evident on their faces. Emma's cheeks turned pink.

Sidney grinned. "To be entirely truthful, I should amend that statement. It was Lady Emma and the princesa that rescued me." He indicated Serena, who stood next to Jim, holding Nico's hand.

William turned. "Perhaps you would introduce us to your companions?"

When Sidney had executed the formalities and Emma introduced Nico, William said, "Clearly you are hungry and tired. And I assume the ladies would like to wash. I have a missive to send to Henry Wellesley, who has been doing everything in his power to discover what happened to Emma. But with the attack, the enemy is allowing nobody to leave the city. We were preparing to sail to Tarifa tomorrow to go ashore and search for you ourselves."

Emma hung her head. "I am so sorry, William. I am so sorry to have worried everyone."

"A few days ago, I debated locking you in the brig for the journey home." He rubbed his eyes and pulled Emma into another embrace. His voice trembled. "I am so relieved that you are safe."

Sidney raised an eyebrow and did not miss the surprised looks on the face of the crewmembers at the tenderness the typically gruff man was showing his sister. The last week must have been terrible to have changed him so.

William made arrangements for hot water to be brought to the cabins below so that the women could bathe and wash their hair, and a few hours later, William, Sidney, Jim, the officers and marines from the *Venture*, Riley, and Nico sat around the large table in the officers' ward room. Sidney held Nico on his lap. The men pestered Sidney and Jim for the account of their adventures, but Sidney insisted they wait for the women before beginning what was to be a long story.

William only raised his eyebrow, and a few moments later, Emma and Serena entered, both wearing gowns that Emma must have brought from London. Emma wore her hair down, no doubt to obscure the bruises on her face and neck. The golden tresses shone in the lantern light, and Sidney's fingers itched to brush his fingers over the soft strands.

Emma moved to sit next to her brother, and Sidney felt a small pang of loneliness. He had become accustomed to having her at his side. Truly, he considered her to be a partner in their journey. An exceptionally lovely partner.

Supper was served, and Sidney told their story to the spellbound audience. The others interjected frequently. Between the four of them and the questions William and the others posed, the account took well over two hours. When they finished, the room was silent, and Riley burst into applause, quickly joined by the others.

The men continued to discuss the battles and politics of the war, and Emma excused herself to put Nico to bed. Serena left with her, and soon after, Jim followed, a little less green but still pale. The others trickled out one by one, and finally, William and Sidney were left alone.

"Sidney, I cannot even begin to express my gratitude for the safe return of Emma," William said, pouring Sidney a drink from the decanter on the side table. "Amelia was beside herself when we'd heard you had been killed. If I had to return without my sister too . . ." He coughed, and Sidney turned away for a moment to allow him to compose himself.

"Emma told me she stowed away," Sidney said, hoping to lighten the mood.

William rolled his eyes. "Yes, and I have my suspicions that my darling wife may have been a party to the deception."

"I would not put it past her. The two of them together—it chills me to think of the schemes they could come up with." Sidney set the glass carefully upon the table, keeping his hand near in case the ship dipped and sent it sliding. He cleared his throat. "William, I have something to tell you, and I know you will quite likely slash my gullet to ribbons." He attempted to smile but felt too nervous to rally more than a weak lift of his lips. "I fear that I am in love with your sister." Sidney watched William's reaction, fully prepared to jump out of the way should he reach for his sword.

William, however, did not appear surprised. "And I assume you'd like to offer for her hand?"

"There is nothing I would like more, but I cannot. I've nothing to recommend myself." He shrugged his shoulders in defeat. "With the obligations to my family, I cannot leave the navy and ensure that she has the life she deserves."

"If it is a matter of money, Sidney, you do not have to worry. Emma has plenty—"

"I cannot live off your charity, William." The idea of relying on his wife's dowry to support them was humiliating.

"Even though it would mean hearing your annoying witticisms on a more constant basis, I would rather see Emma happy," William said in his typical dry tone. "There are other options."

"I am not an earl, William," Sidney said quietly. "I do not have the resources you do."

"That is incorrect. You are my closest friend, my brother. My resources are yours."

He spoke frankly, but Sidney was surprised by his words. He had certainly never voiced such a high regard for their friendship before. While he *felt* the closeness between himself and William, his friend showed his fondness through sarcasm and insults. Sidney again wondered how the week of agonizing for his sister had affected William.

"Thank you." Sidney stood and returned the glass to the cabinet in the side table. His mind was in turmoil. "If you will excuse me, I will retire. I am to report to the *Calcutta* in the morning." As he voiced the words aloud, a pain blossomed in his chest.

The men shook hands, and Sidney walked slowly to his quarters, wondering for an instant who had given up their berth that he might have a good night's sleep. He entered the small cabin and paced, though there was only room for three steps in each direction. He hadn't even made five revolutions when he heard a small knock, and Emma entered, closing the door behind her.

"Emma, what are you . . . ?" It would be the height of scandal should she be discovered in his quarters, but every inch of him ached to hold her.

She rushed into his arms, and the sight of her eyes shining up at him was nearly his undoing.

"I wanted to share one last moment of our adventure before we re-enter society and are restricted to speaking reservedly in parlors," she said, making an exasperated expression and then laying her head upon his chest. "Or a dull carriage ride around Hyde Park."

As if his arms had a mind of their own, he clung to her, feeling the way her soft body molded to his and inhaling her smell. If he wasn't careful, he wouldn't be able to let her go.

He stepped back, holding her at arms' length. "Things haven't changed, Emma."

Her eyebrows pinched together in a look of confusion. "What do you mean?"

"I am not returning to London. I leave tomorrow to join my ship in Portsmouth. We . . . can't . . ."

Emma stepped back. Her face paled. She shook her head. "But you said . . . you told me—"

"I know what I said. I do love you. But it doesn't change the fact that I have no means to support a wife."

The wounded look upon Emma's face hurt Sidney worse than if she had wept. She looked utterly betrayed. She did not look at him again and turned to go.

"I am sorry, but I—"

Emma held up her hand to stop his words. She paused before returning, pressing something into his hand, then closing his fist. "I wish you would have chosen me," she whispered and was gone.

He sat on his berth, opening his hand to find the jade bracelet and Spanish coin. He squeezed his eyes shut, pushing the heels of his hands into them, feeling as if his heart was shattered.

The next morning, the crew turned out to bid him and Colonel Stackhouse farewell. He would see most of them in a few weeks when the HMS *Venture* had finished undergoing repairs. William shook both men's hands, thanking them again for bringing his sister safely home and admonishing Sidney to visit. Amelia was certainly anxious to see him.

Serena embraced them both, weeping as she said farewell. Emma merely stood holding Nico. She bid Jim good-bye and allowed Sidney to kiss her hand, though she did not look at him when he attempted to catch her eye.

He picked up Nico and kissed his cheeks, explaining that he was leaving. Nico broke into sobs, clinging to Sidney's neck until Emma pulled him away. Sidney could still hear his small voice calling as they rowed away in the dinghy.

He choked on the swelling in his throat and coughed to mask the sound.

"You know yer making an enormous mistake, I'm sure," Jim said.

Sidney turned to him, blinking away the moisture that had begun to pool in his eyes. "I must, Colonel. I have obligations to my family."

"And what do ya call that woman and child?" Jim asked, clinging to the sides of the boat.

His chest hurt so badly he looked down to make sure he was not injured. Sidney looked back to the *Lady Jamaica* bobbing in the water and realized the ache only grew the farther away he got from Emma and Nico—his family.

Chapter 27

EMMA HESITATED AS SHE FOLLOWED William and Amelia up the grand stairs into the duke's ballroom. It was the last ball of the Season, and Emma's mother and Amelia had insisted she attend. She smoothed down the gossamer netting over her pink satin gown. Anna, Amelia's lady's maid, had taken great pains to weave matching ribbons through Emma's hair. The bruises on her face had faded. She wished she could say the same about her heart.

"Are you ready?" Amelia linked her arm through Emma's and smiled. "You look beautiful," she said. "That gown is the perfect complement for your skin."

Emma didn't care, and Amelia knew it. She would much rather be home reading a story to Nico or even playing marbles, but the Duke of Southampton was a dear friend of the family, and she knew he would feel badly if she did not attend.

As she reached the top of the stairs and surveyed the crowd, waiting to be admitted to the ballroom, her eyes fell upon a group of soldiers in Spanish uniforms. As the men parted, she recognized Princesa de Talavera, and accompanying her was a tall handsome man with the same thick dark hair, who Emma assumed to be her brother. Serena looked beautiful. She wore an elaborate and exotic gown, as suited her station, and a small tiara had been woven into her dark hair. Emma felt a thrill of joy at seeing her dear friend.

When Serena saw Emma, she hurried closer, and the women embraced.

"You remember my brother, Lord Lockwood," Emma said. "And allow me to introduce Lady Lockwood. William and Amelia, Princesa Serena Antonietta de Talavera of the two Sicilies.

"My brother, Principe Rodrigo Fernando de Talavera." Serena turned to her brother. "Rodrigo, this is my dear friend, Lady Emma Drake."

Rodrigo took Emma's hand and bowed elegantly. "I must thank you for assisting in the safe return of my sister, Lady Emma. She has spoken of little else since arriving from España."

Emma curtsied. "Thank you, Your Excellency."

"Here comes the duke," Amelia said.

"And you are waltzing with *me* this evening," William told his wife.

The duke greeted his old friends, and William introduced Serena and Rodrigo. When the duke turned toward them, his typically genial expression froze on his face as his eyes met Serena's. For an awkward instant, he seemed unable to speak. But he seemed to collect himself, bowing to the principe and princesa. He offered his arm to Serena, whose face he could not seem to take his eyes from as she accompanied him into the ballroom. The sight made Emma smile, but at the same time, her heart felt heavy as she recognized the look of adoration in the duke's eyes. She took Rodrigo's offered arm and entered the room.

Rodrigo was charming. He wore a sash from his shoulder to his opposite hip, making him look every bit the foreign prince he was. He carried himself proudly and conversed politely, but Emma sensed he was decidedly uncomfortable with the young ladies who practically threw themselves in his path to get his attention. She watched Serena and the duke, who seemed to have forgotten that anyone else even existed. Certainly a handsome Spanish prince attending a London ball and the duke being smitten with a princess would be the talk of the town for quite some time.

The remainder of the night consisted of the same people sharing the same intrigues and gossip. The same gentlemen attempting to catch her eye and filling up her dance card. She listened with a wandering mind and a simulated smile as a group of her friends chattered about the disgraceful dress Olivia Dewitt had worn and how it did nothing for her figure. Emma felt frustrated. It was as if the world had changed, but the *ton* had not. Finally excusing herself, she stepped out onto the balcony, inhaling the cool night air.

A moment later, Amelia joined her. "You do not seem to be enjoying yourself."

"Amelia, why is it so different? The women argue over which lace collar is a la mode while there are people across the sea who are not safe in their own homes. All of the gossip and scandal, and none of it matters when there is real suffering. I hear the officers telling glorious battle stories, but I know better. This"—she waved her hand to indicate the ballroom behind her— "none of *this* is real. And I do not feel as though I belong here anymore."

Amelia turned to lean her back against the balcony railing. Emma continued to look out over the duke's gardens. "The *ton* has not changed, Emma. It is *you* who have changed. You are not the same woman who followed her heart across the sea. You are strong, and you can see the truth behind the façades. It is a gift you have been given, and you must decide what to do with it."

Emma sighed. "And what am I to do? Return to Spain and fight the French? I feel as though I do not belong anywhere. I cannot play this game any longer, pretending to be something I am not."

"You are already doing something. What would have happened to Nico if not for you?" She laid her hand on Emma's arm. "In a few weeks, we will be back at Lockwood Manor, and you will not have to worry about all of this. You will take Nico for walks in the forest, William can teach him to fish . . ." Amelia's voice trailed off.

Emma glanced up at her then followed her gaze to the doorway where William stood, and next to him . . . Sidney.

Emma turned away and clenched the railing so hard she feared she would tear her gloves. She was vaguely aware of Amelia and William leaving but did not dare to turn around. Her stomach churned as every possible emotion fought for supremacy—hurt, anger, hope—and she waited to see which would win.

"Emma." His voice was soft, and the hair on the back of her neck prickled at his nearness. "Will you not turn around?"

She shook her head, not trusting her voice. Why was he here? Did he not know that it would tear her apart to see him again only to say farewell once more?

He stepped closer, reaching his hands around her to detach her from the railing and turn her to face him. His crooked finger lifted her chin, and she allowed her eyes to meet his.

"Emma, please forgive me. As soon as I left you, I knew I'd made a terrible mistake that I have spent the last three weeks trying to rectify. What you said—I made the wrong choice." He closed his eyes and took a breath, letting it out slowly. "I choose *you*. Please give me another chance to make this right." His fingers traced along her jawline and down her neck, finally resting upon her shoulder.

Emma's mind tumbled. She had been hurt so badly. Could she forget all of that and allow him back into her heart? "What about your family?" she asked, trying to keep her voice impersonal.

"William has helped me hire a solicitor to look into the financial situation. I think the Viscount of Stansbury and his household will be forced to tighten their purse strings, but I am assured they will survive. And they are my family in name only." He leaned close enough that their foreheads nearly touched. "You and Nico, you are my family, or I hope you will be."

Emma opened her mouth to answer, but Sidney kept speaking. "I have resigned my commission and taken a post as a commander upon a merchant vessel. Perhaps you have heard of it, the *Lady Jamaica*?"

"William's ship?" Emma was beginning to wonder how long her brother had known what Sidney was planning. She just now registered the fact that Sidney was wearing a waistcoat and jacket instead of his uniform.

"The plan is to sail to Jamaica twice a year, at least for the time being, and of course, when the war is over, I intend to return to Spain to search for the treasure. My only problem right now is that I need to recruit two more crew members. I hoped that you and Nico might fill the last vacancies. That is, if you were my wife. What I mean to say is—" He rubbed his hand over his cheek. "This speech was perfect in my mind."

Emma merely raised an eyebrow. She was not going to make it easy for him. "I think you did a much better job earlier when you proposed by accident." This was certainly not the most polished proposal she had ever received, but somehow, his clumsy words still had her knees turning to jelly.

Sidney grinned, and the sight made Emma's heart jolt. She allowed her face to soften into a smile.

"Will you be my wife, Lady Emma Drake?"

"Of course I will, Captain Sidney Fletcher."

"Even if I cannot offer you a traditional noblewoman's life?"

"After everything, how can you believe I would ever be content with something so boring as a traditional noblewoman's life?"

Sidney brushed the tears from her cheeks with his thumbs, whispering against her lips, "*No eres solo. Me preocupo por ti. Voy a mantenerte a salvo.*"

Heart pounding and stomach fluttering, she tried to think of the words to express her utter joy, the ache of missing him, and just how much she was in love with him. But his lips upon hers banished the need for words, and she simply clung to him, allowing herself to drown in the sensation that the very thing she had wished for had at last come true.

Epilogue

EMMA STEPPED INTO THE UPSTAIRS hallway of the manor house, pulling her wrap close around her shoulders. After the warm sun of the Caribbean, she did not think any number of blankets or knitted shawls would be able to keep her warm in an English winter. She peeked in the doorway of Nico's bedroom and saw that his bed was empty. *He and Sidney must already be at breakfast,* she thought.

When she reached the staircase, she heard whispers and hushed laughter, and a moment later as she entered the main hall, she saw why. Sidney and Nico were covered in pine needles, and every doorway and mantel was decorated with greenery and ribbons.

"*Feliz Navidad!*" Nico cried, running toward her.

She snatched him up and kissed his cheeks. "Merry Christmas, my darling. But you must be quiet, or you will wake the baby."

Nico pointed to the sitting room doorway just as William walked out holding a small bundle.

"Lady Charlotte has been awake for hours," her brother said. "Apparently she prefers the early-morning patrol, though we have assigned her the dog watch." He gazed lovingly at his child. "The two of us have been having a talk about allowing her mother to sleep." He tucked the blanket around her little body, and Emma smiled. She did not think there was ever a man who doted upon a child as much as her brother.

Sidney took Nico from her arms, setting him upon the floor, and pulled Emma toward the dining room doorway to stand beneath an enormous kissing bough. "Are you sure you are happy to have Christmas here at Lockwood Manor with your brother instead of in our own home, Mrs. Fletcher?"

"Of course I am. I would not wish to miss Baby Lottie's first Christmas, and these rooms are full of memories—such as my first kiss beneath the kissing bough."

Sidney got a wicked gleam in his eye. "First, perhaps, but I wager you'll not consider it your best. Some things only improve with practice." He leaned toward her, and Emma closed her eyes, waiting for the touch of his lips that had become so familiar, yet even after months did not fail to send a thrill down to her toes.

"But it will have to wait," Sidney said, smiling at her pout when she opened her eyes. "I have a Christmas gift for you." He produced a small box from his pocket, and Emma opened the lid. Inside, wrapped in a piece of cloth was a golden chain attached to a pendant in the shape of a ship's anchor.

He lifted the necklace and fastened it behind her neck, tracing his finger over the chain to where the pendant rested beneath her collar bone. "Emma, when my damaged mind sinks into a dark space of nightmares and bad memories, I have only to think of you, and . . . You are my anchor. I did not ever think I would depend upon the strength of a person so small," he said, allowing a small smile to bend his lips.

Emma's throat was tight. Tears stung the backs of her eyes. "Sidney, I—"

He placed a finger over her lips, winking. "And now, where were we?" He glanced up at the kissing bough, and the mischievous look reappeared in his eyes. He pressed his lips against her softly and then burrowed his fingers into her hair, holding her head in his hand and molding her body to his. When he finally pulled away, Emma's mind was muddled for a moment, and she looked up at him, blinking away the haze in her eyes.

"I have half a mind to hang these bits of greenery from every inch of our home. This one, in particular, seems to be especially potent," Sidney said in a breathless voice.

Emma wrapped her arms around his neck, gazing into his darkened eyes, knowing with a certainty that that particular expression would never fail to send her heart fluttering as long as she lived. "Perhaps we should put it to the test one more time?"

The words were barely out of her mouth before Sidney happily obliged.

No eres solo.
Me preocupo por ti.
Voy a mantenerte a salvo.

Posttraumatic Stress Disorder affects millions of people worldwide. To recognize the symptoms, understand causes and treatment, or learn how you can help, visit the National Alliance on Mental Illness at www.NAMI.org.

Author Bio

JENNIFER MOORE IS A PASSIONATE reader and writer of all things romance due to the need to balance the rest of her world, which includes a perpetually traveling husband and four active sons, who create heaps of laundry that are anything but romantic. Jennifer has a BA in linguistics from the University of Utah and is a Guitar Hero champion. She lives in northern Utah with her family. You can learn more about her at authorjmoore.com.

Lady Emma's Campaign is a regency romance that takes place in Spain during the Napoleonic wars of the early 1800s.